"Look," Zoe said, "this walking-me-home business was your idea. I appreciate the gallantry, even though that sort of thing isn't usually all that appealing to me. If you've changed your mind, Spencer, take off. Nobody's forcing—"

And that was the moment I kissed her, as much to shut her up as to keep me from changing my mind about kissing her at all. But then she kissed me back. Zoe was, is and will always be a world-class kisser. In less than ten seconds I was a goner. Judging by the turnaround in her disposition, the kiss worked for her, as well.

In that instant I knew I'd never be able to get enough of her—whatever might happen in our future, no matter how different we clearly, irrevocably were.

Dear Reader,

I couldn't be more delighted that Harlequin has created a "home" for love stories that take the reader—and the author—beyond "happily ever after." For those women (like me) who have spent decades with the loves of their lives, facing life's unpredictable and sometimes unimaginable challenges, "happily ever after" can sometimes seem a great deal more like a line from a fairy tale than real life. But when two people who truly are meant for each other find ways to survive and thrive— together—who needs the fairy tale? There's a line that Spencer Tracy delivers to his daughter and future son-in-law in the classic film *Guess Who's Coming to Dinner*. Paraphrased, it's something like this: "If what you feel for each other is even half of what your mother and I feel, then that's everything." I've been blessed to find that kind of deep love in my life, and my hope for you is that you will not only have it but treasure it, as well.

All my best,

Anna

(Write to me at www.booksbyanna.com, or
P.O. Box 161, Thiensville, WI 53092.)

THIS SIDE OF HEAVEN

ANNA SCHMIDT

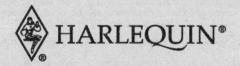

HARLEQUIN®

TORONTO • NEW YORK • LONDON
AMSTERDAM • PARIS • SYDNEY • HAMBURG
STOCKHOLM • ATHENS • TOKYO • MILAN • MADRID
PRAGUE • WARSAW • BUDAPEST • AUCKLAND

ISBN-13: 978-0-373-65425-3
ISBN-10:   0-373-65425-1

THIS SIDE OF HEAVEN

www.eHarlequin.com

Printed in U.S.A.

ABOUT THE AUTHOR

Anna Schmidt is a two-time finalist for the coveted RITA®
Award from the Romance Writers of America, as well
as twice a finalist for the *Romantic Times BOOKreviews*
Reviewers' Choice Award. The most recent Reviewers'
Choice nomination was for her 2006 novel *Matchmaker,
Matchmaker....* The sequel, *Lasso Her Heart*, has inspired
readers to write to Anna and declare that its theme of recovery
from tragedy brought them comfort in their own lives. Her
novel *The Doctor's Miracle* was the 2002 Reviewers' Choice
Inspirational Category winner. A venture into screenwriting
also brought kudos when her screenplay, entitled *For Patriot's
Dream*, was a finalist in the Wisconsin Screenwriters Forum
2003 Contest and a quarterfinalist in the respected Nicholl
Fellowship Awards sponsored by the Academy of Arts and
Sciences, sponsors of the Oscars.

Anna has published a total of eighteen works of historical and
contemporary fiction. Watch for two more 2008 novels from
her: *Seaside Cinderella*, which brings her back to historical
writing, and *Slingshot Moves*, which gives her the opportunity
to explore the wild (and sometimes wacky) world of racing.
A transplant from Virginia, she now calls Wisconsin home—
although she escapes the tough winters by spending three
months in Florida.

Books by Anna Schmidt

STEEPLE HILL LOVE INSPIRED
CAROLINE AND THE PREACHER   MATCHMAKER,
A MOTHER FOR AMANDA   MATCHMAKER...
THE DOCTOR'S MIRACLE   LASSO HER HEART
LOVE NEXT DOOR

For Larry

ACKNOWLEDGMENT

To my agent, Natasha Kern,
and my editor, Beverley Sotolov

To everything there is a season
And a time to every purpose under heaven
A time to be born
And a time to die
A time to plant
And a time to uproot
A time to kill
And a time to heal
A time to pull down
And a time to build up
A time to weep
And a time to laugh
A time to mourn
And a time to dance
A time to scatter stones
And a time to gather them
A time to embrace
And a time to refrain from embracing
A time to seek
And a time to lose
A time to keep
And a time to throw away
A time to tear
And a time to mend
A time for silence
And a time for speech
A time to love
And a time to hate
A time for WAR
And a time for PEACE

Adapted from Ecclesiastes 3:1–8

Summer, 2007

Spencer

"Spence?"

I had been turning the pages of a six-month-old copy of *The New Yorker*. My colleague and friend, Dr. Elizabeth Simmons, stands before me, her hands fisted in the pockets of her white lab coat. She is smiling, but I'm not fooled.

"What is it?" I ask, standing and nervously rolling the magazine into a tube, which I proceed to tap against the side of one thigh.

"Come on back. Zoe's getting dressed." Liz nods to the sole other patient in the waiting room. "I'll be with you in a few minutes," she promises, then holds the door for me that leads to the inner sanctum of her practice. We walk down a long hall, past examining rooms, some open and empty, others with their doors shut, signaling occupancy. Zoe is in one of them and I am tempted to try each door until I find my wife. Instead I follow Liz into her office.

"Have a seat," she says. "I'll get Zoe."

Before I can say anything, she's gone, closing the office door behind her with a soft click. I hear the murmur of her voice in conversation with a nurse or assistant as she retraces her steps down the hall. I fight the urge to go after her, grab Zoe and get the hell out of here before Liz can say whatever she clearly does not want to say.

Like Liz, I am a physician and member of the medical faculty at the University of Wisconsin. Like most doctors I am not good at being on the other side—as either a patient or family member. Liz is a gynecologist. I am a psychiatrist. We have often joked that between us we treat the whole person—body and mind. Zoe always reminds us that there's a key third component to any human—the spirit.

My wife is what many would call a Renaissance woman—a lawyer by trade, although she hasn't practiced law in years and that credential only scrapes the surface of all the roles she has assumed in her life. She is endlessly fascinated by the human drama that is inevitable in any gathering of one or more people. She is especially curious in medical settings. Perhaps it's all the years of living with me and listening to my "shoptalk" about patients.

I have watched her take lost souls under her wing and guide them through the chaos that is any hospital emergency room. And more than once I have arranged to meet her in the hospital coffee shop, only to arrive and hear her deeply engrossed in conversation with a stranger whose family member has been admitted for treatment. Once I walked in and found her leading everyone in the place in an impromptu toast to the first-time father who had burst through the door to announce the birth of his son. Everyone is drawn to Zoe. People love her. Trust me, I did not miss the averted but sympathetic looks of Liz's staff as we made that endless walk to her office.

"Old age. It's nothing I haven't experienced before," Zoe told me after I noticed her breathlessness as she climbed the stairs from our boathouse—a trip she usually made far more easily than I did. "I see Liz for my annual checkup day after tomorrow. If it'll make you happy, I'll ask her to schedule a stress test."

"It's not about me," I said peevishly.

Zoe smiled and ruffled my hair. "Oh, Spence, it's always about you," she teased, then added quickly, "because I love you, and if you're worried—"

"Concerned," I corrected.

"Then that's reason enough."

"Thank you." I leaned in to kiss her lips.

"But it's nothing," she repeated before accepting the kiss. Over nearly four decades of married life, Zoe has almost always gotten the last word.

We agreed to meet at Liz's office at the appointed time. I had arrived twenty minutes early and assured the receptionist that Zoe was on her way. Just as I was beginning to feel a prickle of irritation at Zoe's habitual tardiness, she burst through the door.

As usual she arrived in a whirlwind of activity, balancing magazines for Liz's waiting room with her usual shoulder satchel—which was always overflowing with folders and letters—as well as her wallet, glasses and cell phone. She was babbling a litany of excuses—meeting ran late, got hung up in traffic, couldn't find her keys.

"Sorry," she said once she'd run out of both words and breath. The singular word, accompanied by a genuinely apologetic smile, swept through the waiting room to include the receptionist, the other patient and me. Zoe sat down next to me, arranged the magazines on a side table and unbuttoned her light denim jacket with the word *Joy* embroidered down one sleeve.

"No problem," the receptionist replied, absolving Zoe of all responsibility. "She's running a little behind."

"She's worth waiting for," Zoe assured the young woman sitting across from us. The woman responded to this announcement with a blank stare.

"Dr. Simmons—Liz," Zoe explained. "I'd trust her with my life." Then she laughed and squeezed my hand. "Actually, I already have. I was diagnosed with breast cancer nearly five years ago and look at me now."

There is no denying that Zoe is the picture of health, glowing with a zest for life that belies her sixty years. Her skin is smooth and the pinkish tint of her cheeks along with the pixie cut of her hair make her appear a decade younger than her chronological age of sixty-two. When Zoe's hair came back as snow-white instead of the brown of her youth, she was delighted. "Gives me character, don't you think?"

The young woman's eyes widened with interest. "It's my first appointment," she admitted, then laughed nervously. "I like your jacket," she added after a brief pause.

Zoe grinned. "Tag-sale purchase," she said. "One of my treasures."

"Oh, I know," the young woman replied, clearly relieved to have settled on a topic of conversation other than medicine and doctors. "I furnished my entire apartment from stuff I got at garage and estate sales."

I've often thought that Zoe's personality should be considered for use as a weapon to disarm terrorists. Once she focuses her attention on you, she is impossible to resist. Complete strangers tell her things about themselves in that first half hour that they are loath to tell their dearest friends.

"I found this—thing," the young woman confided, lowering her voice and gently touching her own chest. "It's probably nothing but…" She blushed.

Zoe moved her chair closer to the young woman and took her hand. "And even if it's something," she assured the young woman, "the cure rate is really in your favor. You did the right thing scheduling this appointment."

She passed the woman a tissue and continued to stroke her hand, while I flipped through my magazine.

"Mrs. Andersen?" Liz's nurse has known Zoe almost as long as Liz has but maintains decorum in the office.

Zoe headed for the door. "There's a sale Saturday at one of the churches on Johnson Street," she said to the young woman. "Maybe I'll run into you there."

The young woman smiled. I got up to accompany my wife into the exam room, but she stopped me with a quick kiss on my cheek. "Susie will get you once we get past the physical, won't you, Susie?"

Liz's nurse grinned. "This wouldn't be about your not wanting your husband to be present at the weighing in, would it?" she asked, and I heard the music of Zoe's laughter as the two of them disappeared down the hall and the door to the waiting room swung closed behind them. I checked my watch and then settled in to await my summons.

But I realize now as I pace Liz's office, rhythmically tapping the rolled magazine against my palm, that from the moment Zoe disappeared behind that closed door I felt uneasy. As if I were the one who had trouble getting my breath. Zoe and I are certainly no strangers to tough times, and something about this whole scenario is all too familiar. On the other hand, Zoe would laugh if she could see me now. "And you counsel patients with anxiety issues?" she would say.

Liz's office is on the tenth floor of a professional building near the heart of campus and offers a bird's-eye view of some of the landmarks that are unique to Madison, Wisconsin. From the corner window, I make out the dome of the State Capitol building, reflecting the bright afternoon sun in the distance. Then I allow my eye to follow the length of State Street—a pedestrian shopping street that Zoe loves to frequent, lined with an assortment of merchants peddling everything from upscale clothing to trendy beverages to T-shirts and other logo-enhanced paraphernalia—to where State Street ends and the campus of the University of Wisconsin begins. Zoe, born and raised in Manhattan, nevertheless considers this small midwestern city, with its unique mix of youth and politics, home.

Liz's office affords a magnificent view of several of the oldest buildings on campus set along the shore of Lake Mendota. Today the calm blue water is speckled with the colorful sails of windsurfers and a few kayaks. Below me is the Memorial Union, with its popular terrace—a tiered outdoor gathering place cluttered with its trademark jumble of colorful metal chairs and café tables.

I'm mesmerized by the terrace, lost in memory, when I hear voices outside the door and turn to see Liz and an abnormally subdued Zoe enter the room. My heart goes into overdrive as I step around Liz's desk and take Zoe's hands. She's dry-eyed, but her smile wavers as she sits in one of the chairs facing Liz's desk. My knees feel suddenly filled with water and I collapse into the remaining chair.

Liz assumes her place at her desk and fumbles with her computer, bringing up Zoe's medical records. "I'm scheduling a few more tests," she begins.

"Just tell me," I demand between gritted teeth.

"The cancer's back," Zoe says, stroking my hand with her thumb. "It's spread."

"Where?"

"Let's not—" Liz begins.

"Where?" I ask again.

"A spot on my lung," Zoe says, then clears her throat and smiles. "Guess that shortness-of-breath thing was a wake-up call. At least it's not just old age." Her voice cracks on the last word.

I focus my attention on Liz, studying every nuance of her expression. "Prognosis?"

Liz blows out a breath she might have been holding in anticipation of a question she really doesn't want to answer. "Spence, you know that I can't—"

"Best guess," I say.

"Definitely treatable," she replies.

I have built my entire practice out of counseling patients suffering from post-traumatic stress syndrome. More than once I have heard them describe the kind of terror that is a physical reality, clawing at your insides until you think you can't endure it. In that instant in Liz's office, I finally understand what they mean.

"Spence?"

I realize that my eyes are shut tight. When I open them, Zoe is on her knees next to my chair, her hand slowly massaging the length of my back. "Whatever it is, we can deal with it," she says, and I notice her voice has dropped a register. It's raspy with her fear.

"Let's not get ahead of ourselves, here," Liz advises. "I've set up more tests. They can run them today if you like and I can push through the results. Or if you'd like to take a few days to digest this…"

"Let's gather all the facts," Zoe says.

Liz stands. "Susie will get everything set up for you. I wish—"

"I know." Zoe stands, as well, and gives Liz an awkward hug across the expanse of Liz's cluttered desk.

"I have other patients." Liz is apologetic. I see that she is fighting to control her emotions. "But I'll stop by the house tonight and we can talk some more, okay?"

"Of course." Zoe glances around the office. "Should we just go on over to the hospital?" The uncertain waver has returned to her smile and permeated her voice, and I realize that for all her bravado, Zoe is every bit as scared as Liz and I are for her.

Liz nods, unable to make a sound. Then she hugs me and flees the room.

Zoe and I focus on the closed door, dimly aware of Liz's muffled instructions to Susie, the distant sound of a passing fire engine and the soothing splash of the small fountain in the corner of Liz's office.

Without a word, Zoe puts on her denim jacket, the embroidered *Joy* mocking us now. She hooks the strap of her bag over one shoulder and laces her fingers through mine as she starts for the door with the determination of a soldier headed into battle.

Zoe

I can practically hear the wheels grinding in Spence's brain as he drives me across campus to the hospital complex. As a psychiatrist—the best—I know that trying to figure out ways to get us both through this is as natural to him as breathing. He returned from Vietnam determined to complete his residency in short order and then devote his practice to establishing a center for counseling veterans, especially those returning from 'Nam. Because of all that he had seen and experienced over there in the relative safety of a medical unit, Spence was eager to help his comrades in arms get through reentry into "the world."

"You're right. We'll go at this one step at a time," he says to me now, and I understand that he is talking more to himself than to me. "It's one spot, right? Caught early…"

I reach over and lay my hand on his knee. "I'm not worried about the tests," I tell him. "After all, it's nothing I haven't been through before."

He concentrates on the road ahead. I notice how his hands grip the steering wheel correctly, positioned at ten and two, the way he taught the kids to drive. "Last time," he begins, and his voice cracks. He clears his throat. "Last time we caught it early," he says.

"Hey," I say softly, moving my hand to the back of

his neck and rubbing it to ease some of the tenseness that is visible in the hunch of his shoulders. "It is what it is."

Spence

By the time we are finished at the hospital, Zoe is exhausted. I know that it's more than physical exhaustion from the battery of tests—a bone scan, MRI, CT scan and blood work. We're both emotionally drained.

"How about a little drive?" I suggest because going straight home means actually facing this news. "I'll handle dinner."

She cups her palm to my cheek and kisses me. "Good-looking and he cooks," she says. "How did I get so lucky?"

The wave of emotion that hits me is as tangible as someone kicking me in the gut. I pull her into a full hug so she doesn't see and I hang on—we both do.

"Okay, doctor's orders," I say in what Zoe has always referred to as my "overly hearty doctor voice." "Sit back and enjoy the scenery."

For once she does not protest. In a matter of minutes her breathing is deep and even. She has always been able to rejuvenate herself through what she calls power naps. After just fifteen or twenty minutes of deep sleep, she will suddenly sit up, fully refreshed and announce, "Power nap over," as she heads off to tackle whatever is next on her agenda.

I use the time she is sleeping to try to steady the hammering of my heart. After everything we've been through together, surely there's a way out of this horror, as well.

I drive below the speed limit and without destination, earning for myself the irritated honks and gestures of fellow drivers. By their furious glances and rolled eyes, they have labeled me as some old man, and I wonder how they might react if they knew the news we'd just been given.

"Power nap over," Zoe announces as she sits up straight and stretches. "Any chance of something to eat?"

"How about Thai?"

"Perfect. How about ice cream at the Union to top it off?"

"Liz was going to stop by the house," I remind her, hating myself for bringing us back to the one topic she'd obviously put aside for a moment.

She holds up her cell phone. "Marvelous little invention," she says, and grins. I bless her for not allowing me to spoil her upbeat mood.

While she calls Liz's office and leaves a message, I find a parking place near our favorite Thai restaurant.

"Remember that time," I begin as we walk arm in arm the half block to the entrance.

Zoe laughs, already picking up the story. "I decided to learn to cook healthy, and got a Thai cookbook and spent a fortune on a wok and a rice steamer and what I swore were authentic and necessary utensils."

We are laughing as we enter the restaurant. The hostess recognizes us by sight and smiles as she leads us to a booth.

"The usual?" the waiter asks.

Zoe giggles. "Oh, my, we *have* been coming here way too much if they know we have a 'usual.'"

"Fried rice chicken—no MSG—for the gentleman.

And shrimp—steamed, not fried—with vegetables for the lady," the waiter quotes.

"Plus two spring rolls," I add, and he disappears to fill the order. "As I recall, I had to make a run to the Asian market to pick up some spice that night."

Zoe's still laughing. "And then I burned the oil and the smoke alarm was going off when you got back and the rice stuck and—"

"You certainly gave new meaning to 'pot stickers.'"

We are laughing so hard that tears are twinkling on Zoe's cheeks when the waiter brings the food. He smiles and shakes his head, as do the few other diners around us. Little do they imagine...

Zoe

We linger over dinner long enough that we decide to postpone the ice cream until after we've met with Liz.

"We have ice cream at home," I say.

"Not the same. We'll come back later."

I laugh. "We are not going to drive all the way home and then all the way back here just for ice cream, Spencer Andersen. You were the one complaining about the price of gas this morning."

"We'll see."

When Liz arrives at our house, our friend and another of Spence's colleagues is with her. Dr. Jonathan Nelson is an oncologist specializing in lung cancer. He has a lousy poker face, never more evident than when I open the door, and he plants a quick kiss on my cheek without allowing his eyes to meet mine. Obviously the weight of his combined role as a doctor and our friend for the past thirty years makes it impossible for him to hide his feelings. Our children grew up together. Jon and his wife, Ginny, have traveled with us all over the country with and without kids. And almost five years ago, when I was originally diagnosed with breast cancer, Jon and Ginny were the first people Spence and I called.

As soon as he and Liz walk into the family room and take their places next to each other on one of the sofas paralleling the fireplace, I know that the news is worse than we had first thought. Spence and I sit down opposite them. Spence reaches over and holds my hand so tightly that I think my fingers might be permanently welded to his.

Jon fumbles with his glasses, clearing his throat and nervously fingering the file that holds the results of the tests I went through earlier. Amazingly, I feel no panic or fear, only irritation.

"Oh, for heaven's sake. Whatever it is, Jon, let's hear it and then figure out where we go from here," I snap. Spence eases the death grip he's had on my hand and begins stroking my palm with his thumb. "Sorry," I murmur to Jon.

Jon glances at Spence, and I do, as well. Spence is ashen and I realize that he's also read Jon's hesitation. When I see the expression on Spence's face, I start to shake, but my anxiety is all internal, as if my insides are about to explode, while externally I remain perfectly still, perfectly calm.

Jon takes me at my word, and because we're all familiar with medical jargon, he makes no attempt to explain the technicalities of what the various scans and tests have undeniably shown. I watch his lips move in what appear to be complete sentences, but hear only selected words.

"Distant recurrence…irreversible…CEA markers… metastatic…pharmacological options…"

"What about surgery?" Spence asks.

At this last I hear something I can latch on to. "You mean to remove the damaged parts of the lung?"

"In some rare cases that might be an option," Liz replies in that measured way I know doctors use when there's more to the story.

"But?"

"In those cases," Jon explains, "the metastasis is localized. In your case…" Jon glances down, sorting through data on the chart.

"It's spread throughout my lungs," I say, horrified as I guess the end of the story.

"No!" Liz almost shouts. "It's just that there's a second spot—tiny."

I turn my attention to Jon. "A few hours ago I was working in the garden, planning what to serve this weekend when you and Ginny came for dinner so we could talk about our trip to Vancouver." I pause, glancing at Spence. "Can we still go to Vancouver?"

"Of course," Jon and Spence chorus as Spence sits closer to me.

"Whatever you want," Spence promises.

"Be careful what you offer, farm boy." I touch my hand to his cheek. "We city girls can have some expensive tastes."

Spence has heard something in my tone—in the gentle teasing—that has finally offered some relief in the face of the oppressive and bleak news Jon has just delivered. "We'll be okay," I tell Spence as if he and I are suddenly the only two people in the room.

Spence focuses his attention on Jon and Liz. "So how do we fight this thing?"

Back on the firm ground of his expertise, Jon provides us with available medical interventions, not very promising and definitely no magic potion for a cure, but options that could prolong life nonetheless. A combination of medications that has shown some success in slowing the growth or even shrinking tumors. Chemo—

"No chemo," I say, and feel Spence seek Jon's help. "Look, if I have a finite time here, whether that's a year or a decade, I want every minute I can have to be spent living. Unless you can assure me that chemo will…"

Jon shakes his head. "Don't rule anything out, Zoe. There are pills now without a lot of the side effects you went through five years ago. Some patients demand to try everything," he says.

"Yes, let's consider everything. Let's read everything. Let's beat this thing," Spence says fiercely.

"I can bookmark some articles for you," Jon offers, getting up and going to our computer. While he brings up various resources online and adds them to our "favorites" file, I take notes.

"I can e-mail you some journal articles once I get back to the office tomorrow," Jon promises. Then he hesitates as if unsure of what he should do next. "I should let Ginny know I'm running late," he says, reaching for his cell phone. "Will you excuse me?"

"You can tell her," I say. "Just ask that she not tell anyone else for now. I'll call her tomorrow or the next day."

Once Jon returns from speaking with Ginny, Spence

and I walk Liz and Jon to the door. "Thanks, Jon," I say, and hug him as Spence holds Liz's coat for her. When I turn to Liz, we both have tears in our eyes and smiles on our faces.

"Well, kiddo," I say, "ready for round two?"

Wordlessly she hugs me, then Spence, and follows Jon down the front steps to where their cars are parked on the driveway.

Spence stands at the open door for a long moment, his back to me. I hear the slam of two car doors, and at first I assume that Spence is watching Jon and Liz drive away. Finally he steps back inside, and closes and locks the front door. He performs this routine task with such concentration and precision, checking his work when it's done. *Doors closing—one by one,* I think.

Spence looks at me and two large tears fall in unison onto his shirt.

I wrap my arms around him. "Hey, we can do this. This is not our first war, after all."

Spence draws in a long shuddering breath. "We'll need to call a family meeting, and you'll need to call your mom."

"Tomorrow. Tonight you promised me ice cream. Let's sit out on the Union Terrace together and think about how two people from polar ends of the spectrum found each other—and stuck...."

1967

Spencer

The first time I saw Zoe Wingfield she was standing on an orange metal café chair on the terrace of the Memorial Union, a bullhorn in one hand and a small placard decrying the war in Vietnam in the other. At the time I had no idea that she was the sister of a guy I'd gotten to know through the Reserve Officers' Training Corps, Ty Wingfield. So it wasn't recognition that made me stop that day and listen to her. It was the sheer magnetism of this compact dynamo surrounded by an impressively atten-tive—if small—audience. Zoe Wingfield was a presence, a force like a sudden and unexpected shift in the weather that would not be ignored.

I was finishing up my internship after completing med

school and I was on my way to the hospital and a double shift in the emergency room. Zoe was using the bullhorn to full advantage, as she exhorted every passerby, including me, to get involved in protesting the war in Southeast Asia, a war that she considered both unjust and illegal. Her East Coast accent was apparent. It was surprising me the number of students from New York and other points east who had decided that a university in the heartland of America was a good choice. The attraction varied—the exceptional curriculum or the reputation the university had as a liberal and progressive institution. Some even made no secret that the attraction was UW's reputation as a bona fide party school.

Since the woman with the bullhorn did not strike me as anything close to a party animal, I assumed that UW's initial appeal for her might well have been the academics. I wondered if the campus's perfect environment for rabble-rousing had figured into her decision from the start or was an unexpected bonus once she arrived. Either way, her intensity was a magnet, whether you agreed with her politics or not.

More students stopped to listen. Among them was a heckler, who taunted her with comments about her looks, her dress and what he assumed were her sexual preferences. She handled his taunts by pointing the bullhorn directly at him and continuing her harangue against the government, the war and those who, according to her, were getting rich off the war.

It was October, and she wore jeans and a thick cable turtleneck the color of split pea soup. Her hair was suede brown and thick—a fact not at all enhanced by how she'd styled it in fat braids wound round her head like skeins of bulky yarn. Although she was not more than five two, in spite of the stacked heel of her laced boots, and weighed not much more than a hundred pounds, she had the aura of a much larger person.

"Get laid," the heckler shouted, and others who had paused to listen snickered. Some of them took this as their cue to move on.

"Get smart," she fired back. "What's your draft number, frat boy? Think you can't be sent? Think you're safe? Think again."

The heckler threw her the finger as he sauntered past her and joined his friends at a distant table.

When I saw Zoe home in on me, I chickened out and took off. I stopped at my apartment building, where I lived in a basement studio and did maintenance chores to offset some of my rent. The mail was in, and as I had hoped, there was a letter from Ty in the batch. After Ty and I met in ROTC, my deferment to finish medical school had been approved, while Ty had received his orders to ship out. Six weeks had passed with no news. I tore open the envelope and read as I walked:

Andersen,

I made it. I'll spare you the details of the trip over—you'll have the pleasure of that soon enough, Dr. Deferment.

First impressions? Chopper ride into base was all rattle-your-bones vibrations and eau-de-kerosene. Hot air and fine powdery dust blasting our faces because door has to be open so gunner can sit there at the ready. Charming. On the ground things go from thick jungle foliage to a kind of beige landscape where everything's been cleared away with napalm to expose the enemy and keep him from establishing positions in the jungle. On the road into base camp, we were always dodging craters left by bombs and mortars. Then we'd round a curve and there would be a burned-out farm or even an entire village blown to kingdom come. In the distance the drumbeat of artillery fire is constant, as is the whup-whup-whup of helicopters.

Hey, Doc, what's the nutritional value of dirt? You are not going to believe this, but I would happily eat campus food for the rest of my life over the stuff they serve here. Dirt permeates everything—food (even pudding) crunches.

Almost forgot to tell you. My sister, Zoe—the rebel—is there on campus. She got into law school. Could have been at Harvard, but she likes the "political" climate better at UW. Look her up. The two of you could be an interesting pair. I'd love to be a fly on the wall for that meeting!!

Well, Uncle Sam calleth. Later. Ty

It was the one letter I got from Ty. Several weeks after I received that single letter from him, Zoe and I finally met. I had meant to call her as Ty had suggested, if for no other reason than to have some story to tell him in my next letter. But the days had flown by, and between my duties as an intern and the extra shifts I took to cover my bills, I hadn't found the time. Then I'd gotten word that he was KIA— killed in action—trying to rescue a Vietnamese woman and her children from their burning village. After my duty at the hospital, I tried to find Zoe—to introduce myself and offer my sympathy. But when I called the number I'd been able to get, I was told that she'd already left for New York and the funeral.

So the setting for the introduction that Ty had imagined taking place on campus was the spacious and elegant Upper East Side penthouse apartment that her parents, Mike and Kay Wingfield, owned in Manhattan. The occasion was the gathering of friends and family following Ty's funeral, and so in some ways he was there to see the meeting—at least in spirit.

Earlier at the cemetery, while keeping a respectful distance from the open grave and watching as family members and friends tossed flowers onto the top of the rosewood casket, I couldn't help remembering Ty's laugh the day we parted.

"Big mistake, man, accepting that deferment," he'd said. "I'll be back home and you'll just be getting there."

"Maybe it'll all be over," I countered.

Ty's perennially boyish features had sobered. "Not going to happen—not that fast. Things are gonna get a lot worse before we can make them better. Zoe's got that part right."

His elder sister's name had been a regular topic in our conversations. Ty idolized her, even if he felt her view of the war out of synch with his own sense of patriotic duty.

On that blustery late-November afternoon I stood off to the side in a cemetery where gravestones soared like monuments to the rich and famous who were buried there. All the mourners had their coat collars pulled close around their throats. Then a woman stepped up to the edge of the open grave, a white rose in one hand. Even though her hair was down and she was dressed like every other woman in heels and a black cloth coat that was at least a size too large for her, I recognized her as the girl with the bullhorn on the steps of the union. I realized that this must be Ty's sister—this was Zoe Wingfield.

The wind whipped her hair—loose and striped with the waves of days spent in braids, it fell almost to her waist. With her free hand she fought to contain it and keep it from becoming entangled with the frames of her small round wire-rimmed glasses. She paused for a long moment at the grave, staring down at the cold pewter gray of the steel lid of Ty's casket. Then she tore the rose petals free of the stem and scattered them as she walked slowly around the perimeter of the open grave. Her father shuddered and let out an audible sob and her mother wrapped her arms around him, but Zoe's eyes were dry.

I had felt compelled to attend the funeral, if for no other reason than to serve as a representative of that part of his life that Ty had devoted to ROTC and serving his country. Most of the rest of our group had already shipped out to 'Nam, so I was pretty much it. But it didn't take long before I realized that no one gathered around Ty's grave much cared who I was or why I was there. I could have just as easily sent a card or flowers.

I couldn't have said why I decided to go to the gathering at the house. I certainly hadn't planned on it. Following the service at the graveside, I had made my way to the entrance of the cemetery and was figuring out the best way to get to the bus depot for the overnight trip back to Wisconsin. Then a car stopped and the man I recognized as the minister rolled down his window.

"Need a ride, son?"

"Thanks," I said, and got in, happy to be out of the cold. "I'm catching a bus back to Wisconsin at nine," I explained. "So, anywhere in the city that's convenient, sir."

"You're not going for the wake?" he asked after we'd formalized the introductions.

"I just came for Ty," I said. "I never had the opportunity to meet his family. I don't want to intrude."

"Spencer, here's what I've learned about things like this. What matters here is that you knew the Wingfields' son. They are trying to deal with the fact that he's gone, and frankly, anyone who can give them another little piece of him would be welcomed today. Your choice."

His logic made a lot of sense, so I agreed to go with him to the wake. After parking in his reserved space at his church, the minister and I walked the four long blocks to the stately building where the Wingfields lived.

The air inside the spacious apartment was close with expensive perfume, cigarette smoke and too many people, even for such a large space. The expansive rooms were jammed with family members, friends and business associates of Ty's parents, and younger people I assumed to be Ty's friends from childhood and the private schools I knew he'd attended. It was apparent that this was a close-knit community of people who had some connection not only to Ty but to the rest of the family, as well. The minister was pulled aside to console Ty's father the minute we walked through the door, leaving me to fend for myself. Once again the feeling that I shouldn't have come washed over me. I considered making a quick exit, but the door opened and a group of people pressed forward, forcing me farther into the room. I decided the least I could do was take the minister's advice and share a memory with Ty's parents that might offer them some tiny measure of comfort.

Bits of conversation floated above the general funereal hum as I moved around the room, trying to think of something meaningful and comforting. The comment I heard repeated most often was "What a waste!" In second place was "He had his whole life in front of him."

Not really. He had lived his whole life. It ended in a jungle in a country he'd never seen before at the hands of a people he knew next to nothing about as he fought a war that did not follow traditional rules of encounter. In that moment in a jungle made eerily naked by the tons of Agent Orange dropped from the skies, Ty had faced death. That moment and the nineteen years up to it constituted a life—Ty's life.

I spotted a photo of Zoe and Ty in their early teens. They were on a beach. He was taller. She was older, and in spite of the height difference, she looked it. I remembered him reading me parts of the letters she sent him in the days before he left college for basic training. Letters that used a kind of code urging him to defect to Toronto, where he would live with his Aunt Vivian and Uncle Harry. Her code for Toronto was Toledo.

Auntie Viv and Uncle Harry send regards from Toledo, she wrote. *They've just finished the papering and the new furnishings are all ready to move into the new space.*

"Papering means she's got fake ID for me," Ty explained.

"And furnishings?"

Ty shrugged. "Total makeover probably—change the hair color, contacts, that sort of thing. She's mentioned that I might look good in a beard."

"Are your aunt and uncle really on board with this?" I asked.

Ty laughed and shook his head. "Man, I keep forgetting just how green you are, having lived your whole life out here in the hinterlands. There is no Aunt Viv. Vivian is a friend of Zoe's. They met at some civil rights rally and found they shared similar politics related to the war. I assume Vivian is setting up the underground that will spirit me over the border."

"So no Harry, either?" On some level I was disappointed. Harry sounded like a good guy.

"Harry is the family dog—Zoe's dog, really." He grinned and shook his head. "That mutt goes ape if Zoe just walks in the room."

Ty was right. We were definitely from different worlds. For me it was a farmhouse in the middle of Wisconsin twelve miles from the nearest town. And for Ty it was this penthouse across the street from Central Park—the penthouse where I stood uncomfortably in the background, wondering what had possessed me to come here. Oriental rugs, any one of which might be worth enough to buy my family's farm, softened the shine on the highly polished original planked floors. Then there were the antique furnishings—the kinds of pieces that would make my aunt Rose hyperventilate—and the priceless paintings, each illuminated with its own little lamp. Interesting paintings, very contemporary but perfectly at home in the company of the priceless antiques.

"Thank you for being here."

I turned from my survey of a painting to face Ty's mother, Kay Wingfield, standing next to me. She was tall and slender, with white-blond hair that skimmed her shoulders and a deep tan that one day she might regret. The same clear gray eyes Ty had had met mine. She extended long, perfectly manicured fingers and offered a smile that took some effort to produce.

"Forgive me, but your name…"

"I'm Spencer Andersen, Mrs. Wingfield. Ty and I were friends at UW."

"Ah, yes. The doctor."

"Mrs. Wingfield, I am so very sorry for your loss. Ty was—"

She cut me off with a nod, a waver of the smile and a slight pressure on my fingers. "So good of you to come," she said in a voice made raspy by ceaseless crying, and focused her attention on a gathering of mourners behind her. It was as if she saw her role as one of consoling others rather than the other way round. Manners and breeding, my mom would have said with admiration.

I edged toward the foyer, a good fifty feet and two large people-filled rooms away, acknowledging other mourners. Some of them looked at me—and any young man in the room below the age of thirty—with the clear understanding that it could have been me who'd been killed—it might yet be me.

"Why did you come?"

Without the bullhorn, which had seemed like a permanent extension of her arm during that rally on campus, Zoe's voice was soft and husky. I leaned closer. She did not retreat. "More to the point, why didn't you talk him out of going?" she added, stabbing one nail-bitten finger at my chest. "He respected you. He would have listened to you."

I put down the framed family photo I'd paused to study until I could slide past a group of guests blocking my escape. It was another of Ty and Zoe. The rooms were filled with these images from the family's past. In this one Ty was in full dress uniform and Zoe was standing next to him, but staring off-camera. He was smiling; she was not.

I saw Kay Wingfield watching us and surmised that she had sent her daughter over. I offered Zoe an introduction and my hand. She ignored both and gave me a mock salute, instead. "I know who you are. Answer the question." Her features were drawn tight from exhaustion and her eyes were swollen and red, but she was not crying now.

"I came because your brother was my friend," I said. "You see, Ty was—"

She raised herself to her full height, which put the top of her head just level with my chin until she tipped her head back and fixed me with a glare. "Don't you ever presume to tell me who my brother was," she said in a voice that was barely above a whisper but that sounded as loud as a scream. She turned and would have stalked off but that same gaggle of people was still blocking the way.

"Too bad," I said quietly. "Because my friend and your brother are the same man, and we'd both be a lot richer if we could share what we remember of him."

The twitch of one shoulder in contrast to the total stillness of the rest of her was her only response before she excused herself and made a path through the group. I saw her head for the foyer, grab a brown corduroy men's jacket from the closet next to the entrance and leave.

Mrs. Wingfield and I seemed to be the only ones who noticed. Zoe's mother sighed and focused on her guests, while I—for reasons I thought had something to do with my loyalty to Ty—decided to go after Zoe.

The elevator doors slid shut just as I reached the hall. A second later a service door at the end of the hall opened. First to emerge was a furry wheat-colored dog the size of a cocker spaniel. He was straining at a long bright-red leash. Attached to the other end was a short rotund woman swathed in a heavy wool coat, mittens and a faded striped scarf wound at least three times around her neck, chin and mouth.

She smiled at me as we both waited for the elevator to

return. The dog sniffed my shoes and pant leg, then plopped into a sitting position and gave me his full attention.

"Harry?" I said, and the dog's tail beat out a response on the tiled floor.

The service door opened again, emitting the chaotic sounds of a kitchen in full battle mode as a tall heavyset woman with very flushed cheeks and the voice of a drill sergeant shouted, "Mariska!"

Both the woman by the elevator and the dog shuddered.

"What do you think you're doing?" the drill sergeant bellowed.

"The dog needs his walk," Mariska replied in a soft accented voice.

"I can't spare you now. The dog can wait. We're running low on glasses and coffee cups. I need you in here." Half a beat. "Now!"

Just then the elevator arrived. I stepped in front of the doors to keep them from closing and said, "I could take him out. I'm a—I was a—I'm a friend of the family."

"Mariska!" the voice boomed through the half-open door.

Mariska thrust the leash at me and hurried back down the hall, shrugging out of her scarf, mittens and coat as she went.

Outside I tugged at the leash and headed down the block. Then Harry pulled a sit-down strike. I remembered Ty describing Harry as being just like Zoe. "Stubborn, smart and just petite and cute enough to get away with it." After my brief encounter with Zoe upstairs, I'd have to think about that one—especially the "cute enough to get away with it" part. She was definitely cute, more than cute really. She was downright intriguing.

"Come on, boy." I tugged at the leash.

"Don't yell at my dog."

Zoe crammed the glowing stub of a cigarette into a sand-filled urn. "What are you doing with Harry, anyway?" She grabbed the leash from my hand. Harry snapped to attention, tail wagging furiously. I—having pretty much had my fill of trying to do the right thing and being treated like a mass murderer—remained silent.

"Well?" she demanded, and I wondered if Ty had ever found her subliminal anger as tiresome as I was finding it now.

I took a deep breath to steady my voice. "I was kidnapping him with the idea of holding him for ransom until someone up there acknowledged that perhaps Ty never thought of his service or his death as a waste. Just maybe he considered doing his duty a real honor, a real part of being an American. He was my friend and I am pretty damn sure that he would have hated it that the sister he loved for everything she was isn't willing to accept that just like her, he knew exactly what he was doing. Just like her, he chose this path."

"And it got him killed," she argued.

"Life happens, lady." I felt bad about that last crack, but I doubted if apologizing would do any good. I started toward the corner, my hand already half raised to hail a cab. Three of them passed with no results.

"Pretty tough to get an off-duty cab to stop," she called as I continued to try to wave down yet another of the yellow machines hurtling by.

I glanced back. She and Harry had followed me from the entrance. She was leaning against the corner of the building, one high heel resting on the toe of the other. Harry sat next to her, waiting to do her bidding.

"Are you laughing at me?" I asked, taking a step toward her.

"Why not? Ty would be." She pushed herself away from the wall and held out the leash—a peace offering or at least a cease-fire. "Take it," she urged, and I accepted the leash. Harry glanced skeptically at Zoe and then trotted along at my side as if we'd done this a thousand times.

We walked for well over an hour. I discovered that, if you knew where to go, Central Park at night was not the war zone I'd been led to believe it was. I discovered that Zoe indeed had a sense of humor. And I discovered, although I didn't realize it until much later, that I was starting on a journey that would last a lifetime and give me the kind of wild joyous ride I'd only read about in books.

1968

Zoe

I took the rest of the semester off after Ty's funeral. Dad was a wreck and Mom was barely holding it together, and frankly, it helped to hole up in the home of my youth and wallow in my grief for a while. By the time I returned to campus, my fury over the war that had killed my brother had exploded, and the only thing I focused on was stopping this madness any way I could. But I kept remembering Spence and that night in the park. His calm assurance that there was another side to a story I could see only one way had rattled me. Nothing I said that night had changed his mind in the least and for me that was a personal defeat. After he got into that cab, I had thought of any number of points I hadn't made—points I was certain would be powerful enough to change his mind.

Still, it seemed pretty moot to even consider pursuing a conversation we had begun two months earlier. I spotted him once, and even at a distance of several yards, I recognized his easy, confident stride, his upright carriage and wheat-gold crew-cut head. In spite of the bitter January winds that bent the rest of us into hunch-backed, stocking-capped robots hurrying to make our next class, he wore no hat. He saw me and lifted one gloved hand. I answered with the mock salute I'd given him that night in New York. I was pretty sure that he was smiling as we headed in opposite directions—a paradox that did not escape me.

Then late one afternoon, worn down by studies, the weather, the whining of my housemates, I sought refuge in the Rathskeller. As I had expected, it was virtually deserted and its cavernlike shadowy recesses suited my mood. I dropped my books haphazardly onto a table and positioned the chair so that I was behind one of the low-arched columns that supported the room.

He walked in, glanced around, didn't see me and chose a table in the opposite corner of the room. After setting his books on the table in an orderly stack, he removed his coat and scarf and hung them with great care on a chair near the heat register, then headed for the counter. I heard the rumble of his voice as he ordered, before I tried to force my attention back to my notes. But I couldn't seem to stop eyeing that table, that coat, that empty chair across from where he'd placed that precisely aligned stack of books. With a sigh, I got up and crossed the room.

"Hi," I said. He raised his eyebrows, but otherwise gave no sign of surprise to see me there. "I thought of a couple of points I didn't make back in Central Park. You got a minute?"

Spence

Hard to say if it was the times, the tension of the unknown future or the fact that we were two people wildly attracted to each other because our contrasting backgrounds and approaches to life were so extraordinary and fascinating, but by the time we left the Union late that frigid night, neither Zoe nor I was thinking about our philosophical differences.

In spite of my own niggling doubts about what the engagement in Southeast Asia had morphed into, Zoe and I had reached an impasse. While she continued to lay out her best case against the war, I remained steadfast in my belief that love of country included doing one's duty when your country demanded it. Zoe argued—convincingly—that it was precisely because she loved America that she was protesting the involvement in Vietnam. "Why isn't it just as patriotic that I want to keep our soldiers from having to go as it is for them to 'die with honor'?"

"Serving to defend freedom is one of the responsibilities we have as Americans," I said. "Freedom really does come at a cost, you know—and a high one."

"Of course it does," she agreed, resting her chin on the palm of one hand and blinking up at me. I wasn't fooled. I saw this for what it was—a break to permit her to reload. "On the other hand, doesn't it make at least as much sense to believe that one of the duties of a free people is to be very sure that the battle cry is valid?"

"What makes you so sure this one isn't?"

She raised her eyebrows. "What makes you so sure that it is?"

I was out of my league trying to match wits with her knowledge of history and political philosophies. Zoe had graduated summa cum laude from Columbia, with dual undergrad degrees in political science and world history. "My country, right or wrong," I quipped.

"You can't believe that," she protested, and launched into a fresh harangue about past wars and people standing on the sidelines.

Finally I clasped the hand she waved to make a point and held it, tracing my finger across her palm. It was the first time I had actually touched her and the moment silenced us both. It was a little past eleven and I was exhausted just thinking about the on-call duty I faced starting the next evening. I asked Zoe if I could walk her back to her dorm.

"I'm not some freshman. I live off-campus," she said as she gently dislodged her hand from mine.

"Not an answer," I replied.

She shrugged. "Okay. Walk me home, farm boy."

She gathered her things from the table across the room while I did the same, although it took her several minutes longer. Books and papers were scattered across the table, and more books and notebooks had toppled to the floor. She crammed everything into a huge, sturdy, basketlike shoulder bag and plopped it on the table while she wrapped a long black-and-white plaid scarf around her head, throwing the ends over her shoulders. I reached for her jacket—the same brown corduroy she'd worn that night for our walk in Central Park.

"You could use a warmer coat," I said, holding it for her.

"I like this one." She zipped it shut and her eyes met mine. "It was Ty's favorite jacket whenever he came home."

We remained silent as we left the Union and walked up State Street. I can't say for Zoe, but there was only one thing on my mind—somewhere in the seconds after I grabbed her hand I had made a decision. I was going to kiss her. The only question was when and where.

"Are you mad about something?" she asked after we'd trudged along through the icy muck of three weeks of snow for several minutes without speaking.

"Just cold." I hoped that would explain my hunched shoulders and the gloveless hands clenched into fists to keep them from grabbing her right there on the street. "How much farther?"

She stopped. "Look," she said, "this walking-me-home thing was your idea. I appreciate the gallantry, even though that sort of thing isn't usually all that appealing to me. If you've changed your mind, take off. Nobody's forcing—"

And that was the moment. I kissed her as much to shut her up as to satisfy my own fantasy. But then she kissed me back. Zoe was, is and will always be a world-class kisser. In less than ten seconds I was a goner.

"Come on," she said, tugging at my sleeve and grinning as she headed down a side street at a near run. "Well?" she called when I hesitated.

I didn't have to be invited twice. I fell into step with her, and with little traffic, we jogged down the middle of the street, our footsteps muffled by the unplowed snow, and our laughter rising on the clear night air. I had no idea what time it was. I barely knew what day it was. What I did know beyond any doubt was that the world as I had viewed it before kissing Zoe Wingfield had shifted on its axis.

Zoe shared a small house on Mifflin Street with four other postgrad students. Judging by the placards and piles of wooden sticks ready for placards piled haphazardly on the tiny front porch, it also served as headquarters for the group's antiwar campaign. She was still giggling as she stumbled up the icy steps to the front door. This unexpected girlish side of her personality was incredibly arousing, and I kissed her again there on the porch.

"I thought you were freezing," she murmured against my neck as we clung to each other.

"Not anymore," I said, and pressed her against the wall of the house as I kissed her a third time. In that instant I was certain I would never be able to get enough of her—whatever might happen in our future. "What about your housemates?" I asked after coming up for air.

She tugged at my coat, pulling me closer. "Just how far do you want this to go, farm boy?"

I leaned back just enough to see her face in the dull light spilling out from inside the front hallway. "That's for you to decide," I replied, and backed away half a step. I saw her consider and then decide in my favor. I grinned and reached for her again.

"Not here," she whispered, dodging my kiss as she led the way into a foyer that smelled of recently cooked onions and curry. As soon as we stepped inside, a blast of warm air hit us, along with a chorus of male and female voices from the living room off the hallway. "Shut the damn door!"

She slammed the door and, without acknowledging the two guys and one woman sitting on broken-down furniture in the living room, led me up the narrow stairway. On our way to the end of the hall, we passed one open door and one unseen room, where the protest music of Phil Ochs blared. Finally we arrived at a door that revealed a steep narrow stairway to her room in the attic. At the top of the stairs, she shrugged out of her coat, kicked off her boots and waited. The next move was mine.

I glanced around, getting my bearings—a double

mattress on the floor, covered in a batik fabric and multi-colored pillows; an overturned orange crate with small table lamp serving as a nightstand. A rocking chair in the alcove next to the dormer windows and bookcases filled to overflowing, forming temporary walls under the eaves of the sloped ceiling. I took off my pea jacket, folded it and laid it on the rocking chair.

Zoe lit a candle on the nightstand, then sat cross-legged on the mattress, facing me and the rocking chair. The position she took gave us a choice—it was casual without being provocative. There was still time to reconsider. If I took the chair, we would talk some more and then I would go. I hesitated.

"The idea of a coed house bothers you, right, farm boy?"

"Just caught me off guard," I said, lying through my teeth. Ty had always teased me about catching up with the times.

"It's the sixties, man," he'd say. "You know—free love as in freedom to love?"

I wondered if he'd ever talked about my old-fashioned ideals with Zoe.

"I don't sleep with them, Spence."

"Okay."

"I just don't want you to think that this—" she waved her hand back and forth between us "—that if we… It's not just routine for me, you know."

I knelt on the floor next to her and removed the pins from her hair, smoothing it over her shoulders and the outline of her breasts beneath the bulk of her sweater. She cupped my face between her hands. I closed my eyes and she kissed my eyelids. It was as if we were each taking one last moment before diving into the deep waters of an affair that neither of us was sure was a good idea.

"No strings," she whispered, running her tongue over the rim of my ear.

I pulled her around for a kiss, but she held me off, her eyes probing mine. "No strings, okay?"

I had assumed her statement was a promise she was making not to expect more of me than I could offer when it came to commitment. But in her dark eyes, I understood that we weren't talking about no strings for her. She was asking me to agree that I had no ties on her, either.

"Deal," I managed to get out before dragging her back to me. I hoped I hadn't just lied for the second time in the last ten minutes.

For the rest of that night our only communication was a touch, a look, a smile and the more than occasional moan of pure ecstasy. Permission and acceptance found voice through our hands and mouths and eyes. We were neither of us innocents, but we took turns leading as we stumbled through the steps of the dance that would be uniquely ours forever.

In the weeks that followed we made love every night and fell into a routine of going about our separate lives during the day. She had law-school classes and her protest meetings, while I divided my hours between rounds at the hospital and the maintenance duty I had signed on for to help cover my rent. She dashed off papers and other assignments almost absentmindedly, while I spent hours going over and over patient notes and preparing for the complex diagnostic and treatment option questions the senior resident would throw at me on rounds.

We spent our nights in Zoe's attic room mostly because my basement studio was dark, dank and frankly depressing. If I saw her housemates at all, it was to nod in passing or mutter a polite "How's it going?" After several weeks of this, I arrived at the house early one evening in late April before Zoe had returned. I had rescued some early-blooming spring flowers from discards at the university greenhouses and was anxious to get them in water before Zoe arrived.

I had tagged Zoe's housemate Peter Quarles as the leader of the revolution shortly after meeting him for the first time the morning after Zoe and I spent that first night together. He had obviously tagged me as an intruder, since he rarely acknowledged my existence. On this evening he was sitting in the cramped living room shared by all the residents of the house, and on very rare occasions by me. His long legs were thrown over the arm of the thrift-shop sofa I had helped Zoe haul home a week earlier. Peter was a grad student in international studies, although when he went to class or did anything other than prepare for the next protest or campus rally was a mystery to me. Every time I entered the house, he was there, usually holding court in the living room as two or three new recruits to the cause sat enthralled, hanging on his every word.

Like Zoe, Peter exuded a kind of intense fervor that could not be ignored. Zoe's was tempered by her natural sense of humor and innate charisma. Peter's was constantly on full-beam passion for the cause. The only person capable of breaking through his messianic demeanor was Zoe. And it was pretty obvious to everyone—except perhaps Zoe—that he was madly in love with her.

Three of Zoe's other housemates—a music major named Sara, who lived in a dining room turned bedroom on the first floor, and one of the two guys I'd seen that first night—had accepted my presence in the house as a normal thing. Peter had made it clear by his silence and his habit of always seeming to be around on the mornings after I'd stayed over that he did not.

Zoe assured me that the problem was that Peter didn't trust me—yet. "He'll come around," she said.

I didn't think so.

Now I felt him studying me, noticing the flowers.

I nodded and headed for the attic.

"Andersen?" he said as I started up the stairs.

I reversed my route and entered the living room. The couch was far too short for Peter's lanky frame and yet he occupied it with the same authority he brought to everything he did. Just by his presence Peter had a way of filling up a room, making anyone else the interloper.

He continued to study me. It was a little like being under the scrutiny of somebody's father. I half expected the man to quiz me on my intentions, but I understood that Peter's interest in Zoe was anything but paternal—or even fraternal. Zoe thought that it was really sweet that I was actually jealous but assured me that her relationship with Peter was of the "just friends" variety. Maybe for Zoe. Definitely not for Peter.

"Zoe tells us you're pro-war."

This was hardly news. I'd been staying at the house for weeks by that time. I had to assume that my background had been thoroughly scrutinized long before now. I decided to play along until I could figure out where this conversation was really going.

"Is that the way she said it?" I asked calmly.

Peter pushed himself to a half-sitting position. I accepted that as a sign of semirespect that I hadn't caved or gone ballistic as he might have anticipated. "It's just that—in this house—well, all I'm saying is—"

"Look, Quarles," I said, sitting on the arm of a thread-bare wingback chair across from him, "if you guys are plotting the overthrow of the government, I couldn't care less. I came here to be with Zoe, nothing else."

"It's just awkward, man."

"Why? Because I represent another side of this debate?" I took a deliberate breath, then added, "Or is it because I'm with Zoe?"

To his credit, he didn't play coy. "Can't it be both?" He stood up. So did I. We locked eyes.

"You're in love with her?"

He blinked.

"Thought so," I said, and left the room.

That was also the night when Zoe came back from a rally where she'd learned that troop buildup was escalating beyond predictions and showing no signs of slowing down. She had barely cleared the top step before she began lobbing statistics at me. Her eyes glowed with the zeal of her newfound evidence in her case for getting me to defect.

"Zoe, it's a moot point—at least where I'm concerned. I made a deal. I have to go, so there's no sense debating it." The truth was that I was tired of debating it with her. These philosophical arguments seemed to energize her, but they simply drained me.

"You give up too easily," she said as she plopped onto the middle of the bed and sorted through the contents of another of her collection of large, colorful satchels—a cloth one she'd declared her "spring" bag. "Just be open-minded about this." She passed me a flat, unmarked manila envelope.

I opened it. Inside were documents—driver's license, birth certificate, the works. The description of the person fit me—at least, height, weight, eye and hair color. I was well aware of where she was going with this and wanted no part of it. I tossed them back onto the bed. "I'm not going to desert, Zoe," I said quietly.

"It's not deserting if the war is proven to be illegal. And it will be. You have to think past now, Spence."

We did not speak for several minutes. It wasn't like her not to hammer away at me, so finally I looked up. She was sitting with her back against the makeshift headboard—a painting she'd done directly on the wall. Her knees were drawn up to her chest and she had her arms wrapped around them. Her chin rested on her knees and her eyes glittered with the fire of her fury. "Why can't you understand that this is personal for me?" she said, releasing her grip on her knees and raising both fists to the ceiling in utter frustration.

I joined her on the bed as I caught her hands and stilled them. Then I gently stroked her cheek with my thumb. "I get it," I said.

"No, you don't. You think this is about Ty, and maybe in a small way it is, but it's also—"

"Zoe, don't do this," I said, hugging her. "Let's not spoil the time we have."

She pushed me away and scrambled off the bed. "Why can't you be reasonable?"

"Why can't you?" I shouted back, surprised at my loss of temper.

She continued to stalk around the room, while I lay back on the bed.

"I thought you were starting to love me," she said, her back to me and her voice unusually quiet.

"I am—I do—but loving another person doesn't mean giving up everything you believe in. I wouldn't—I don't ask that of you," I argued, and felt a tingle of pride at making what I considered to be a really strong point.

"I'm not the one who seems determined to go off where I can get myself killed," she said, her voice now so low I had to strain to hear the words.

"That's not fair and you know it," I replied.

She stood for several minutes, staring out the window into the black night. I longed to take her in my arms. I wanted to assure her that this would all turn out fine. I wanted to tell her—no, show her—how much I loved her. I stayed where I was and waited, fingering the bracelet in my pocket—the one she had admired at a craft fair the weekend before. The one I had bought to give her when I told her I loved her.

"Zoe?"

"You know something? You should just go, okay?" she said, her voice flat—dead. "It's been fun, and after all, that's what we agreed to, right? We're just kidding ourselves with the idea we can ever be on the same page. So let's just end it here—quick and clean, the way it started." She delivered this little speech without moving or turning to face me.

"'Same page'? 'It'?" Was that all I had meant to her? Had what we had shared been reduced to such an inanimate, impersonal void? "It?" I repeated savagely, trying hard to get a rise out of her, wanting the fight now because I knew it was the only way back from this brink.

I got up but took my time putting on my jacket, gathering some things I'd left there in the weeks we'd been together and throwing them into the small duffel I carried between my place and hers. I kept walking past her more than was necessary. She remained silent, not moving a muscle, her arms wrapped around herself.

"Zoe," I said when I'd run out of things to do to keep me there. Her name was a plea on my lips.

She didn't answer, didn't move.

I removed a single daffodil from the bouquet she hadn't even noticed, laid it with the bracelet on her pillow and left.

Peter stepped out of his room just as I rounded the corner and headed for the stairs to the main floor. He glanced at me and then to the attic. He smiled as I passed. *You can have her,* I thought bitterly, even as I recognized the childish annoyance in that thought. I slammed the front door loud enough to rattle the ill-fitting glass and send a final message to that attic room. If she was still standing at the window, I never found out. I was damned if I was going to give her the satisfaction of looking back.

Weeks passed. I buried myself in work and stayed away from anywhere I was likely to run into Zoe. Finally the day came for me to leave for 'Nam, with a stop at Fort Sam Houston, in Texas. The bus station was busier than I'd ever seen it and I was far from the only guy in uniform. Mom and Dad had worn their Sunday best to see me off on a Tuesday. Dad was pacing and smoking, glancing out the station window repeatedly, watching for my bus to arrive at the station. Mom talked nonstop, a nervous chatter filled with homilies about eating properly and writing regularly and such. Her normally calm, measured speech was high-pitched and nearing hysteria. Her fingers clenched and unclenched the handle of her purse as if wringing out a dishcloth.

In spite of myself I kept one eye on the door. I could think of nothing but Zoe. Earlier I had stopped by the house to leave a letter for her with Sara. Had Sara delivered it? Had Zoe read it? As the days dwindled to nothing, I realized that I didn't want to leave things between us unresolved. In the letter I'd asked her to come to the station and see me off. Would she?

Everything happened at once. The bus pulled in and there was a surge of humanity toward the door. Families waiting to welcome incoming passengers. Families moving together to board the bus. Military families like mine, trying to hold it together for another ten minutes while the driver tossed duffels into the baggage bins under the bus.

Mom touched my cheek, her eyes brimming with tears. Dad crushed out his cigarette with the toe of his brown wing tip. And Zoe ran through the station and out the side door to the platform, peering left and right, a bouquet of daisies clutched in one hand. When she spotted me, she straightened her shoulders and strode toward me. She wasn't smiling.

"Excuse me a minute," I said to my parents, and made my way through the crowd to her.

We met and waited for the other to speak, then spoke in unison.

"Those for me?"

"Hey, farm boy, I just…"

I grinned, forgiving her everything because she had come. She glanced over my shoulder. "Well, do I finally get to meet the folks?"

Taking her hand, I led her back to where Mom and Dad waited. Mom was smiling—a genuine smile that seemed to say everything would be all right now. "Zoe Wingfield, my mother, Marie Andersen."

"Hello, Mrs. Andersen," Zoe said shyly.

"It's Marie, Zoe, and it's wonderful to meet you." She gave Zoe an awkward hug and released her. "We've heard so much about you."

"And my dad, Hal," I said.

Dad looked Zoe over. "So you're the revolutionary," he said, holding her hand between both of his.

Zoe, for once in her life, was speechless.

"Gotcha," Dad said and chuckled. He put his arm around Mom. "Let's give these two a minute alone, Marie."

Alone was a relative term in the throng on the platform, but I took a step closer to Zoe and she closed the gap a step farther, until we were standing so all we could see was each other.

"You're really going," she said. It wasn't a question.

I rejected any number of snappy retorts including "Duty calls," and settled for resting my forehead against hers.

"It's not too late," she muttered, clutching the lapels of my uniform. "You could stay and…"

"Or you could let me go," I said, lifting her chin so that her eyes met mine.

She shook her head vehemently. "Why are you so stubborn about something that might save your life, that might at the very least keep you safe, that might—" She drew in a deep, shuddering breath, swallowed hard and looked away. "That might be our chance."

I wrapped her in my arms. "Let me go, Zoe. When I get back, then—"

"What if you—"

I shushed her with a finger to her lips. "You should think about seeing others," I said. "Peter's in love with you and—"

She stopped me in midsentence. Her eyes flashed with tears and anger. "You don't get to decide that," she said, her voice cracking. "I thought that asking me to come here meant… Well, hey, if you really want out of this thing we have—had—don't let me stand in the way." Her voice was low and raspy.

I lowered my voice, as well, in spite of wanting to shout at her and shake some sense into her. "It's not like that and you know it. You're the one…."

"Really? How is it then?"

I took her shoulders and forced her to look at me. "Of course I want you to wait, but I won't ask that of you. It's selfish of me and unfair to you, and frankly, it would be worse to have it end while I'm over there."

"Well, obviously I don't get a say in this," she said, and focused on her shoes, her body stiff under my grasp.

The bus driver sounded the last call for boarding. Mom and Dad were still watching us. Mom frowned and said something to Dad, who nodded. "I have to go," I told Zoe, meaning I owed it to Mom and Dad to get back to them. "I'm offering you an out, Zoe. Think about the fact that once I do this and come back—if I come back—neither one of us will be the same person we are today."

I kissed her hard and then walked over to where my parents waited. Dad started to shake my hand, then grasped me into a bear hug before pushing me in the direction of Mom and turning away.

Mom stood on tiptoe and put her hands on my cheeks. "We love you. Call as soon as you get to San Antonio for training, okay?" She smiled and let me go, and I understood that she had given me the gift of making this aberration normal. It was what she always said whenever one of us went away—even if it was just across town.

"I will," I promised, and kissed Mom's cheek.

Then I was caught up in the tidal wave of passengers boarding the bus. I found a seat by a window near the rear.

Mom and Dad followed my progress, moving along the platform until they were outside the window. Dad pressed his hand to the glass, while Mom waved as the bus driver shut the door with a vacuumed *whomp* and released the air brakes. Zoe stood apart from them, deliberately allowing herself to be outmaneuvered by others as she lost herself in the crowd.

I waved to her and she offered a smile and weak imitation of her usual mock salute. She was wearing the bracelet and tears streamed down her cheeks unchecked. I matched my palm to Dad's pressed against the outside of the tinted glass and, as the bus picked up speed, looked down at the crushed daisies on my lap.

1968-69

Letters from the Front

June 1, 1968

*C*aptain Andersen, I presume?
    After our less-than-sweet parting, you probably thought you'd never hear from me. Guess again, and don't think I've forgiven you—yet—for ignoring all my hard work in attempting to keep you safe. But you're there—and I'm here. So be it.
    Things on campus are about the same. I go to class, volunteer at the legal aid office and spend the rest of my time trying to drum up support for the cause. Remember the heckler who kept showing up every day and making disparaging remarks about my sexual preference? (He should

be so lucky—but that's another letter.) Anyway, his number came up, and get this—he called me, asking for help to skip the country! I made him listen to several lectures about why there is absolutely no connection between being in Vietnam and saving the world for democracy and then sent him to see Peter. If Peter helped him, I really don't want to know. Yes, you should read between the lines here and understand that Peter and I are not now, never were and never will be an item—at least, not in the romance department.

After you stormed out—okay, calmly left—that night, Peter did drop by to check if I was okay—a gesture I choose to view as old friends being there for each other. After that we had a couple of what you would undoubtedly call dates, but nothing ever developed—at least for me. A couple of beers, walks on the lake path, some aborted kissing attempts in the shadows, but that was all. Not sure why, but it's really important to me that you know that.

Summer has truly arrived to Madison. I've been thinking about driving up to the farm to see your folks, milk a cow in your honor or something. Did they tell you that after you left the three of us had lunch? Your mom's idea. It's like she's decided to adopt me. Yesterday I got a care package complete with homemade brownies, a small framed photograph of you that she felt I'd like and this really sweet chatty letter filled with news of your dad and brothers.

I miss you—more than I realized I would. And if you write one word about my dating other guys, this correspondence will cease abruptly. Do I make myself clear? Stay low, stay back and stay safe. Be a doc—not a warrior!

Zoe

P.S. Oh, yeah, almost forgot, Now that you're there, the least you can do is furnish me with unbiased reports of the "real" story. As Ty liked to say, when you're shoveling manure, there has got to be a pony somewhere nearby. (Note how I cleaned that up for you, farm boy.) What do the locals think of Americans? Are we viewed as liberators or occupiers? What about the GIs on their way home? Tell me everything. Z...

June 16, 1968

Dear Zoe,

As soon as your letter arrived, I grabbed the first chance I could to answer. It turns out that moment is now at three in the morning, after I've just finished the latest round of patching up wounded. Hopefully that will give you some idea of the importance of your writing to me. I was so happy to hear from you. How stupid was I to ask that you not wait, when the very idea you might have decided to take me up on that has been driving me nuts?

I'll start with the easy stuff—I'm the GMO (general medical officer) for a battalion (that's about 800-1000 soldiers)—can't tell you exact location or they'd have to shoot me, but trust me, it's not San Francisco if that's the postmark on this letter the way it was on yours. It's a hilltop surrounded by thick jungle. A village of canvas buildings—the hospital has a big red cross on top of it. It's supposed to keep us from getting shot at—pray that works! Inside, the equipment is a couple of decades shy of being state-of-the-art—my guess these are leftovers from Korea or—in some cases—WWII. But the medics and nurses are first-rate, dedicated and innovative when the situation calls for thinking on their feet (which is where we seem to *spend the better part of every day—not to mention most of the nights).*

It's hot—110 degrees today—humid—and they tell me the rainy season should hit any day. You asked about the Vietnamese people—inscrutable is the word that comes first to mind. On the face of it they are friendly and certainly more than a little exotic—especially for somebody like me. I'm a giant here, a big, blond giant—a real novelty. Kids follow me around, expecting I don't know what but keeping their distance. Just staring at me with those incredible black eyes.

Those who have been here awhile warn us to not get sucked in by the sweet faces and aim-to-please smiles. They can apparently be deceptive, even treacherous, and it's very hard to tell North (enemy) from South (ally). If that seems racist, so be it. The Vietcong are—in my opinion—masters of guerilla warfare since they are more than holding their own against the best trained and supplied fighting force in the entire world. And families can be split—some for the North and others for the South. Sound familiar?

Got to close and try to get some sleep—even though I have to be back on duty at dawn. Like I said, on my feet all night, and we never know when the next load of wounded will arrive, but it's been pretty steady ever since I got here. By the way, the food is lousy and even your cooking would be a feast. Oh, and the water is like drinking from a cesspool. When you talk to Mom—and I have no doubt that you will—ask her to send Kool-Aid packets so we can disguise the taste, and tell Dad I want pictures of you with that cow!

Miss you...only 335 days to go till I'm back in the world again.

Spence

Howdy, Farm Boy—Say hello to Pseudo Farm Girl!!

Went to see your folks over the weekend. LOVED everything about life down on the farm. The quiet, the colors—red barn, fields that range from emerald green to golden brown (do not ask me to name which crops produce which color). I even got used to the smells, although that took some doing.

Marie has planted this amazing herb garden, and she gave me a few recipes plus some fresh herbs to try. Who knew food could taste so incredible? Hal insisted I help with milking. (You failed to tell me that this takes place before dawn every single morning, including Sunday.) Polaroid proof that I actually performed this charming daily ritual enclosed!

Your "little" brothers are delightful—quiet and gentle giants but with that same subtle humor you have. We all went to church on Sunday morning, and I still can't believe how welcomed everyone made me feel. It was as if they just assumed that because I was with your family, I must be "good people."

When I left, your folks loaded me down with enough homemade soups, breads, cookies and such to feed me through the summer. And get this—Marie asked if I was free to come back next weekend and help the church ladies make pies for the annual bake sale. So you might want to warn your mom about my cooking skills—or lack thereof. More later...

Zoe

June 30, 1968

Dear Zoe,

Thanks for going to visit the folks. Mom wrote that you are "just delightful"—must have been some act you pulled! Dad thought you were potential farm-girl material—not sure whether that's in reference to your helping him and the boys with the chores or his way of saying you have the body of the farmer's daughter of all the jokes. Knowing Dad, it's a combo. The man has an eye for the ladies, but more than that, he respects women who aren't afraid to get their hands dirty. Would have loved to see you slopping those hogs! Mom writes that little brother Willie has a major crush on you—better watch yourself around all those raging teenage hormones!

We've had a change in command here. There's a big push to get this thing finished, which usually is a sign that things are not going well and Washington wants us to mop up and get out. Now, don't get all excited and figure I've surrendered to your side. It's just that I'd like to watch those Washington bureaucrats hack their way through a triple canopy of jungle in foot-gripping mud, four-foot, razor-sharp grass and such thick humid air and fog that the only thing you can see is the soldier to your immediate front or side.

In a war like this, there is no "front"—no real battle strategy other than search-and-destroy. Day after day we see guys go out in search of the enemy with no other plan than to make contact. Night after night we see them brought back by chopper for us to patch up and send on to Saigon for surgery or rehab—or worse—in body bags.

Then this morning we got the villagers from down the

road—more kids, babies some of them—full of shrapnel, covered in burns from the napalm and… Got to stop—not sure I can make you understand that this isn't meant to indicate a change of heart with regard to my view on duty and patriotism. You and the Peters of this world are really only making things worse, Zoe. You give the enemy hope.

Midnight…

Zoe, what I didn't—couldn't—finish above is that after that parade of wounded I got the news that Corporal Greg Rockwell, a medic—and a good friend—was killed in yesterday's battle. Greg's number came up early in the draft and he enlisted as a medic because they allow conscientious objectors to be medics. Greg was a Quaker. The unit was on patrol and got ambushed. Greg observed an officer down, and five other guys provided cover while he crawled to get the guy. All five were shot and wounded. Greg popped a smoke can to call in the chopper but died before it could arrive. The officer and others will make it, but Greg is gone. He hated this war, but he loved his country. Can you understand that? I know you said that you consider yourself a patriot, a lover of everything America is and stands for, but can't you understand that all your flag-burning and marching and protesting isn't doing us any good over here? People—good people—are dying here, Zoe—dying to defend your right to speak out. Greg could have probably gotten out of this, but as he told me, "Then somebody else would have had to take my place. Why's my life worth more than that other guy's?" That's a real patriot. That's how Ty looked at this thing. Think about that the next time you and your cronies decide to help somebody over the border.

Spence

P.S. Later. Sorry for the outburst. It's just so fricking hard. Don't stop writing. Please. I need you to be there.

July 10, 1968

Dear Spence,

I am so sorry to hear about Greg's death and I understand your anger—I do. It's just that some people choose to fight in the streets, while other choose to fight in the Congress, and some—like you—have no choice but to continue the fight there in Vietnam. We're all on the same side, Spence. We are. Please know that the work I'm doing here has only one purpose—to bring you and the others home safe and alive. Whatever happened to "Blessed are the peacemakers"?

Okay, enough. I'm going home tomorrow for the rest of the summer. Dad isn't doing well—he's just never gotten over Ty's death. Mom is at her wit's end trying to hold everything together. Maybe I can help. And maybe there are things I need to say to them—things I never had the chance to say to Ty. Things we think we have time to say, questions we think we have time to ask, history we think we will learn—someday.

I miss you, Spencer Andersen, more than I thought possible. I'm lonely and horny and cranky, and here's a really scary idea—I might be truly—as in till death do us part—falling in love with you. I would have preferred to admit that in one of those predawn lover moments, but there you have it. Don't get all nervous on me now—it's probably not a sure thing. Could be the times and the separation and all…still, what do you think?

Z

August 17, 1968

Dear Zoe,

Just back from Saigon, where I was sent to deliver a report at a conference of high-ranking officers and government types (members of Congress and Department of Defense, etc.) at the U.S. Embassy. As much as it pains me to admit this, you and your followers might just be starting to have some effect—still can't say if that's a good thing. The central message of the meeting was the need for a real PR effort in selling this war back home. Bigger battles and bigger victories. Less pessimistic in reporting losses—I am not making that up. When questioned by the panel, I tried to make them understand that it's hard to fudge the numbers when there have been more casualties in the past six weeks than there were in the previous six months combined. I also pointed out that most of the soldiers I know just want to get out of here alive and couldn't care less about politics. I was not a popular guy.

On the brighter side, it was an escape from life in camp. Saigon was—on the surface—almost luxurious. But there's this undercurrent of desperation—I swear you can smell it, touch it, feel it from the moment you arrive. At first it's hard to define. Then you notice people working to make every dollar they can from the Americans. And you realize that in spite of the constant arrival of fresh troops, the locals seem to assume we will just one day give up and leave. We see the same thing in camp—the black market is its own industry over here and trust is the item in shortest supply.

Speaking of supplies, thanks for the school supplies for the kids. I'm still teaching English to the locals who work at the hospital and their kids. And I'll admit that I use that time to try to show them the importance of questioning and gathering information before making blind choices—your influence, no doubt. In return they've educated me, as well. I'm learning so much more about their history and culture and everything begins to make more sense.

Choppers! That means incoming wounded—oh, yeah, about that "falling in love" idea? Definitely interested in pursuing that. Hold that thought and I'll write more soon.

Spence

Continuing above on August 20…

Dear Zoe,
Didn't mean to belittle your question about falling in love. I know what it cost you to be the first to bring that up. So, here's a letter with no war, no politics, no philosophical debates—here is a love letter from a farm-boy soldier-doctor to his rabble-rousing city-girl almost-lawyer.

I've always thought of real love as finding that single person you instantly knew you could trust with every thought or dream you might ever have. For me, you are that person. For me, love is also about respect—embracing differences, finding them interesting and unique rather than threatening. It's about caring—even when the other person is pushing you away. It's about making allowances, forgiving, sharing, laughing, grieving. It's about life and living it together in all its imperfect glory.

I love you, Zoe, in all those ways. I want to share whatever life we have left with you starting the day I come back to the world. Please give this more thought and be very, very sure that this is what you want, as well.

Spence

September 12, 1968

Wow! You really know how to write a love letter, farm boy!

Okay, all silliness and nervous chatter aside, here's my answer—yes.

Yes, I love you.

Yes, we're finally on common ground—at least when it comes to defining love.

Yes, I felt the same connection from day one.

Yes, I want to be together for the rest of our lives.

Yes, yes, yes!

Hurry home to me, Spence. We are going to be incredible together!

Love, Zoe

October 12, 1968

Zoe,

Tired beyond tired today, so what follows may not make much sense. But the more time I spend patching up the bodies of these soldiers, the more I find myself wondering about the wounds we can't touch—the mental and emotional scarring, the aftermath of fear and loss these men will carry with them even after they are safely back home. What happens then? I've been giving some thought to pursuing a residency in psychiatry. What do you think? I mean, maybe having been here and seen what they've seen and experienced some of it, maybe I can help them. I'm not sure. Maybe what I'm really thinking about is who is going to help me forget all that I've witnessed over here—all that lies ahead? Talk to me, Zoe. Bring me back to the world, because this unending chaos and pandemonium can't possibly be the real world, can it?

Spence

October 31, 1968

Spence,

Before I tell you what's happening here, just need to say that if you're serious about this psychiatry thing, I think you'd be wonderful. Of course, I think you'd be wonderful at whatever you decided to do, but this fits you so well.

As for bringing you back to the world, not sure you'd be any better off over here—at least right now. I'm okay— that's just so you know before you read on.

A few weeks ago Peter and I decided it was time to organize a peaceful protest—peaceful at my insistence. Peter wanted to blow something up. He said it would be ironic symbolism. Always the grand gesture. But I persuaded him that following the example of Martin Luther King was a better way to go. Anyhow, the plan was to stage a sit-in at the Commerce Building, on campus. The turnout was the best we'd had—dozens of students (even a couple of faculty) packed the building and hundreds more gathered outside. No one was surprised when, after attempting to wait us out, the chancellor announced that he was calling in security to clear the building unless we left peacefully.

We held our ground, never once dreaming that instead of campus security, he'd called for the Madison city police. You know how the townies feel about us—especially people like me—interlopers from the East Coast. The police showed up in riot gear—helmets, billy clubs, the works—and used a bullhorn to order us out immediately or they were coming in. Only, they didn't wait. They moved through, stepping on and over people, clubbing students who were trying to get to an exit, stacking wounded bodies, chasing down those who rushed to leave and beating them. Outside they used tear gas!

I have six stitches in my forehead and three in my chin, but the doctor says I was one of the luckier ones. There is good news in all of this—news of this unprovoked attack (although the police swear that the students attacked first and were led by a few East Coast rabble-rousers—Peter's bloody face was all over the news) has spread. There's been a noticeable escalation in the number of demonstrations, sit-ins and riots on campuses across the country. There are even plans for a second massive march on Washington! I think the tide is finally turning, and maybe we can get you back here safe and sound at last.

Love,
Zoe

Thanksgiving Day, 1968

Dear Zoe,

Got your letter. Thank God, you're all right. That also makes it easier to write what I must tell you if we are to have any chance for a future. It's possible that through my letters and reports about things over here you have gotten the idea that I have come full circle and agree with your assessment of this war. But that's not really true.

I'm not so naive as to believe that we are over here to make the world safe for democracy. But as our purpose here becomes less clear and the light at the end of the tunnel dims, what am I—and the thousands of others like me who are here—supposed to think? Those of us over here have no political agenda—we just want to get out alive, as do those on the other side. And what of those who have already been sent home in flag-draped coffins or missing an arm or leg or half a face? What would you say to them and their loved ones? Sorry? It was all a misunderstanding?

Maybe getting involved here was a mistake, but there are ways—built into our system of government—to rectify that. Elections and the order of law to name two. If, as you believe, our only recourse is to take to the streets, then God help us all. And Zoe, if you and I can't reach some understanding and respect for our differing points of view on this thing, then I can't help but wonder if we'll be able to pick up the pieces of our lives once I am back in the world. In spite of our differences, knowing that you are there has gotten me through the endless days and nights of this thing. I do love you, and whatever happens, I will always love you.

Spence

December 26, 1968

Spencer Andersen—

I hate these letters! I want to talk to you, look into your eyes, hold your face between my palms and tell you that if I lose you, whatever windmills I may have tilted at in pursuit of justifying my existence in these chaotic times will have no meaning at all. Please don't give up on us, Spence. Please just stay safe and get back home and we'll work it all out. Just get back here, okay?

All my love,
Zoe

January 2, 1969

Zoe—

   Dictating this to a nurse, so pretend this is one of those telegrams delivered by the guy in the funny costume in the old black-and-white movies: On my way home STOP Wounded in operating room STOP Not serious STOP If you love me DON'T STOP
Details will follow. Spence

1970

Zoe

On my wedding day, I was awake before dawn. Lying in the bed of my childhood, I couldn't help thinking of the biblical advice to "put away childish things" as I reminded myself that next time I slept in this room it would no doubt be with Spence as a guest in my parents' home. The subtle light from the rising sun played over the things I had left behind even before I headed off to college. The expensive and collectible dolls—more Mom's attempt to "normalize" me than a reflection of my own interest—are gathered on the shelves that Dad built for me.

Our little girl—all grown up and soon to be married.

In so many ways my parents are the products of another era—an era of rules and order rather than the chaos that seems to rule my times. They built a life based on certain values, certain beliefs. Dad's inherited fortune from his father and grandfather, who made their money in the stock market, has given us a life most people only dream of living. Yet every Monday through Friday morning, Dad heads downtown to his office in Lower Manhattan to play Monopoly with real money, and helps out the economy by employing several dozen people to play the game with him.

Meanwhile, Mom has filled her days and weeks and years with traditional roles of her era—raising two children, lunch with "the girls," bridge in the afternoon and the opera at night and enough hours spent in charity work to qualify for a full-time career. Theirs is a solid marriage—a fine example for me to follow. I couldn't help but wonder if Spence and I had any chance of being so lucky. The fact was that ever since I'd gone out to California with Spence's parents to welcome him home, I had been wrestling with second thoughts. Prewedding jitters, my mother assured me. Nothing so frivolous, I told myself.

Spence has changed. Or maybe the world has changed us both. Outwardly, he's still the same quiet, patient, gentle man I've been unable to stay away from since Ty's funeral. But inside, the man who got off the plane in San Francisco and limped across the tarmac to where I stood with Marie and Hal was not at all the same man who had boarded that bus in Madison. It was as clear to me as if he had worn a billboard.

Even his physical appearance has changed—it's more mature and hard, all traces of the boy gone. His features have lost a little of that original tightness and suspicion he wore in those first days back. But that day of his return the deep furrows and valleys of his face were a road map of everything he'd seen over there. Even now the change is still there in him. He's lost that certainty and assurance of who he is and what he believes that I'd come to respect.

After a few weeks I finally understood that what I was really seeing that day was disbelief. I'll never forget how he described it when I was finally able to get him to talk about how it felt to be home. "It felt like stepping off that plane into a world as foreign to me as Oz was to Dorothy."

Of course, I didn't know any of that as we stood on that tarmac, and I hesitated, afraid that everything had changed. That we would never find our way back to each other.

"Go," Marie urged when I glanced her way, wanting to give her the first chance to hold him. "Go," she said again, and smiled as Hal took her arm.

I didn't need to be told three times. I ran toward Spence, my sandals slapping crazily on the pavement, my long skirt tangling around my calves and ankles until I grasped the folds of it in one hand and raised it to my knees so I could cover the distance faster. When I reached him, he wrapped his arms around me and buried his face in the crevice between my shoulder and cheek. The cane clattered as it hit the hard pavement.

When his parents joined us, Spence released me and folded his arms around first his mom and then his dad. Marie blubbered her relief and fussed over the obvious aftermath of his wound, while Hal retrieved the cane and handed it back to Spence. Spence laughed as he assured all of us that the cane was window dressing. "I've got some physical therapy ahead of me, but I'm luckier than most."

Perhaps realizing that he'd dampened the spirit of the occasion, Spence struck a pose and grinned. "Makes me look dapper, don't you think?"

Then he focused on his father. The two men stared at

each other for a long moment. Hal's eyes were red-rimmed but dry as he straightened and offered his son a military salute. Spence returned the salute, and as he hugged his father, I saw the shuddering sob that rocketed across his shoulders and down his back. He was home. He was safe. But how could he ever be the same? And how could I ever be anything but a constant reminder of the other side— those who had protested and defected and refused to serve?

At the hotel, where Marie and I shared one room and Spence and Hal took the connecting room, I begged off joining the three of them for lunch and headed upstairs. I told myself that I wanted to give Spence this moment with his parents. I told myself that we would have plenty of time now—years and years together. But when I entered the room and closed the door, I started to shake and then I started to sob.

"Zoe?"

I didn't answer. Spence tapped again and opened the connecting door between my room and his. "Zoe." This time the speaking of my name was an overture, a gesture toward peace. I turned but didn't look at him, certain that my face would reveal just how frightened I was for us now that he was back.

He crossed the room and put his arms around me. "Let's go for a walk," he whispered and I nodded.

We walked mostly in silence, occasionally commenting on one of the many painted-lady houses that lined the streets or the quaint sound of the cable-car bells. Later at a café table in Ghirardelli Square, we shared cups of rich, foamy hot chocolate. In spite of the fact that it was June, the breeze off the bay was chilly. Spence pulled his chair close to mine and draped his arm around my shoulders.

"Zoe, it's going to take me a little while to…" He shook that thought off and began again. "It all seems pretty unreal right now." He smiled and ran his fingers over my face. "I keep thinking that all this is nothing more than a dream and I'll wake up—back there."

I caught his fingers in mine and kissed them. "I'm here," I promised him, "for as long as you want me to be."

"How about forever?" He fumbled in his pocket and produced a ring box. It was old—royal blue velvet rubbed threadbare on the corners.

He fumbled with the box, opening it and removing a simple silver band engraved with intertwined vines and flowers. "I asked Mom to bring it along with her. It was my grandmother's," he explained, holding it out to me. "Or we can buy you what you want—something more traditional with a diamond," he hurried to add as he searched my face for some response. "I just thought…"

"When have you ever known me to be traditional?" I held out my ring finger. "I love it," I whispered as he slid the ring into place. "And more to the point, I love you." I threw my arms around his neck and kissed him.

When the kiss ended, he was grinning—a flash of the man I'd known before. "So that would be a 'yes'?"

I kissed him several more times and punctuated each with a "yes." And I ignored the niggling doubts that earlier had taken root in the recesses of my heart. The doubts that had warned me we'd both changed and would need to get to know these two new people shaped by a war we had each fought on different battlefields.

So now the day is here. At sunset Spence and I will be married in Central Park under the arching canopy of an oak tree. After dinner and dancing at the Tavern on the Green in the park, we will spend our wedding night at the Waldorf Astoria—Spence insisted.

"It's the best, right?" he asked, and my parents had assured him it was, indeed.

Tomorrow we'll leave for a honeymoon in Paris—a gift from my parents. By this time in three weeks, we'll be back in Madison, where Spence will start his residency in psychiatry. I'll go back to my job at the Legal Aid Society and set up a home for us in the small apartment we've found just off State Street. We'll be married—and for the first time since his return from Vietnam, we'll be truly alone "back in the world."

Spencer

In the year since I'd returned from 'Nam, the sheer normality of my daily routine made my stint over there exist only in the nightmares that haunted me when I least expected them. I would dream that I was in the fields, harvesting the corn or baling the hay with Dad, and then everything would change and I would be performing surgery in a paddy. The water running with blood, the rice field littered with wounded soldiers or villagers I couldn't rescue because my boots were mired in the muck of the field. I would wake suddenly, sitting upright, gasping for air, my body bathed in sweat. I told myself—and Zoe—that in time the dreams would go away. Normal, I assured her, laughing off her suggestion that maybe I should see about getting some help.

Zoe had moved in with Sara and two other women her last year of law school, and had decided to stay with them until after we were married. She had taken a full-time job with Legal Aid, which limited her on-campus protest activities and time with Peter Quarles and his group. I couldn't deny that I was relieved.

For the first several months after I got back to the world, I stayed on the farm whenever I could be away from the hospital. I told Zoe that it was because I had noticed a change in Dad—he had aged and the heavy chores took a lot out of him. I told her that they were struggling—which was true—and Zoe agreed that my place was with them.

"Besides," she joked, "the bride and groom aren't supposed to shack up before the wedding."

"I thought that was just the night before," I replied with mock surprise.

"We'll start a new tradition," she said, and I loved her more for accepting that for the moment my folks needed me more than she did.

But my parents were only part of my reason. The truth was that I couldn't get used to the way things had changed. The television news, the campus, everywhere I looked it seemed that people were up in arms about the war—and blaming those of us that had served. The antiwar movement even infiltrated the small rural community I'd grown up in. People who had known me my whole life were polite enough when I ran into them in the grocery or stopped for gas, but few showed any real appreciation for the job that I'd gone to do.

"It's the times," Dad maintained. "The war—well, folks are confused. Nobody seems able to tell us how we got mixed up in this thing to begin with."

But in spite of all that, I kept finding new things to love about Zoe. Away from campus and the politics of war, she was the girl Ty had told me about—sweet, loving, completely unselfish in giving her help and understanding, and in sharing her obvious joy in planning the wedding. It was Zoe who was adamant that my older brother's wife, my younger brother's girlfriend and even my aunt Rose must have a role to play at the wedding. It was also Zoe who insisted she must have a full year to put this thing together.

"What's so complicated?" I protested. "You get a dress and I get a suit and we book the church and minister and—"

"I have dreamed of this day practically my whole life," Zoe replied, and when my eyebrows must have shot up in astonishment at that admission, she added, "Go ahead and laugh. Go ahead. Ty would. But the truth is that I only plan on doing this once and I want stories to tell our grandchildren."

"Yes, ma'am," I said, holding up my hands in surrender and ignoring the grin that spread across Mom's face just before she turned her back to me and continued slicing strawberries into a fruit salad.

I expected Dad to offer some male support, but he was no help. He just shrugged and went back to his newspaper.

And over the next several months the traffic between Wisconsin and New York became a fairly regular thing. Zoe's parents came to Madison and then ended up staying on the farm when the hotel overbooked and didn't have a room for them. They returned for Thanksgiving, and we all went out there for New Year's. Dad was blown away by the very idea that Zoe's parents had lived in NYC practically their whole lives and never once seen the ball drop in Times Square. The six of us spent New Year's Eve in Times Square dressed in silly party hats, rattling noisemakers and tossing confetti as the countdown began. Afterward we feasted on Nathan's hot dogs while Dad and Mike Wingfield discussed the economy, Mom and Kay Wingfield discussed the latest doings on the soap opera they had discovered they were both devoted to and Zoe and I sat on the sidelines beaming like proud matchmakers.

On our wedding day Zoe arrived by horse-drawn hansom cab and then walked down the aisle created by the rows of white folding chairs where our guests stood and smiled and murmured their comments to one another. Sara sang the song she'd written for the occasion—her wedding gift to us—as Zoe's dad offered his arm and led her toward the altar.

After years of turmoil and chaos, once again everything seemed possible. Once again the world felt the hope and promise that had been wiped away in the hail of bullets that had taken the Kennedys and the Reverend King. It was a new world, I thought, as my eyes met Zoe's. And there was no one I wanted to share the adventure of discovering this new world with more than this woman. I stepped forward a minute before my cue and, without my cane, walked more than halfway up the aisle to meet Zoe.

Fall, 2007

Zoe

In some ways those first nights after we learned that the cancer was back were the hardest times for me. Lying there next to Spence, aware of the steady rise and fall of his chest as he slept, I felt more alone than at any other time. For as I lay there, awake in the dark, my fears were as real as the monsters our daughter, Cami, had once declared lived in the shadows of her room.

"No, darling," we had assured her, switching on lights and opening closets and drawers to show her. "There are no monsters, see?"

Cami had crossed her chubby four-year-old arms and observed us with what could only be described as a look of pity. "Well, of course you can't see them,

Mommy," she had explained. "They're indivisible, but they're real."

"Invisible," Spence had automatically corrected her, scratching his head as he'd tried to find the words to comfort her.

"You're the shrink," I had murmured. "Do something or none of us will get any sleep."

His solution had been inspired.

"Cami, have I ever introduced you to my friend Leonardo, here?" Spence had indicated a vacant space next to him on Cami's bed.

Cami had eyed him suspiciously.

"He's a lion I met when I was in the army and living in the jungle. He went everywhere with me while I was over there and kept me safe so I could get home to Mommy."

"There's no lion," Cami said, crawling closer to Spence and peering around him.

Spence laughed. "Well, of course. He's invisible. I forgot that part."

Cami frowned.

"How would it be if I ask Leonardo to sleep here on the foot of your bed? That way if any monsters start acting up, you can just ask Leonardo to take care of it."

Cami was skeptical, but finally she rearranged her menagerie of stuffed animals to create room for Leonardo. I edged toward the door as Spence gave Leonardo his instructions.

"What's that?" Spence said to the thin air at the foot of Cami's bed. "I'll ask." He turned to Cami. "Leonardo would like to know if just for tonight you might keep the lamp on. He thinks the monsters might not like the light."

Cami focused on the empty space she'd made for Spence's imaginary lion. "I think that's a good idea, Leonardo," she said.

Spence turned on the small lamp next to Cami's bed before snapping off the ceiling light.

"All set," he said, and kissed Cami's forehead as he tucked her in.

Tonight, just before switching off the lamp, Spence had kissed me and positioned the covers around my shoulders. "All set?" he had whispered, and I had nodded.

Now, in the dark, I pulled my knees to my chest, making room for Leonardo at the foot of the bed.

Spence

As the news of the recurrence of Zoe's cancer spread, family and friends tripped over one another trying to do something for us. At the same time, Zoe was determined to get through the initial treatment on her own.

"If I accept rides or hand-holding now, where will it all lead?" she asked when I suggested that letting a friend take her to lunch or go with her to a doctor's appointment when I couldn't wasn't the worst thing.

"There are lots of people who would love to have the kind of support you have, Zoe," I reminded her.

"I know," she admitted. "I just—it's just that—"

Zoe has always been a giver and finds receiving next to impossible. She's never quite understood why she is so admired and loved. "I'm a pain," she has said more than once. "I am stubborn and controlling and—"

"Loving and generous," I remind her.

"I don't want pity," she finally admits.

"Oh, sweetheart, they aren't doing it because they pity you. They want to do something because they love you—and because they are scared for you and for themselves."

She blinks.

"If this could happen to SuperZoe," I remind her softly, "then what could happen to the rest of us mere mortals? Do it for them, Zoe. Let them in and let them help."

She frowns and eyes me suspiciously.

"You have a golden opportunity here, Zoe," I add.

"To teach my friends and family maybe how to die bravely?"

I shake my head. "To teach us—as you always have—how to live fully."

Zoe

By Labor Day, it was clear that the medication regimen Jon had originally recommended wasn't having the effect we had all hoped for. As the days and weeks passed with little change, we sat down with Jon and Liz for some straight talk. Spence wasn't happy with what Jon offered.

"We'll get another opinion," Spence declared. "No offense, Jon, but—"

"Listen to me," I said quietly. "What we have learned today is nothing we didn't already suspect. We have always known that time—anybody's—is finite. So, get this straight, farm boy, I will not spend whatever months or years I have left chasing doctors. I—we—will spend every minute of every day and night we have living."

"I'll request a leave of absence," Spence said. "We'll travel. You've always wanted to go back to Paris. The house—maybe we should sell and get into something more manageable. Maybe full-time help. Maybe—"

"Stop it, Spence," I whispered. "We'll get through this as we always have—together." I squeezed his hand.

I pulled my hand free of Spence's and wrapped my arms tightly around my middle as if to hold myself together, for surely Jon's answer to what I was about to ask would break me in half. "How long have I got?" It sounded like dialogue from some bad tearjerker movie and yet there seemed to be no more original way of putting the question that was the two-ton elephant in the room.

Jon watched as Spence got up and walked to the door leading to the sunporch and back. He was standing behind me then, his hands on my shoulders.

"It's early, Zoe," Liz began, her mouth refusing to utter the *but* that must have been there.

"How long?" I repeated, and was not at all sure I had uttered the words, even though they were a constant drumbeat in my brain.

"The average—and I am saying *average*—is three to six years after onset of symptoms," Jon replied.

I did the math. My shortness of breath first appeared at least a year and a half ago, even though I hadn't mentioned it to Spence or allowed myself to credit it as anything more than lack of proper exercise.

Jon was still talking, so I forced my attention back to his moving lips. "There's significant spread, Zoe, and while we don't have a magic pill or surgical procedure to fix what's there, we can treat it, contain the spread."

If we can went unsaid.

He glanced down at his hands and I found myself

wanting to reach out to him, to console him and let him know it wasn't his fault that he had little to offer.

Liz—bless her—tried to half fill this rapidly emptying glass. "On the other hand, you are anything but normal, Zoe. You quit smoking nearly forty years ago. You eat right and exercise regularly. You're in good health…."

A sardonic laugh escaped my tightly pressed lips. "Yeah, except for the fact that you're telling me that my lung capacity is already compromised, which has to mean that my heart will need to keep working harder than it should. Yeah, great health will definitely help here."

Liz looked as if I'd slapped her. *Don't shoot the messenger,* I thought and forced myself to calm down. "Sorry. Reflex action."

Liz accepted my apology. As my best friend, she's well aware that my weapon of choice when I need to gear up for a fight is pure unadulterated rage.

In spite of all attempts to put up a brave front, I was terrified and I fought back in two ways. First, I became manic, filling every hour with activity no matter how meaningless. Anything so I would have a few seconds or minutes of respite from worrying about the fact that the new medicine might not work, either.

Second, I got angry—at everyone and everything. I began with me. How stupid had I been five years earlier when I had blithely assured myself that skipping a couple of annual mammograms was not a problem. There was no family history of breast cancer. I had none of the risk factors beyond having breasts and being a woman, and who could blame me for not exactly embracing a situation where my small breasts had to be smashed and flattened by a torture machine while I held my breath and waited for the camera to click? I would have the test next year.

On top of that I had little patience for others—especially my friends and family—getting on with their lives. Of course, I had insisted on just that. "Please be normal," I had begged. "Go to work. Talk about the future. Tiptoeing around doesn't help."

They had taken me at my word—even Spence. He would come home from the counseling center filled with stories of patients or new ideas for programs they might institute to help victims of natural disasters like Hurricane Katrina. I would sit across the dinner table from him, nodding and smiling and occasionally offering a comment. But inside I was seething. It wasn't fair. I knew it was a cancer cliché but, *Why me?* I had so much left to do.

Spence

The medicine isn't working. Not only is Zoe not getting any better, but lately the number of days when she has no energy—or real belief that there's any purpose to any of this—has been on the rise. And yet she insists on doggedly sticking to the regimen that Jon originally prescribed for her.

"There are other options," I've tried suggesting.

"I know what I'm doing," she always replies, without looking up from feeding herself her morning brew of medications.

This wasn't the first day we'd had this conversation. It wasn't the twentieth time, either. It was more like the fiftieth. Each time, I try a different strategy. Today, it was,

"Maybe we should drive up to Rochester and see what the folks at Mayo Clinic recommend."

That gained me direct eye contact. Zoe was horrified. "The folks at Mayo? Do you hear yourself? You make it sound like we might go out to the farm and see if the corn grew another inch."

"I'm just attempting to—"

"Well, don't," she growled, returning to her breakfast. "Just don't," she whispered, touching my face in apology.

At their annual Labor Day potluck, Jon had told me about a new combination of medications that had had promising results with others in Zoe's situation. A few days later I ventured to ask Zoe if she had come to a decision about switching to the new regimen.

"It's probably all palliative care," she said. "Prolong the quality of life," she added bitterly.

I swallowed the anger and frustration I'd been fighting for weeks. In spite of all my training and research as a psychiatrist, I had been helpless to stem the tide of Zoe's rampant depression.

"Are you saying you're ready to give up? That you won't even consider Jon's recommendation for treatment?" I asked, working overtime to maintain calm and civility.

Zoe continued to pick at the food she was moving around her plate without eating. She eyed me sharply. "That's not at all what I said and you know it."

I felt the spurt of a break in the dam I'd built around my emotions and fought it by getting up on the pretense of taking my dirty dishes to the sink. "Are you finished?" I asked, indicating her full plate. She pushed it away, folded her arms and sat back in her chair. "I'll take that as a yes," I said, and removed her dishes, as well.

"I don't know what your problem is," she began as I stood at the sink with my back to her, rinsing the plates. "All I'm saying is that—"

I wrenched the faucet lever off and spun around. "My 'problem,' as you call it, is you. More specifically, my inability to do anything or say anything to help you—to make you want to fight this thing. My problem is that Dr. High and Mighty Psychiatrist here has not the vaguest notion of how to heal his wife. My problem is that I have become the very thing I warn all my patients not to become—I have become your rescuer and enabler."

"Meaning?"

"Meaning that I am working a lot harder than you are to fight this thing and I flatten like a cardboard box every time you get on your soapbox about living every day but refuse to even consider other treatment options."

"I don't ask you to do any of that and I certainly don't require rescuing." She left the kitchen and a minute later I heard the back door slam and the car engine fire.

As I watched through the kitchen window, Zoe roared out of the driveway. In that moment, it flashed through my professional mind that bringing it into the open was exactly what was needed.

We had to stop dancing around the fact that we were both terrified and filled with the bile of panic and anxiety. We needed to face the fact that we both were helpless to reach out to the other for fear of infecting the person we loved most with our rage and our fear. And most of all we needed to bring into the open the pure dread that this might tear us apart before we realized it was too late to fix it.

How many times had I assured my patients that confronting the issue—bringing it out into the open—was best? How stupid and misguided had I been not to realize how gut-wrenching that could be?

Learning Zoe's cancer has returned should have brought us closer. Instead it's driving us apart. I try to remember how we survived this distance five years ago—how we found our way back to each other from the brink before it was too late.

Zoe

After I slam out of the house and race the car down the driveway, leaving tire tracks on the pavement, I force myself to swallow the nausea of my rage and guilt and slow down. I wind through the streets of this neighborhood I love. I notice every house and remember everything Spence and I have shared in the nearly forty years we have lived here. We are the old-timers now. Several of the houses I pass are newly occupied, our former neighbors having moved on to warmer climates or downsized once the children left home.

I drive past Liz's and see a single light burning—a sure sign that she's away for the evening. If she'd been there, would I have stopped as I might have before when Spence and I argued? Probably not. In the weeks since it became obvious I have a tough road ahead, I have withdrawn into my shell, pushing friends away with a tight-lipped smile that screams, "Leave me alone!"

What's the point? I think.

Half an hour later, I've run out of neighborhood so I circle the block and find myself sitting in front of our house. Light streams from every window, even in those upstairs rooms we rarely light until we go up to bed for the night. I realize that Spence has done this. He is telling me to come home—that we will work it all out as we always have.

I pull into the garage. As I cut the motor and turn off the headlights, the back door opens and Spence is standing there.

"I made popcorn," he says, handing me his mug of hot herbal tea. "Want some?"

I run my fingers across his thinning hair. "I'm sorry," I whisper. "It's just that I'm so tired of the fight."

"Then I'll fight for you," he promises as he wraps his arm around my shoulders and leads me into the kitchen. "All you have to do is agree to take the meds."

"Oh, Spence. Maybe—"

He stops my words with fingers pressed to my lips. "Not yet," he says hoarsely. "Not until we've looked under every rock, tried every possible treatment. We can do this, Zoe."

1972

Zoe

It had never occurred to me that trying to have a baby could be so difficult. Spence and I were surrounded by people who seemed to merely state their intention to start a family and—zap—they were expecting. Not me.

Six months almost to the day after our wedding Spence and I agreed that it was time. We had settled into the small one-bedroom walk-up above a bookstore in Madison, halfway between the Capitol and the campus. With Spence's psych residency nearing completion, he'd been offered a faculty position at the medical college, a position that would allow him to focus on the research into postwar psychosis that he'd begun during his residency. I continued to work at Legal Aid. Money was tight, because we were determined not to accept any financial help from my parents. So we spent hours dreaming of the future we were building. Spence dreamed of one day establishing a center for counseling veterans and others who had suffered from the aftermath of war. For me the plan continued to be some nonspecific form of saving the world. But in those days the all-consuming dream we shared was having a family of our own. We wanted the whole Norman Rockwell scene— kids, a house of our own with a yard, close neighbors, and our parents and friends gathered around a huge old farm-style dining table with Spence ready to carve the turkey on Thanksgiving.

"How many?" Spence asked one night as we lay in the waterbed we'd thought was a good idea at the time we bought it. We'd celebrated that first half year of marriage with a candlelight dinner on the fire escape landing outside our bedroom window.

"A dozen?" I replied, smiling to myself in the dark as I felt him stiffen in protest next to me.

"Tell me you're kidding," he said.

"Well, how many, then?" I said, turning on my side and propping myself on one elbow to watch his expression in the street light finding its way through the blinds.

He waited for the rocking of the bed to calm. "How about two?" he said uncertainly.

"A boy for you and a girl for me like the song lyric?"

He smiled, obviously relieved that I had decided not to push the even dozen. "Or the other way round." He reached up and cupped my face with his palm. "Are you sure?"

"About the number?" I shrugged. "Let's try one and see how it goes."

"About the timing," he replied, and his tone told me we

had switched gears. He was serious about this. It was no longer "someday"—it was "how about now?"

I kissed him. "Now is perfect," I said.

And because the bliss of my life had apparently made me stupid, I assumed that "now" was a reasonable goal. After we made love that night, I lay awake listening as Spence's breathing settled into the even rise and fall of his chest that told me he was sleeping soundly. I mentally toured the apartment and began rearranging things to accommodate a baby. I thought about my job and made a mental note to ask my boss about perhaps bringing the baby with me to the office sometimes or working from home part-time. I ran through what I assumed would become Spence's schedule of lectures, labs, administrative duties and the constant pressure for him to publish journal articles and present at various medical meetings. And I assumed that if I wasn't already pregnant, I would be shortly.

"What did the doctor say?" Spence asked a year and a half later after we had separately and together gone through just about every test available and experimented with every method currently in fashion for getting pregnant. I had taken my temperature eighty gazillion times a day. More than once Spence had rushed home from campus so we could mate at the optimum moment. I had begun to feel like some sort of rare zoo animal, and although he never said a word, Spence had to be feeling like a thoroughbred who'd been put out to stud.

"What does she always say?" I replied bitterly. "Give it time."

I knew I wasn't being fair. It wasn't Spence's fault. It was no one's fault, everyone assured me. But I felt— What did I feel? Inadequate? A failure? Sad as I mourned the life

I wanted so much? All of the above. What scared me the most was that the plans Spence and I had dreamed for the future had included not only children but grandchildren—generations of Wingfield-Andersens carrying forth a legacy of my fiery independence mixed with the reassuring calm that was Spence. It wasn't fair. We would be such good parents. Our children would surely make the world a better place.

Spence patted my hand. "I've got an idea," he said.

"What?" I snapped, irritated at anyone who had one more well-meaning suggestion for me. "It's not my fault, you know," I shouted, and burst into tears.

Spence held out his arms to me, but I couldn't stand the expression I interpreted as pity and I pushed away from him. "And don't suggest adoption. I want my own baby. If that's not possible, then…" I faltered and looked around wildly. Then what?

Spence handed me my coat. "Come on," he said, shrugging into his own jacket and grabbing the car keys. "Let's go for a ride."

Feeling guilty at striking out at him, yet not ready to apologize or back down, I jammed my arms into my coat and walked into the hallway. In silence I followed him down the dim stairway and out to the alley where we parked our car. In silence Spence opened the passenger door for me. In silence he got in and drove.

"Where are we going?" I asked finally. I had assumed that we were headed for a movie or perhaps a walk on the lake path on campus, followed by cups of hot tea enjoyed on the nearly deserted terrace outside the Union. All were therapies that had worked in the past. But by now I couldn't be pacified.

"I've got something to show you," he said. His voice

was perfectly calm. He could be maddening that way. While I would stew for hours or even days if he snapped at me unfairly, he took it all in stride.

I folded my arms tightly across my chest and stared out the window at the gathering twilight. We hadn't eaten. I'd come home upset and exhausted and then realized I had meant to do the grocery shopping after work. We were saving for so many things—the baby, a house, a future. We couldn't afford to go out, but he deserved better than the can of tuna waiting at home.

"Just something quick," I muttered. "Barney's or fast food. Let's don't make a big deal." Translation—let's don't make me feel even guiltier by spending more than we can afford on dinner just because you think it's going to cheer me up.

"Who said anything about dinner?" he replied evenly as he turned onto a side street I'd never been on before. He followed its winding path and stopped the car under a gigantic elm tree. "Well," he said as he pulled me closer and pointed out the window on his side. "What do you think?"

I followed his gaze. Across the street from us sat a house on a hill, every window lit and that warm golden glow spilling out onto a lawn sprinkled with mature trees dressed in all the golds and reds of their autumn splendor. In the center of the lawn was a For Sale by Owner sign.

I blinked and looked more closely at the neighborhood, considering the route we'd taken to get here. "It's on the lake?"

"Yep." Spence grinned. "Has a boathouse and everything."

It worked. For the first time in weeks I was not constantly obsessing about getting pregnant. Before me was the kind of house—the kind of *home*—I'd always dreamed of. "But—"

"Want to see the inside?"

Before I could answer, Spence was out of the car. I opened the door. "We can't just—"

"They're sort of expecting us," he said.

On the way up the cobblestone walkway to the front door, Spence said, "Remember Professor Kent?"

"Philosophy 101 and one of the prime backers of the antiwar effort," I replied. "Of course I remember Professor Kent, Spence. In case you've forgotten, we attended his funeral last spring."

"Right. Well, I ran into his son on campus today. The kids are here to try to sell the house. They all live out of town and Mrs. Kent is moving to California with one of the daughters and—"

The front door swung open and a man in his forties stepped forward to greet us. "Dan Kent," he said, extending his hand to me. "Come in. Come in. I thought maybe you'd decided tonight wasn't good."

He took my coat and hung it in the hall closet, then stood aside while Spence hung his jacket, as well.

"It needs work—a lot of work." Dan glanced around. "Funny how when you grow up in a place you forgive so much, but then when you try to sell it…"

I wanted to warn him to stop talking so much about the downside and focus on the good stuff—like the Arts-and-Craft-style moldings and doorways and windows I could see in the rooms leading off the hall. For that matter the stairway itself was an architectural treasure. On the landing—large enough to accommodate a small writing desk and mission-style rocker with a reading lamp—there was an incredible window seat beneath a span of three tall, thin leaded-glass windows.

"Make yourself at home," Dan urged. "I'm just going

to attend to a couple of calls and start a pot of coffee. You two take your time touring, okay? I'll be back in the kitchen when you're ready and we'll talk."

With Dan gone, I abandoned any attempt to remain cool and calm. I clutched Spence's arm. "Oh, my stars, Spence, look at this place." Before he could reply, I was already across the hall, examining the living room. "That fireplace," I whispered excitedly.

"Definitely works," Spence said as the logs snapped and popped. But I was already into the adjoining dining room, with its built-in china cabinet, scarred wood floors that could be sanded and refinished and more windows.

"Both rooms have a view of the lake," I observed, my voice rising now as I hurried on to the pantry, with its glass-front floor-to-ceiling cabinets and enough counter space to hold a buffet for all our friends.

I could hear Dan on the phone, so I skipped the kitchen and retraced my steps through the living room and across the foyer to a long, narrow room that the professor had obviously used as his office and library. On one side were French doors that led to a screened porch large enough to hold a worn but magnificent wicker settee and two matching chairs. Images of lazy summer evenings sitting in a darkness lit only by fireflies skittered across my mind.

"Let's check out the upstairs," Spence said, grinning as I emerged from the porch, my mouth agape. He led the way.

I paused on the landing and ran my fingers over the chintz fabric of the window seat cushions, already imagining myself curled there on a rainy Sunday afternoon, working the *Times* crossword puzzle.

"There's more," Spence said from the top of the stairs. I hurried to see what marvels waited there.

The master bedroom and its adjoining old-fashioned bath were enormous. The Kents' large four-poster bed fit easily, with plenty of room to spare. The bathroom was tiled in a sort of peach-and-green combination that would take some getting used to, but I barely noticed when I walked in and saw Spence sitting, knees to chin and fully clothed, in the old-fashioned claw-foot bathtub.

"And check this out," he said, scrambling from the tub and leading the way across the hall. "One, two, three more bedrooms, plus another full bath," he announced as he dashed from one doorway to the next. "And an attic—" he opened the last door and flicked on a switch "—with its own cedar-lined closet."

"We don't have enough furniture to fill half the rooms," I protested, but I was laughing, and even the sight of the extra bedrooms did not ignite my sorrow at failing to become pregnant. This was like Christmas morning and Santa had dropped off an entire sleigh full of goodies.

"Wait," Spence said mysteriously. "It gets better. But first let's go hear the bad news."

In the kitchen—sorely in need of updating, not to mention a really thorough cleaning—Dan laid out the downside. "Okay, start with a new roof and furnace. The windows are all wood, with separate storms and screens that have to be put up and taken down every season. Likewise the screened porch. The gardens are nonexistent. Once Dad got sick, Mom gave all her time to him and the outside pretty much went to pot."

"The boathouse?" Spence asked.

Dan shrugged. "I walked down there earlier—the steps are rotting and that roof also has to be replaced."

I glanced at Spence. This was my dream house—our dream house. If there was any way…

"Look," Dan said, "there are four of us kids all with jobs and families of our own and all hundreds of miles away. After the funeral we each chose the furniture pieces and sentimental items—books and knickknacks and such—that we wanted. The plan is to try to sell the place ourselves this fall. If that doesn't work, we put some money into fixing it up and list with a Realtor in the spring. Frankly, we'd rather get a deal done before the holidays and not have to fool with it for the next six months."

I cradled the mug of coffee and blessed Dan for the cheese spread and crackers he'd set out, as well. "So, what you're saying is—" The phone rang.

"What I'm saying is make us an offer—any reasonable offer," Dan replied on his way to take the call in the professor's study.

"What's he asking?" I whispered.

Spence named a figure and my heart fell. "It's fair, but we can't afford that, Spence."

"Actually, we can. I had Zach run some numbers earlier and—"

"But there's the roof and the furnace and the painting and the lawn and…this…" I finished, weakly motioning to the kitchen.

"Do you like it?"

"I love it. You knew I'd fall in love with it. That's why you brought me here, but—"

"Well, so do I. Let's make a fresh start, Zoe. This is the home we've both dreamed of and it's here for the taking. Let's do it."

"It would be fun," I said, glancing around, ideas for

paint colors and new kitchen curtains and how our things might fit spinning through my brain.

"Did I mention that the price includes the furniture that's here?" Spence said casually as he got up and rinsed the empty coffee mugs in the sink.

"What? You're kidding."

He turned and he was grinning like a kid. "That's what I meant upstairs when I told you it got better. Let's do it, Zoe."

And within the month we were the proud owners of a 1920s two-story house overlooking the lake, the campus, the Capitol building and, somewhere in there, our old apartment.

Spence

Over the next several months, the house claimed all our time and most of our money. Zoe's parents gave us a sizable check for the replacement of the roof and furnace. "An early Christmas present," Kay said when Zoe protested.

"Christmas, birthdays and anniversaries for the next decade," I said when Zoe showed me the check.

"Are you okay with accepting it? I can give it back."

"They'll just find another way. I just wouldn't want my folks to be upset that they can't do as much."

Zoe whirled, her eyes wide with genuine shock. "Are you nuts? Hal and your brothers have climbed all over the outside of this place patching and painting, replacing cracked windows and adding insulation so that our heating bills—even with the new furnace—don't bankrupt us."

"Yeah, but—"

"And Marie? Don't get me started on what your mother has done for us. The new drapes for the library, the wall-papering she did in the bedrooms, the..."

I could see that this was a conversation likely to go on for some time, so I did what I always did in the face of Zoe's one-sided debates. I surrendered. "Okay, you win," I said with a grin.

"It's not a matter of winning—this isn't a contest," she huffed, and went back to painting the woodwork on the sunporch. "We're incredibly lucky to have your parents and mine in—" She stood and swayed slightly, then immediately sat on the edge of the wicker ottoman.

"Zoe?"

"Paint fumes," she said with a smile that didn't quite extend all the way to her eyes. She put down the brush and held her head.

"Enough," I declared, relieving her of the paintbrush. "Go inside and lie down." I gave her my support as I walked with her into the library and led her to the worn leather sofa. She didn't protest and that worried me. "What can I get you?" I asked, covering her with the afghan Mom had made especially for this room.

"Maybe a little white soda," she said, her eyes closed. "I'll be fine."

But she slept the rest of the afternoon, and when I gently shook her to see if she could eat a little chicken soup, she moaned and closed her eyes again. The idea of Zoe any less than hale and hearty was the scariest thing I'd ever considered. "I'm calling the doctor," I muttered, more to myself than to Zoe.

"No. It's a touch of the flu or else the paint fumes got to me. I'll be fine. Just need some sleep."

I pulled a chair close and read while she slept. Near eleven she woke and sat up. "I could use a little of that soup now," she said. "And maybe a couple of saltines," she added as I hurried to the kitchen to do her bidding.

It should have occurred to me that what we were seeing were the classic symptoms of pregnancy, but we had both begun to accept the idea that perhaps children—at least of our own making—were not in our future. So, as the evidence mounted, I found every possible cause other than pregnancy, because frankly, I didn't want to get my hopes up.

The next day she was her old self—off to work for ten long hours, then home to make dinner and start in on the next project on her list. I had insisted that any more painting be put on hold until the weather permitted open doors and windows and proper ventilation. For once, Zoe hadn't argued—which told me just how lousy she'd been feeling the night before.

But when it happened again two days later—same time, only no paint fumes—I refused to listen to her protests as I went to the phone and called Elizabeth Simmons—my colleague at the medical college and our neighbor two doors down.

"Liz, tell him he's overreacting," Zoe pleaded as Liz arrived ten minutes later and calmly performed her examination.

"Here's what I'm going to tell both of you," she said quietly as she put away her stethoscope. "I'm ninety-nine percent sure that you're pregnant."

"But…" Zoe started to protest.

"Probably a couple of months—that's usually when morning sickness hits."

"It's nine o'clock at night," Zoe pointed out.

Liz shrugged as she packed up her stethoscope. "Tomorrow I want you in the office first thing so we can run a proper test." She stood up and grinned down at Zoe. "Congratulations."

Speechless, I walked with her to the door. "You're sure?"

"As sure as I can be under the circumstances," she replied as I held her coat for her. Then something in my expression must have made her reconsider the flippancy of her tone. "Spence, I'm sure enough that I said it outright in there instead of waiting until tomorrow. I would never want to disappoint either of you after all you've been through wanting this news."

"Thanks." I opened the door for her. Then, overwhelmed with the realization that this was almost certainly for real, I hugged her. "Thanks," I repeated joyfully.

"Oh, sure," Zoe announced from the doorway to the library, "I'm barely pregnant and you're already making moves on another woman." Then she grinned and held out her arms to me.

I caught her and swung her round and round as we repeated the incredible and completely unexpected news. "We hadn't even been trying," she said at the same time that I shouted, "A baby—*our* baby."

Somewhere in there Liz let herself out and gently closed the door.

After these initial bouts of morning-in-the-evening sickness, Zoe sailed through pregnancy as if she'd already done it a dozen times. And if brides are radiant, they are pale and bland compared with a woman anticipating her first child. Zoe had always been beautiful, but now there was a kind of ethereal luminosity that took my breath away.

"Spence?" Zoe whispered one night about six weeks before her due date. "It's time."

I had just gotten to bed after working most of the

night completing a journal article on my theory on post-traumatic stress syndrome. I had fallen into bed and instantly into an exhausted slumber. "Just got here," I mumbled, and pulled the pillow over my head.

"For the baby," she said calmly.

Her words registered and I was immediately wide-awake, grabbing for my trousers and shoes without bothering with socks. Zoe sat across from me on the chair next to her dresser. She was dressed, her hands folded primly in her lap and the bag that Mom had helped her pack was at her feet.

"I have to call Elizabeth," I said, stumbling about like a drunken sailor, grabbing for glasses, wallet, the sweatshirt I kept on the back of the closet door.

Zoe stood up and held out the car keys. "Calm down. I called Liz when the contractions started half an hour ago. They're still at least fifteen minutes apart—in fact, this may be what they call false…"

Her voice trailed off and her face went white as she dropped the keys and grabbed her protruding belly. "Right," I muttered as I picked up the keys and scooped Zoe into my arms. "Let's go."

"The bag," she protested.

"I'll come back for it after we see why this kid is in such a rush." I carried her down the stairs and through the house to the garage, where I deposited her in the car and raced around to get in myself.

"The lights," she said.

"Leave 'em," I said, and then cursed as I flooded the engine.

"Tender ears," she warned, pointing to her tummy. Then she gasped again. "We'd better hurry," she admitted.

If sheer will can start a car, it worked that night. The VW Bug we'd bought when we got married finally caught and I roared out of the garage and down the winding street.

"You're going to get a ticket," Zoe observed, her voice sounding far away and weaker by the minute.

"Then the kid gets a police escort. Hang on," I ordered, and floored it.

Liz was already at the hospital, gowned and ready for anything. I could see that she was worried and trying not to show it.

"It's too soon," I protested.

"We'll see," was her noncommittal response, and in that moment I vowed to reexamine my own script for reassuring family members, because I definitely was not reassured by Liz's words or her expression.

"Spence?"

Zoe's voice trembled.

"Right here, love." I grasped her hand as the aides wheeled her along the corridors as if they were doing time trials for the Indy 500. "Everything's going to be fine. Liz is right here."

Zoe nodded and then smiled. "Your daughter's in a hurry," she said.

"Our *son* takes after his mother," I replied as the double doors at the end of the hall opened with a pop, exposing an operating theater where nurses and others immediately went into action with no direction from Liz.

"You guys have done this before," Zoe observed, her words already beginning to slur from the drugs they were pumping through the IV a nurse had inserted into her arm almost before the gurney came to a halt.

"Oh, honey, we're the best," the nurse assured her.

"That's why they pay us the really big bucks." The orderlies transferring Zoe from the gurney to the table laughed.

Liz examined Zoe, consulted quietly with two other doctors, gave some orders to the staff and then turned to Zoe. "Your baby is coming. It's early, but you're both strong. The problem is the position, so we're going to put you under and perform a cesarean. That—"

"No." This was Zoe—a single word, strongly stated and undebatable.

"But, Zoe," Liz began again, lifting her eyes to mine, pleading for help.

"Can you do it without doing the C-section?" I asked.

"Well, sure, but…"

Zoe gripped my hand so tight I thought at least two fingers would crack. "She's waited a long time for this and it's important to her. It's her call," I replied.

Zoe's fingers relaxed, then tightened again as the next contraction hit. "Jeezle Pete," she yelled, and then blew out her breath in the panting sounds she and I had learned in our prenatal training. "Check again," she said to Liz when the contraction passed. "I'm pretty sure the kid just stuck the landing on a triple somersault."

Liz did as Zoe asked, then looked at me and shook her head once.

I bent close to Zoe, turning my back on everyone else. "Zoe, you don't have to do this. You're not going to be any less a great mom just because you—"

She grabbed the front of my sweatshirt and pulled me closer. "Now, you listen to me, farm boy. Unless you want to trade places and lie here on this gurney with eighteen people checking out your privates, every few minutes followed by repeated karate kicks to your gut, you don't get to decide what I can and cannot do, okay? As long as I'm not endangering our child—and I'm not, right?" She glanced up at Liz for confirmation.

Liz hesitated, then sighed and shook her head. "No, you're just being stubborn and putting yourself through more than you need to."

"But I can do this—we can do this, right?" she asked, gently running her hands over her extended belly.

"You can do it," Liz agreed.

Zoe smiled and released me. "Then let's have ourselves a baby."

Camilla Louise Andersen—named for two of her great-grandmothers—entered the world some eighteen hours later. She weighed just over five pounds, had a full head of black hair, my eyes and her mother's temperament, stating her needs from the start. But she was also a miracle—a tiny being who would settle into what Zoe called "coo" stage, sleeping or simply lying quietly and taking in the world around her.

"Hey, Cami," Zoe said softly as she studied the miracle that was our firstborn. "Welcome to our world."

1976

Zoe

It didn't take long for me to realize the upside of waiting so long to become a mother. My friends had learned from their mistakes and couldn't wait to fill me in on the basics—what car seat was the best for infants, what formula to use, what diaper service was the best deal. For another thing, I'd had plenty of time to observe and figure out how Spence and I would do things differently.

Of course we failed to count on the fact that Cami might have her own ideas about how this relationship was going to work. I should have suspected that she had her own agenda when she hit every baby milestone—crawling, solid food, walking, talking—well ahead of schedule. She redefined the concept of "terrible twos," stubbornly refusing to even consider the logic or reason behind a normal routine of eating and sleeping. At three she did an abrupt about-face, becoming such a sweetheart that at one point I asked Spence, "Who is this child and what has she done with Cami?" In fact, she was so well-adjusted that I was able to return to work full-time. Then six months after that she morphed into Daddy's little tomboy—fearless and oblivious to the possibility that she might be hurt.

"Camilla Louise Andersen," I said, and Cami froze, her back to me, her feet dangling from the low willow tree branch she'd managed to inch her way onto. Now that she was four she was well aware that anyone who used her entire name meant business.

Spence had persuaded me that spending an unexpectedly mild winter weekend on the farm was a good idea. Never mind that I had cases up the wazoo at Legal Aid. Never mind that caring for Cami was a full-time job when she wasn't in preschool or being watched by one of the college students we used as sitters. Never mind that Spence seemed to just assume that the house would get cleaned at least semiannually and the food would appear in the cupboards and refrigerator. Never mind that...

"Where's your father?" I asked as I strode across the lawn, my leather briefcase with its full load of homework smacking at my side with each step. *And where's your coat?* I wanted to add.

"He went to help Grandpa."

She nodded toward the field beyond the house. Hal was sitting on the ground leaning against a fence post. Spence was kneeling next to him. I turned back to Cami, torn between my daughter in a tree and my father-in-law on the ground.

"I'm okay, Mama," she insisted as she leaned forward

and wrapped her short stubby arms around the branch. "See?" she shouted down at me as she swung one leg over the branch.

"Wait," I cried, dropping the briefcase and running toward her.

In true Hollywood slow motion, the weight of her swinging round the limb broke her hold and she was falling. My feet seemed set in concrete and in the background I could hear Spence yelling. Just before I reached for her, my shoe caught on a rock hidden in a pile of frozen leaves and I fell forward, landing on my chest, the wind knocked out of me. A split second later I felt Cami land on top of me and in that second there was the most astonishing silence, broken only by the lazy drone of a distant tractor.

Then Cami wailed and Spence shouted for his mother to hurry, and suddenly I was surrounded.

"I broke…" Cami bawled as she lay on top of me and clung to me, sobbing.

"Come on, honey," Marie said. "Let Grandma have a look."

"No!" Cami screamed, and clung tighter to me. "I broke Mommy."

My chest hurt and I felt as though my breathing would never again be normal, but of course I knew better. "I'm fine, Cami," I managed as I attempted to roll over.

"Lie still," Spence ordered before focusing his attention on our daughter. "Cami, Mommy is going to be fine. Let Daddy check her for owies, okay?"

I both heard and felt through the light fabric of my jacket a noisy, wet sniffle, then I felt the weight of her lifted away from me.

"Can you turn over?" Spence asked, his fingers already

gently probing here and there, checking for broken or dislocated bones.

I eased onto my side and saw Hal standing next to Marie.

"See?" Marie told Cami. "There's Mommy. You didn't break her at all."

Cami swiped at her eyes with the back of one small fist and stared down at me, frowning. "I'm sorry, Mommy," she said. "I'm sorry I made you fall down."

"I'm fine, Cami. Are you fine, too?"

She nodded.

Spence helped me sit up. "Just stay put," he ordered, and continued his examination. "Mom, would you and Cami get the car keys? I think we should all take a little trip here."

"Ice cream?" Cami guessed, her smile and eyes widening in equal delight.

"Maybe," Marie replied after looking from Spence to me to Hal and back again. "Let's hurry and find the keys."

"Get in the car, Dad," Spence said as he helped me to my feet.

"There's no reason for all of us—" Hal began.

"Get in the car," Spence repeated, and Hal headed back toward the house.

"What happened out there?" I asked as Spence wrapped his arm around me for support.

"He went out to check the field and got dizzy...damn near fainted. Fortunately, he'd stopped for a minute near the fence. Cami saw him sitting on the ground."

"What is it?"

"That's what we're going to the hospital to find out." His face was set in what I referred to as his "doctor-mode"— that serious but noncommittal expression he used with patients. Hal and Marie were already in back, with Cami between them, when we got to the car. Spence half lifted me onto the passenger seat and I couldn't help remembering the night that Cami was born.

Cami's presence in the car made conversation unnecessary. She told every horse, cow and sheep she spotted in the fields along the road that we were on our way for ice cream, that her favorite was peach but Grandma thought they might not have that so she was going to have strawberry, instead. The glances that passed among the four grown-ups spoke volumes. Marie's worried sidelong glances at Hal. Hal watching Spence as he passed a slow-moving hay wagon on a double line. And Spence splitting his time between me to his right and Cami and his dad in the rearview mirror.

Spence looked tired and older. When had those lines around his mouth deepened? Where was the sparkle of intelligence and curiosity with which he viewed the most ordinary everyday events? And why had I failed to notice?

I placed my hand on his thigh, startling him, so that he actually jumped and then glanced at me. "It's okay," I said softly. "We're all okay."

Spence

Maybe and maybe not, I thought. Under other circumstances I would have called for an ambulance, but by the time one could arrive at the farm, I could be halfway to the hospital. Also, I hadn't wanted to alarm any of them, but the facts were that by any standards Dad's heart rate had been off the charts, while his hands and face had been clammy and cold. He had recovered quickly, but still…. Cami had a bump on her forehead that was probably no more than a nasty bruise, but still…. The scariest thing of all, though, was that Zoe was bleeding—possibly internally.

When she'd fallen her skirt had bunched beneath her, and when I turned her over and was examining her for signs of broken bones, I'd seen a couple of spots of blood on her inner thigh. Not a lot of blood, but unmistakably fresh. All I could think of as I raced blindly for the emergency room was, *What if? What if Dad had suffered a heart attack or small stroke? What if Cami was hurt worse than she appeared? What if Zoe…?* I couldn't—wouldn't—think about Zoe incapacitated in any way.

Mom had alerted the hospital when she went to get the car keys, so they were ready for us when we arrived.

"Mom, take Cami inside, okay?" I saw Cami's eyes fill again. "Daddy just wants to be sure Grandpa and Mommy are okay," I assured her, and Mom hustled her off. "Possible heart attack," I barked, nodding toward Dad as he got out of the car on his own. "And a room for my wife," I added as I helped Zoe into the wheelchair the aide had brought to her side of the car.

"Curtain three," the aide said as he pushed Zoe through the automatic doors.

"Go check on your kid," Mark Torres directed as he pushed back the curtain and prepared to examine Zoe. "Go on, Andersen. You're way too stressed out to do this."

"Go," Zoe agreed. "I'm fine, really. Just tape up the ankle and I'll be good as new, right, Mark?" She pressed her hand to my chest and added, "Check on Hal, honey. Marie's really scared."

I kissed her, then gave Mark a flick of my eyes to let him know we needed to talk outside. "Don't go away," Mark told Zoe, and I saw that she wasn't fooled.

Mark listened as I described what had happened, made a couple of notes, then grabbed one of the floor nurses and returned to Zoe. I stayed just outside the curtain and listened.

"We're going to run a few tests just to appease the old man, okay?" Mark told her.

Zoe laughed. "He can be such a baby when it comes to any of us. Sorry to put you through this."

"Hey, you know what they say about us docs loving to run up those insurance charges." Then his tone changed to business mode as he dictated orders to the nurse. Satisfied that Mark was taking this seriously and not just doing me a favor, I went across the hall to check on Dad.

By the time Dad's condition had been diagnosed as dehydration and he'd had a couple of liters of fluids pumped into him, Cami was sound asleep in the tiny waiting room. Her head was resting on Mom's lap. I gave Mom the good news about Dad and her face went from delight to consternation in the space of ten seconds.

"I have told that man a thousand times," she muttered as she eased herself free of Cami and stood up. "Where is he?"

I pointed her in the right direction and returned to my daughter, who was sitting up now, rubbing the sleep from her eyes.

"I thought we were going for ice cream," she muttered irritably when she realized we were still at the hospital.

"We did. You slept through the whole thing," I replied, sitting next to her and gathering her onto my lap.

She giggled. "Daddy, that's a fib," she said.

I chuckled and hugged her a little closer. "Yep, you caught me. We had to wait for the doctors to fix up Grandpa."

She squirmed free and looked around. "Where's Mommy?" Her voice bordered on panic, so I reached for her. She scooted away from me, and in that moment her expression was one I knew all too well. Whenever Zoe wanted an answer and was not getting the answer she wanted, she had that very same expression.

"Mommy's here," Zoe announced from the doorway. She smiled weakly and held out her arms.

Cami shrieked and ran for the wheelchair where Zoe sat, one leg extended with the ankle wrapped. Mark was acting as her driver.

I shot him a look and he grinned. I glanced at Zoe as she held Cami against her.

"How's Hal?" she asked.

"Dehydration," I said. "What's the story?"

"She'll need to stay off her feet for a while," Mark said.

"Is it broken?" *What about the bleeding*, I wanted to say but wasn't sure what Zoe knew and didn't know at this point. I resisted the urge to strangle the guy for being so damn cheerful in the face of my wife's pain.

"It's a sprain. I have to stay off my feet for another—unrelated—reason," Zoe said. She glanced back at Mark.

Now I was fully capable of strangling both of them.

Zoe

I was pregnant. Mark obviously assumed I was aware of that fact as he completed his examination and read through the lab results he'd pushed through.

When he dropped it into the conversation, I smiled, not yet ready to reveal my shock at the news.

"You've had a little spotting, but everything seems to be okay for now. I've ordered an ultrasound. They should be here any minute." He touched my hand. "Does Spence know?"

"Not yet," I replied. *I didn't know so how could I tell Spence?*

"Want me to get him?" Mark asked as the tech arrived to perform the ultrasound.

"No. He's got enough to deal with. He's very worried about Hal—and Cami."

"And you," Mark added. "Okay, I'll go check on Hal and Cami and be back in a minute. You stay put."

He returned with the news that Cami would have a bump and bruise for a couple of days. "She probably cracked heads with you as she landed," Mark said. "She'll be fine," he added with a reassuring squeeze of my hand. "She's out in the waiting room with your mother-in-law."

I exhaled my relief. "Two hardheaded women. And Hal?"

"They're still running some tests, but it appears that he's going to be fine, as well. Spence, on the other hand, looks like hell. I passed him in the hall as he was running between Hal and Cami. Pretty clear that he wants to be here with you, but Spence can't help himself. He always has to be where the need is greatest."

I thought about all the nights I'd held dinner because a student needed him or a journal article needed a rewrite that couldn't wait or… And I hated myself for wondering, *But what about me? What about what I need?* Now we were going to have more children. It was what we had dreamed of in the early days of our marriage, but over the past four years I had gotten used to having just Cami. Truth was I couldn't imagine caring for multiple children, when it seemed every waking moment was spent meeting Cami's needs—or Spence's. And yet I wanted this child. I just wanted Spence to want it as much—enough to step away from some of the demands of his career and be there more—for this child, for Cami and for me.

"Spence is going to be thrilled about this news," Mark said, now examining the printout from the ultrasound. "He's been talking about having more kids ever since Cami arrived."

He has? Sure, he'd mentioned the idea once or twice but not in the way Mark saw it—not as if this was something he'd been really wanting.

"I didn't know that," I said, and immediately wished I hadn't.

Mark studied me for a long minute. "Well, you've been pretty busy yourself, from what Spence tells me. Working long hours and then managing the house and Cami. Spence talks like there's nothing you can't do." He waited a beat and added, "You know, Zoe, after my divorce the one thing I realized is how little I paid attention—to Carol, to what she said, to what she thought…."

We are not you and Carol, I wanted to shout, but his words had touched a nerve. The truth was that lately a big part of my frustration and irritability with Spence had to do with fear. All around us couples who had seemed joined for life were coming apart at the seams, and I couldn't help but wonder if it could happen to us.

"What does that thing tell you?" I asked, changing the subject by pointing at the ultrasound printout.

Mark grinned. "It tells me that you'd better be everything Spence says you are and more because, superlady, in about six months you are going to have twins."

"Twins?" I gulped. "You're sure?"

Mark laughed. "See for yourself." He handed me the ultrasound printout.

Twins. I felt a twinge of delight—or was that panic?

Mark commandeered a wheelchair from the hallway and helped me into it. "I want you to spend the rest of this weekend on total bed rest," he instructed. "I'll call Liz and be sure she can see you on Monday—if not in the office, then at home—and we'll let her take it from there, okay?"

"Do I have a choice?"

"Not really. Not if you want to hang on to those babies."

And suddenly I knew that I did—more than anything I could have imagined. I hadn't known I was pregnant, and yet now the news held such promise, such joy, such hope. I heard Cami asking—no, demanding—to see me, and then we turned a corner and there was Spence. He was tired and scared, and all I wanted to do was hold him and tell him everything was going to be all right—*we* were going to be all right.

"When did you know?" he asked as he held me that night. We had done the calendar thing and figured out that conception had occurred on a combined holiday and medical meeting in Rome. My purse—with birth control pills—had been stolen the day before. On our last night there the medical society surprised Spence by presenting him their prestigious Healer of the Year award. No stolen purse could take the glow off that for either of us. I was so proud of him. Pills or no pills, we made love.

"I found out about twenty minutes before you did," I admitted. "And yes, I was just as surprised as you were."

He laughed and the warmth of his breath on my nape told me that the news of the babies was indeed good news. "I've been trying to put it together," I said. "I mean, how could I miss it? Three months?"

"You've been busy," he said, and we both laughed at the absurdity of the idea that even at her busiest, a woman wouldn't notice three missed periods. Then Spence sat up. "Unless you've been spotting all along?"

"A couple of times," I admitted, "but they were about when I would have had my period, and I thought that because of the stress at work and everything…"

Spence lay down and wrapped his arms around me. "At least we know now," he said. "We'll just have to be very very careful."

"Meaning no sex?" I asked, teasing him out of this overprotective mood that could become smothering if left unchecked.

He kissed me. "Meaning," he whispered, "no intercourse, but finding new and innovative ways to make love should keep us busy until these guys get here." He lifted my nightgown and tenderly planted kisses over my stomach and hipbones before moving up to my breasts, easing my gown higher and finally off completely.

Spence

"Daddy, what are fireworks?"

"You've seen fireworks before, Cami. They're those bright colors in the sky that make the booms and the crackling sounds."

"I know *that*, Daddy. I want to know what they are."

We were decorating her tricycle for the annual neighborhood Independence Day parade. I looked at my daughter, at the intensity of expression so like Zoe's, and understood that this wasn't just about fireworks. "Well," I began, choosing each word.

"Because Ben says that they're made out of bullets and

that they could *kill* somebody who just happens to get in the way and…"

Ben Fields and Cami had been friends since Zoe had formed a play group with several other mothers when the kids were two. "Well, Ben's only partly right, honey," I said. "You see—"

"And then I heard Grandma talking to Grandpa and I know I'm not s'posed to eardrop, but I couldn't help it…."

"Eavesdrop," I corrected automatically. "What did Grandma say?"

"She told Poppa that she always worries about how you'll do with all these fireworks going off. She said that it had to sound like the war all over again for you. Is that true, Daddy? I thought you liked the fireworks. Mommy loves them and I thought…"

"I like fireworks just fine," I told her. "Not as much as Mommy does, but just fine." *Should I bring the conversation back to her friend Ben or leave it at this?*

"Well, that's what I thought, too," she said, turning her attention back to wrapping crepe paper streamers through the wheels of her tricycle. "But Ben says that this time the fireworks are going to be bigger than ever because of the bikesentinel and—"

"Bicentennial," I corrected while mentally wanting to take Ben Fields aside and give him a piece of my mind.

"Yeah, and Ben says there are gonna be explosions— like bombs. Did you hear bombs when you were in the war, Daddy?"

Almost two years had passed since I'd had a flashback, and yet it hit me with the vividness of yesterday. The noise, the confusion, the yelling, the night sky lit, the smoke that settled over camp like a thick fog, the men staggering out of the jungle—limping, screaming, bleeding....

"Daddy?"

Cami's face was close and her eyes were wide with fear.

I hugged her and held on. "Now you listen to me," I said softly. "Ben Fields is mixed up about some things. He's right that they use a kind of explosive to make fireworks—that's why they make those noises. And he's right that they can hurt someone who doesn't know how to light them properly. But fireworks are about joy and celebration, Cami. They have nothing to do with war, okay? When we watch them tonight, we'll be celebrating the birthday of America—our country is two hundred years old. Can you imagine that?"

"That's older than Poppa," Cami said, her voice muffled against my shirt.

I laughed and loosened my hold on her. "That's more than Poppa and Grandma put together and then some," I assured her.

Cami scrambled down and started back to work on her bike. "I'm going to tell that Ben Fields that he doesn't know *everything* about fireworks," she announced. "*His* daddy didn't even go to the war, so what does he know?" she muttered.

An unexpected conversation with my innocent daughter influenced everything I saw that night as Zoe, Cami and I lay on our blanket in the backyard while the fireworks soared above the skyline and the dome of the Capitol building across the lake. For the first time since returning from 'Nam I felt as though I might finally have turned a corner and started to put the horror I'd witnessed there in perspective.

"Spence?" Zoe squeezed my hand and I assumed that as usual somehow she had tapped into my thoughts.

"That one was a ten, right, Dad?" Cami squealed as a large chrysanthemum-shaped firework spread its golden dust over the sky.

"Maybe an eleven," I replied, and squeezed Zoe's hand in return.

But Zoe didn't let go. "Spence," she said again—a whisper that was a shout.

"Mom!" I called back to where my parents and Zoe's sat in lawn chairs on the patio. Both grandmothers ran to us.

"Whoa!" Cami shrieked covering her ears and laughing as the fireworks went into their grand finale.

I helped Zoe to her feet and we walked back toward the house. Dad had already gone inside for the car keys.

"Where's everybody going?" Cami shouted in the silence that followed the final display of light and color and noise.

"For ice cream," Zoe said as a contraction took hold.

"Oh," Cami said, disappointed. Ever since our trip to the hospital the previous February after her fall and Dad's dizzy spell, Cami associated going for ice cream as adult double talk for seeing the doctor. "Do I have to go?"

"Absolutely not," Mike Wingfield said, scooping Cami high in his arms and swinging her around. "Let's have some of that peach ice cream your Grandma Marie made this afternoon."

"With chocolate syrup," Dad promised her in a conspiratorial tone. Cami squealed with delight and forgot all about us.

"Hey," Zoe said after she was settled in the birthing room, "maybe, given the occasion, we need to rethink the names."

"I am not saddling a kid of mine with Yankee Doodle."

She laughed and then grimaced as a contraction took hold. "What's wrong with Sam?" she grunted. "Sammy?"

"Too close to Cami," I said, coaching her with puffs of breath. "Besides, what would we call the other guy?"

In the end we stuck with the names we'd originally selected for the twins—Todd and Taylor Wingfield Andersen. Todd arrived a few minutes before midnight on the Fourth of July and Taylor followed just a few minutes into the fifth.

"Oh, goody," an exhausted Zoe cracked, "two birthday parties *and* the Fourth."

Mom laughed. "I'll start making cakes."

Later, after Zoe had drifted into sleep and our parents had left, I walked down the darkened corridors to the nursery and stood at the window, watching my sons. Todd was sleeping soundly, while Taylor flailed about in his bassinet. He wasn't crying and didn't seem to be in pain. It was just as if he wanted to get on with it—life. He was here and he had no intention of wasting a moment.

1982

Zoe

I decided not to keep working once the boys were born. Over the course of my pregnancy I had fallen in love with the image of myself as a kind of grand earth mother—raising my children, cooking healthy meals using the fresh produce I would grow in my gardens. And even though the boys meant twice the work, I approached it with more confidence and less angst than I'd had with Cami. Our growing family settled into a lifestyle that I assumed would work for all of us for years to come. Days blended into months and years as we evolved into a routine that on the surface was the realization of everything we'd ever wanted.

But by the time the twins were six and Cami was ten going on eighteen, I had finally accepted that being tagged

"Supermom" demanded a certain level of constant activity that, once completed, returned to be done again within the week, day or hour. Dishes, laundry, carpools, lunches to pack, homework to oversee, shopping to be done, not to mention basic housework like dusting and vacuuming—something that had never been my strong suit. Spence offered to help, but I was determined to live up to the model I'd set for myself—the model set by Spence's mother, Marie.

She had parented three sons, who at one point in her young life had all been under the age of six. She had maintained a spotless home, never missed a game or parent-teacher conference, actually won blue ribbons at the state fair for her baked goods and canning, and somehow managed to operate a successful child-care program in the old farmhouse until Willie was in high school. Through all of this, she did not lose her identity as a woman with opinions and dreams of her own. I should have hated her. The fact was that I adored her.

I, on the other hand, was always falling behind and falling short of the expectations I had set for myself. While my role model, Marie, had managed her child-care business along with everything else, I had told myself that given my true calling as perfect wife and mother, my law degree no longer defined me in any way. And then one day I realized that I'd allowed things to get completely beyond my control. I wasn't Marie—I wasn't even a poor imitation. The truth was that I missed the challenge of working, of being with adults solving adult-type problems.

Worse than that was the growing distance I was putting between Spence and me. At breakfast Spence had been

telling me about the new office manager he'd just hired—
a woman he clearly found to be funny and smart and interesting. I was thinking through my day—fold laundry, call
the kids' schools, load the dishwasher, make the beds,
clean the toilets…

"You would love her, Zoe."

"No doubt," I had muttered as I took T-shirts, jeans and
underwear in a variety of sizes still warm from the dryer
and folded them.

Spence kept singing the praises of the woman and I
kept folding laundry, making a show of each step in the
process, exaggerating the precision of each fold.

Finally, he put down his coffee cup, sat back and
watched me. His silence was worse than his babbling on
about a woman who had obviously captured his interest in
a way I was apparently incapable of these days.

"I'm listening," I said as if he had accused me of not.

"You're steaming," he replied. Sometimes his ability to
cut through the surface to the heart of the matter could be
beyond annoying.

"Don't analyze me," I said through gritted teeth as I
grabbed the laundry basket, swung around, hit the corner of
the table and dropped the whole thing. Freshly folded laundry
flew into the air and settled in a chaotic heap on the floor.

Spence got up and started helping me retrieve the
pieces, making his own clumsy attempt at refolding things
as he went.

"Don't," I said, snatching a towel from him and stuffing
it unfolded into the basket. "You'll be late and you'll miss
your new office manager's latest tale."

Spence dropped the laundry he'd been holding and took
me by the shoulders, pulling us both to our feet. "What's

going on?" he asked gently as I stood there clenched and stoic, trying hard not to scream or burst into sobs.

"Go," I whispered.

"Honey, Irene is in her fifties. Surely you can't think that—"

I met his eyes then. "But she's funny and interesting and she has great ideas and she's going to make such a difference to the office," I said, paraphrasing the way he had described Irene.

Spence looked confused. I could see that he was really trying hard to understand and I was the green-eyed monster, jealous of a fifty-something woman who had finally found a place in the world where she was appreciated. I pulled away and walked out of the room.

It was true, I thought. Without my noticing, my brain had turned to mush. I could quote every line of *Green Eggs and Ham*, but I couldn't find the time for anything that might define me beyond being Spence's wife or the children's mother. I was frankly envious of his research and potential for building something truly life-changing for so many people.

"What about what I could do for the world?" I screamed into a towel as I sobbed in the bathroom. Then I immediately felt the remorse of a woman who on the surface has more than many women ever have. A husband who adores her, gifted and lovable children, a beautiful home on a lake where every room reflected the reality of the dream Spence and I had set forth to achieve. I washed my face and combed my hair and unlocked the bathroom door.

I walked down the stairs, past the twins occupied by television in the family room and back into the kitchen, where Spence had taken the time to gather up the laundry and clear away his breakfast dishes before leaving for work. In the center of the table was a Post-it note. On it was a crude drawing of a closed door and the words *Please let me in, because I love you.*

I picked up the phone and began making the calls to the kids' schools.

"This is Mrs. Andersen—Cami's mom—and I won't be able to chaperone the field trip tomorrow. My sons are ill with the flu."

Then, fingering a T-shirt, rumpled but still folded, I phoned Spence's office at the university and got not the wonderful new office manager but rather the latest in a line of inept administrative assistants for the department. "This is Zoe Andersen. No, not a student. Dr. Andersen's wife. Is he there? Well, when he returns from class, please ask him to call. Yes, his wife." *Mother of his children and—what else?*

As I went about completing the morning chores almost by rote, I found myself focusing in on the revelation that had struck me earlier. Exactly when had my primary identity become wife and mother? Not that those weren't perfectly wonderful roles to play in life, but they weren't the whole of it—were they? They weren't the whole of me, were they? I found myself mentally humming the Peggy Lee song as I scraped the remains of my breakfast—dry toast with jam—into the sink and flicked on the garbage disposal. The twins were still settled on the sofa, watching *Sesame Street.* Earlier—before the scene with Spence—Cami had stomped off to catch the bus after a tearful tirade about my not chaperoning the field trip—a trip I might add that she had originally been mortified to think I might actually want to volunteer to chaperone.

But this wasn't about the trip. This was the same argument she had staged numerous times since her brothers had arrived on the scene.

"You always pick them," she accused, casting lethal glances toward the family room, where the boys could be heard giggling over the latest antics of Cookie Monster. "They don't look that sick to me."

"I do not always choose them," I said reasonably as I spread peanut butter and jam on bread and gathered the rest of her lunch in the pink fairy-princess lunch box she had declared she absolutely could not live without a month earlier.

"I hate this thing," she announced. "It's a baby's lunch box."

Without a word, I handed her a plain brown paper bag. She stared at me as if I had just offered her a liner for the trash. I shrugged. "Make a choice," I said quietly. "Carry the box or take the bag, but understand that in accepting the bag, you are agreeing to have fifty cents deducted from your allowance each week until the lunch box is paid for."

"You're horrible," she muttered as she grabbed the lunch box and slammed out the door.

Later, as I stood at the window, recalling Cami trudging down the drive, I felt a tug at my jeans. Todd was standing next to me.

"Taylor just threw up," he announced, then proceeded— as usual—to repeat what his brother had just done.

By the time I'd cleaned up both boys, the family room carpet, the kitchen floor and myself, it was almost noon. After starting my third load of laundry in two days, I fixated on the refrigerator, trying to decide what the boys could eat that wouldn't bring on a repeat of what I'd just finished cleaning up. I needed to go grocery shopping. I needed to clean the house. I needed to clean the refrigerator. Marie's birthday was a week away and then the holidays. It was our turn to host Thanksgiving.

The phone rang. I assumed it was Spence finally getting back to me and answered it in a tone that would clearly relay my irritation at his taking three hours to do so.

"So, how's your day going?" I said sarcastically.

"Zoe?"

I froze. The voice was familiar, yet hard to place in the context of life as I knew it these days. "Yes?" I answered cautiously.

"It's Peter. Peter Quarles."

I let out a breath and laugh that sounded more than a little hysterical. "Peter!"

"Are you okay? You sound…"

"Frazzled? Welcome to my world," I quipped. "How are you? *Where* are you? Last I heard you were in Boston. Or was it New York, doing the corporate-law thing?"

"Well, yeah, there is a point when a guy has to earn a little serious money, you know," he replied sheepishly. "Actually, I'm here—in Madison. I was thinking we could get together for a drink."

Did people still do that? I wondered. *Go out for a leisurely drink with an old friend?*

"I…"

"Mommy?" This time it was Taylor tugging at my jeans. I covered the receiver with one hand.

"Mommy's on the phone, sweetheart, okay?"

He nodded, then sat cross-legged on the floor, clearly prepared to wait his turn. Automatically, I pressed my palm to his forehead and studied him for signs of distress.

"Zoe? You there?"

"Yeah. Yes. Right here. Sorry, my kids are fighting a bug and—"

"Okay, I'll cut to the chase." Peter drew an audible breath and delivered his message. "I'd really like to get together, Zoe. I want to talk to you about coming to work for—with me," Peter said.

"You're joking."

"Nope. Here's the digest version. I'm running for mayor," Peter continued, oblivious to the scene on my end of the phone. "I'd like to talk to you about being my campaign manager."

"Mayor?" I asked blankly. "Of Boston?"

Peter laughed. "Of Madison. I'm home, Zoe. It could be like old times."

My mind raced with possibilities. If the boys were feeling better, if Cami didn't come down with it, if— Who was I kidding? I couldn't even handle my own household. There was no way that I could reasonably...

"Hey, sure it's been years, and maybe this is not going to work for either of us—obviously I've changed and no doubt you have, as well—but I'd like to at least have a chance to explore the possibilities. Okay? No strings—for either of us."

"How about coffee Friday at the Union—on the terrace?" I proposed.

"Name the time," Peter said, and I could tell he was smiling.

I calculated the morning schedule—school bus for Cami, carpool for the boys. Spence... "Early—eight-thirty."

He groaned. "I never was a morning person, Zoe. You know that."

"Take it or leave it," I said, and I was smiling, as well.

"All right, you win. And Zoe?"

"Yeah?"

"I really hope this works out. All those plans for the greater good that we had before I went radical on you? We could still make them happen, Zoe."

My heart pounded and I understood that it had nothing to do with Peter. It had to do with what Peter was offering—a chance for me to rediscover Zoe again.

I hung up, and having instantly rationalized why adding a more than full-time job to my already overwhelming responsibilities would be a good idea, I gave a whoop of joy. When I turned around, both boys were sitting on the floor, gazing up at me.

The phone rang again and I grabbed for it, smiling at the boys as I tucked the phone between my ear and shoulder and opened a can of chicken noodle soup.

"Zoe? I got your message. Is something wrong? Are you okay? Are the boys worse?" Spence's voice was slightly panicked.

"Everything's fine. The twins are actually better—hungry. I'm fixing them some soup."

A pause, the sound of rustling papers, the tap of keys on a keyboard. As usual Spence was multitasking while we talked. "Oh. Well, good. It's just that I got this message you called and then I couldn't reach you—the line was busy and—"

"Everything's fine, Spence," I assured him, and recognized that I was deliberately avoiding telling him that Peter Quarles had called. "What time will you be home? I need to go grocery shopping. The cupboard is bare." I tried to keep light and teasing, but I knew my words came out only this side of bitchy.

Spence sighed. "I'm not sure. Why don't I pick up pizza and we can watch a movie with the kids?"

"Pizza is not the best choice for kids with queasy stomachs," I said primly.

"I thought you said they were better."

"They are, but let's not push our luck, okay?" I paused for a breath. "I'll phone Jenny. If she can't come over, then when you get home we'll have something and then I'll go shopping later."

"Hey," he said softly.

It worked as it always did. I drew in another deep breath and calmed myself. "It's fine," I told him, and meant it. "I've got enough stuff for supper. Call when you're on your way, okay?"

Jenny, the college sophomore we hired regularly to stay with the kids, arrived promptly as always at three. She was a burst of sunshine for the boys, who'd been figuratively tiptoeing around the foul mood that had replaced my jubilation as reality set in. Who was I kidding? Running a political campaign was about the least Mom-friendly job I could imagine. I told myself to get back to Peter and cancel, but I didn't have his number. Okay. We'd meet for coffee, catch up on our news and go our separate ways.

What will Spence think?

It's just coffee, for heaven's sake.

Cami's bus pulled up just as I was getting in the car. She blew past me as soon as she saw Jenny at the door, obviously delighted at this turn of events.

"Jenny, you won't believe what happened today."

Cami's immediate bond with Jenny played directly into the internal dialogue I'd been having with myself all day. I felt invisible—to my children, to my husband, but most of all to me. As I backed out of the driveway, I caught sight of my reflection in the rearview mirror. And was stunned at the stranger staring back at me. No makeup. Hair hastily caught into a rubber band I'd found lying on the counter with my keys. Baseball cap pulled low. I was almost forty years old. How come I hadn't yet figured out what I wanted to be when I grew up?

The truth was I wanted it all—I always had. Further, I had always believed that it was all possible. I had set out to become three things—Spence's wife, a dynamite mom and a socially responsible citizen. I was not about to admit failure on any level—not yet.

In the forty-five minutes it took me to drive to the supermarket, park the car and navigate the familiar aisles, throwing in items almost by rote, I arrived at a decision. It was time for a change—in fact, change was way overdue, and it was no one's fault but my own. We were a family, but we were also individuals. The balance was off because everyone's individual needs were being met except mine—and whose fault was that?

I studied the food in the cart—staples, along with far too much convenience food. I picked up the bottle of spaghetti sauce and read the label. The salt and sugar alone were enough to send a healthy person running to a cardiologist. I retraced my steps, returning packaged pasta, potato and rice dishes to the shelves, trading the high-sugar-and-fat peanut butter for the spread ground fresh in the deli department and replacing the bottled spaghetti sauce with fresh ingredients from the produce section.

"Wow," Jenny commented as she came out to help unload the groceries. "You really did a major shop."

"Mom, did you get the cookie dough? I promised

cookies for tomorrow's bake sale," Cami announced in a voice that indicated that she was certain I had forgotten.

"We have cookie dough," I said, unpacking flour, oats, sugar, butter, eggs, nuts and chocolate chips and lining them up on the pantry counter.

"This isn't the right thing," Cami said. "Where's the stuff we slice and bake?"

"We are done with slicing and baking. We will be making old-fashioned cookies from your grandmother Marie's recipe after dinner."

Cami rolled her eyes and turned to Jenny for support. "Oh, wow," Jenny said enthusiastically. "It's been forever since my mom made real oatmeal chocolate chip cookies—the dough is just heavenly. I mean, you almost want to make two batches—one to bake and the other so you can just eat the dough."

I could have hugged her. Cami was still doubtful, but then, this was Jenny, her idol talking. "We'll see," she muttered.

A car door slammed and the boys raced to the door. "Dad," they shouted in chorus, and then gave individual versions of throwing up earlier and playing Chutes and Ladders with Jenny.

Spence entered the kitchen with a twin attached to either side and he was grinning widely. "I got it, Zoe," he said, his eyes bright with the thrill of victory. "I got the grant."

Jenny grinned but then realized Spence had shared his news only with me, and coaxed all three children out of the room. "Time for me to pack up and hit the road," she called. "Who can help?" The children clamored to do her bidding.

Spence tossed his coat and briefcase on the bench by the door, crossed the room and wrapped his arms around me. His forehead was resting on mine and he was still grinning from ear to ear. "Zoe, the whole thing—more than the whole thing. They added money to cover some additional research, and here's what I was thinking as I drove home. What if—I mean the kids are all in school now and you could name your hours—you could even work at home. We could wire the boathouse and set up a little office down there, and…"

I was thrilled for him, but his idea of establishing a stand-alone clinic specifically for counseling and research on post-traumatic stress syndrome was his dream—not mine. If we were going to close the distance that had grown up between us, I had to define my dream—and go after it.

"Well, this calls for a celebration," I said with genuine happiness. "Go shower and change while I get dinner started and then I want to hear every detail."

"Let's eat out—just the two of us," he said, nuzzling my neck. "Jenny can feed the kids."

I glanced at the piles of food still waiting to be put away and then into the pantry, where the ingredients for Cami's cookies waited. I thought about the plan I'd developed on the drive home to introduce a new routine during dinner for sharing responsibilities. I weighed all of that against the fact that Spence deserved the chance to celebrate this milestone that was about to change his life in ways he'd been dreaming of for nearly five years. I thought about my resolve to combine finding my own identity with rededicating myself to the Zoe identity project. I thought about Peter's call. *Choose,* my brain demanded.

"I'll ask if Jenny can stay."

While Spence and I celebrated at our favorite French restaurant, Jenny, Cami and the twins made the cookies together. When Spence and I got home, all three children were gathered around the kitchen table, dipping sticky fingers into what remained of the dough.

"This is so cool, Mom," Cami declared. "I called Grandma and told her I'd followed her recipe to the letter. She was superimpressed."

Spence

It was a couple of days after I learned that the funding had come through that Zoe told me about the call from Peter Quarles. I'm not sure if she would have said anything then, but I noticed that on Friday morning she was especially uptight. Usually nothing ruffled her as the kids and I did a pretty good imitation of the Keystone Kops in our frantic attempt to make sure we had everything for the day and get out the door.

"You okay?" I asked as I poured myself a second cup of coffee.

"I'm fine," she replied tightly.

Suddenly I realized how unusually quiet she'd been ever since I'd delivered my news. Ordinarily after hearing something like that, Zoe would have kept me up half the night, spinning ideas for how the program might take shape and expand. But she'd said very little. My idea for her to play a major role in all of this had been met with a slight smile—and nothing more.

"How about meeting me for lunch today? We can sit out on the terrace at the Union." Her back was to me, but her shoulders stiffened and she dropped the plate she was rinsing. It broke into three triangular sections and Zoe swore softly, then braced her hands on the edge of the sink.

"I'm meeting Peter Quarles for coffee this morning,"

she said in a monotone. "I haven't mentioned it because—well, you got the grant the same day he asked and we've been all caught up in stuff with that and the kids and—"

"Peter's in town?" I said.

"Yes." The look she gave me was one of defiance, as if somehow I had challenged her. "I just told you that he called me."

"Well, that's great. It's been—what? Seven or eight years? You two have a lot of catching up to do."

"He's going to run for mayor," she continued in that same tone that appeared to assume I was questioning or accusing her.

"Wow," I said softly, and let out a breath.

"And he wants me to be his campaign manager."

Okay, that did it. Of the two of us, I am the calm one usually, the one who nothing much can rattle. But something in the way she delivered this news changed all that. "Must have been some phone conversation," I said, and turned away to put my coffee mug on the counter because I was gripping the handle so hard I thought it might snap off. "I have to go. Kids!"

Yes, I was deliberately filling the room with our children, using them as a buffer for a conversation I was not yet ready to have. A thousand questions ricocheted through my mind as I hustled them out the door. Why had she kept it from me? What about our plans—my plans—to have her help with the counseling center? *What qualifications did she have for running a campaign? What about the kids? Why would she even want to run a campaign? Would she be at all interested if it weren't Peter? And what was his story? Who just blows back into town and decides to run for mayor? And top of the list: Since when did Zoe keep news like this from me for days and then just blurt it out like I had somehow forced her?*

After fuming my way through the workday, I was sitting in rush-hour traffic late that afternoon when it hit me that hanging on to some ancient jealousy of Peter Quarles was adolescent, to say the least. The realization actually made me smile. Of course he was going to contact Zoe. Of course he wanted her to manage his campaign. The man was smart and used to the best. The only thing I needed to understand was whether Zoe wanted this.

And if she does? Well, what of it? It was the challenge of the work that interested Zoe—not Peter. I was as sure of that as I was that she loved me.

The house smelled of furniture polish and bleach when I opened the door—sure signs that Zoe had gone on a cleaning binge. Also a sure sign that Zoe had had to work through something—I just hoped it was the same thing I'd been working through all day.

"Mom cleaned," Cami announced, glancing up from the computer we kept on the desk in the kitchen. "Touch *anything* at your own risk," she advised, and went back to the game she'd been playing.

"Where are the boys?"

"T-ball practice. Mrs. Logan drove them."

I nodded.

"Mom's in the garden," Cami added. "Planting stuff and then chopping stuff down. Do not ask me to explain the logic of that." She rolled her eyes.

Cleaning was bad enough, but cleaning and gardening on the same day meant something truly major was going on. I reached over and ruffled Cami's short hair. She dodged my hand but giggled. "Good luck," she called when I headed for the garden.

I loosened my tie and turned back the sleeves of my shirt as I followed the sounds of hedge clippers whacking away at some defenseless bush. Zoe's back was to me. She was wearing denim shorts, one of my old T-shirts and a baseball cap. She had the body of a woman half her age, and something about that and the fact that I had some work to do before she was likely to melt in my arms made the challenge before me all the more tempting.

I eased over to a cluster of bushes near where she was butchering her prized Koreanspice bush. "Help!" I squeaked in a high falsetto. "Somebody please stop her before she cuts me to the ground."

The action of the clippers slowed slightly, and I knew she'd heard and was listening, so I kept going. "Oh, sure, Dr. High and Mighty gets his stupid grant and believes he's king of the world, but does he stop to think about her? No! And who pays the price for his arrogance? Me!"

The clippers were silent and still.

"Well, finally," I said, still in that same falsetto voice.

"Do not imagine you are entirely off the hook," Zoe replied in her normal voice. I wasn't sure whether this was directed at me or the bush. She put the clippers down and gathered the pile of branches she'd accumulated.

"The house looks nice," I said in my normal voice as I stepped out of the shadows and relieved her of the branches.

"You're not exactly dressed for gardening," she protested, but handed me the branches.

"Once a farm boy," I replied and left the rest unsaid as I carried the branches to the compost pile we hadn't stirred or added anything to since the fall.

When I finished, she had collapsed into one of two recycled milk carton chairs we'd once bought at an art fair and optimistically positioned on the edge of the bluff near the steps down to the boathouse and the lake. I sat in the other one. We'd rationalized the cost of them by telling ourselves that we would relax out there every nice evening once the kids were settled for the night. As far as I knew this was the first time either of us had spent any time in them since the day we'd brought them home.

"Nice chairs," I said.

"Better view," she replied, stretching her long legs out and kicking off her garden shoes.

"Wanna talk?"

"Do you?"

"Mom?" Cami bellowed from the porch. Zoe and I sighed in unison and looked back at the house. "Mrs. Logan's here. Can the twins and me go out with her and Jamie for pizza?"

"Jamie Logan is the latest fifth-grade heartthrob in addition to being the junior coach for T-ball," Zoe mumbled in my direction.

"Sure," I called.

"Mom?"

"Your father said okay."

Cami hesitated.

"Go," Zoe shouted, and laughed as she clasped my hand, clearly her way of reassuring Cami that all was well.

"I accepted Peter's offer," she said softly, her eyes still on the spot where our daughter had been.

"Okay."

"I'm sorry about turning you down, but I can't work for you, Spence."

"It's not like working for me," I protested. "It's a partnership."

She laced her fingers through mine. "Here's what I figured out today," she said. "Peter has a dream. You have a dream. I need a dream of my own, and accepting this job is a stepping-stone toward realizing my dream."

I didn't fully get how working for Peter instead of working with me was the best path. What I did understand was that the tension that had been building between us for months was suddenly gone. Zoe was happy, and wasn't that what I'd wanted?

1987

Zoe

Peter won the election and reelection. It hardly seemed like a major step to go from campaign manager to chief of staff. I knew that Spence wasn't thrilled, but by then he was so caught up in his work that he could find little basis for his concerns. His counseling center and its program quickly became a model for other such centers springing up around the country. The amount of time we were each devoting to our work made us blind to the chasm that was widening between us.

"Earth to Zoe," Peter said as he placed his hands on my desk and leaned across it. I glanced up and caught a glimpse of the large office wall clock over his left shoulder. It was after nine. The cubicles where the rest of the mayor's staff spent their workdays were deserted.

"I have to get home," I said. "Can we finish this to-morrow?"

"You don't have to get home. The kids are at camp and Spencer is in London, remember?"

I smiled wearily. "Okay, I lied. What I really need is a hot shower, my jammies and a *MASH* rerun. My brain is seriously fried, Peter."

"How about some dinner first—a real dinner, not takeout? A glass of wine maybe?" When I hesitated, he added, "Come on, Zoe, let me treat you. You've worked really hard to get the budget under control and I'd like to say thanks."

"I have to eat," I said with a shrug.

"Gee, don't get all mushy on me, okay?" Peter replied sarcastically, but he grinned and got my coat from the closet and held it for me.

We decided to walk to the restaurant. It had rained hard that afternoon and the sidewalks were dotted with puddles. Peter took my arm once to guide me around one I hadn't seen because I was filling him in on the latest budget cuts. I never gave it a second thought when he tucked my hand in the crook of his elbow as we continued on our way.

The restaurant was one of those hole-in-the-wall Italian places that's everybody's favorite once they try it the first time, though far from a pizzeria. The chef had trained in Northern Italy and prided himself on a menu that was varied and unique. Peter and I had ordered takeout from the place more than once since I'd started the job as his chief of staff.

While Peter worked the room shaking hands with patrons who recognized him, I ordered a glass of wine and settled into a booth.

It was impossible not to wonder how Spence would react to my having dinner alone with Peter. It was clear that both Spence and Peter thought I had capitulated to Peter's unrelenting campaign to have me on his staff once he won the election. My decision, of course, delighted Peter. One night as we lay in the dark, Spence said, "Another stepping-stone to your dream?"

"I hope you can be okay with this," I had said, knowing I didn't have to explain what "this" was. It was lying there between us in the empty expanse between his side of our king-size bed and mine.

"Zoe, you can't blame me for being confused. I thought you didn't want to work for Peter—or anyone. I thought you wanted your own thing."

I propped myself on one elbow so that I was facing him, even though I couldn't read his expression in the dark. "Taking this job as Peter's chief of staff isn't about settling for something, Spence," I told him. "I've been out of the workforce for years now and my résumé has enormous gaps. If I'm ever going to be able to do something on my own, I have to build credentials."

Spence remained silent, but I knew he was listening. I pressed my case.

"I'm not abandoning my dream. It would be my training ground. Then one day down the road, I'll be ready to run for office on my own, or lead a think tank that builds programs to make the world a better place, or—"

"Okay," Spence muttered, and rolled onto his side, his back to me.

"Meaning?"

Silence.

I sat up, wide-awake now, my arms folded across my chest. "So it's fine for you to travel all over everywhere, spreading the gospel of the post-traumatic stress program, but I'm not allowed to—"

"Allowed?" Spence kept his back to me. He laughed. "Sometimes, Zoe, you are such a piece of work."

"All I'm saying is that it seems to be fine when you want to do something…expand the clinic or—"

This time he not only sat up, he stood beside the bed and turned on me. "It's not a contest, Zoe. Stop trying to make it one. I go to work to support my family—this family—our family. That's the best way I know to make a contribution. If you want me to stay at home and play the mom role, then that's just not going to happen, okay?" He grabbed his pillow and left the room.

The following morning I reported to work as the chief of staff for the mayor of Madison. On my desk was a bouquet of mixed colored roses. I knew they were from Spence before I opened the card. Only Spence would know that I loved the idea of mixing every possible color of rose.

I opened the card and read, *What's Peter going to do when you beat him to the White House?*

But we'd both been incredibly naive about the toll my working in such a high-stress job would take on our lives, and over the next two years as the evidence that we were drifting apart mounted—we both just assumed that it was a natural blip in the path of our marriage—short-term.

"I thought you were going to drive the boys to their game," I would say as both Spence and I hurried to get the kids and us out the door in the morning.

"I told you that I have to be in Washington at eight tomorrow morning. I have a flight to catch."

"You're going to miss their game—another game?"

"It can't be helped, Zoe. I'll make it up to them."

This kind of conversation inevitably ended in a shrug, a frown and the banging of car doors as we each sped off to our separate lives.

We smiled and made small talk at social events we cared little to attend but viewed as necessary to further our careers or support the social activities of our children. "Let's call Jon and Ginny and see if they're free for a movie Saturday," Spence would suggest as he gave me a quick kiss and left for yet another dinner meeting—his third that week.

"They're leaving for Cancun on Friday," I reminded him. "I'll call them when they get back and set something up." But I never did.

And night after night one of us stayed up late to finish a paper or presentation while the other went off to bed and was asleep—or pretending to be—when the other, having undressed in the guest room, slipped under the covers. With work and the kids, neither of us had the energy to explore what might be happening to "us." Neither of us understood that choosing to ignore what was right in front of us was a choice each of us was making in the hope that time would solve the mounting problems.

"Zoe?"

Peter had completed his hobnobbing, ordered for both of us and discussed plans for more budget cuts while we ate. I had nodded and even made hopefully appropriate comments, but my thoughts had been back there—with Spence. Back there when Spence and I had been naive about the toll that my working with and for Peter could take on us as a couple.

"Sorry," I said, taking a sip of my wine and giving Peter my full attention.

Peter laughed and signaled for the bill. "You are a space cadet, woman. I'm going to drive you home."

"I have my car," I said smothering a yawn. "And I need to stop back at the office and get my briefcase. And—"

"No more work for you tonight. This is your employer speaking, and you are going home. No arguments."

We walked back to the underground parking garage, and I had to admit that after the day I'd had and two glasses of wine, I was not in the best shape to drive myself home. "Okay," I agreed when Peter held the passenger door of his vintage Mustang convertible open for me. I settled in, leaned back and closed my eyes. The cool night air was like a balm on my face. I could feel tendrils of my hair escaping the confines of the no-nonsense twist I had adopted to assume a more businesslike appearance. I reached up and removed the pins and started to laugh.

"We've come a long way from Mifflin Street," I said as Peter steered left instead of right out of the parking structure. "Hey, home is that way," I reminded him.

"Let's go for a little sentimental journey," he said, and grinned. He maneuvered the car through the nearly empty streets toward campus. We passed the place where we'd all lived—where Spence and I had fallen in love. The house had been torn down to make room for one of the many hideous little strip malls springing up all around town.

"Ugh!" I said. "At least the house had character."

"Characters is more like it," Peter said, and we both laughed.

He continued the tour of our old haunts as we recalled the days and dreams of our youth. Conversation died once we'd paused at the math building and remembered the bombing—the act that had finally made us realize that things could go too far. He found a parking spot at the top of Observatory Drive.

"When's Spence getting back?" he asked.

"Friday."

"He's been traveling a lot lately."

"Well, he's built the prototype for counseling and support programs for treating post-traumatic stress. Everybody wants him—not some associate."

"But London?"

"The IRA attacks have done in a number of people there. Imagine living every day in a place where you might be in a shop or on a bus and suddenly the world around you just explodes. Talk about stress. It must be horrible never knowing whether doing some simple routine thing like going to work or the grocery store might put your life in danger."

Peter didn't say anything for some time. "It's just that he's gone a lot, and even when he's here you're at the office a lot and— Is everything okay?"

Maybe it was that no one else appeared have noticed. Maybe it was that I had held it all in for so long and shut friends out that there was no more room to put my doubts and fears about what was happening to Spence and me. Maybe it was because this was Peter and we'd gone this nostalgic ride down memory lane when, for all its turmoil, life had seemed so simple. I burst into tears and then escalated into full-blown and superembarrassing sobbing.

Peter rubbed my back and then slowly wrapped his arms around me and drew me to him. "I'm here," he murmured again and again, his breath fanning my hair. His hands moved over me, caressing my shoulders, then cupping my chin until I faced him. "I've always been here, Zoe."

The kiss was loaded with his desperation and desire

and my anger and fear. It exploded between us, startling both of us with its power, forcing us to hold on tighter as we tried to navigate our way through the smoke and flame it ignited.

"No," I said, even as he carried me back into the thick of it.

"Let me," he said, his voice hoarse with desire, as he ran his tongue over the rim of my ear. "Let me love you, Zoe," he said just before his open mouth covered mine.

"No," I said, and pushed hard at his chest. "No," I repeated more gently when he leaned back, his eyes heavy with desire, his breath pumping in the steady pants of a marathon runner.

"Why not?"

I looked at this man who had been my friend and co-conspirator in the cause for good, and realized the difference between us. "Because you find nothing wrong with hurting someone else to have what you want," I said, and touched his cheek with my palm. "While even if I were not in love with Spence anymore, I could not—would not—intentionally betray any love he might still hold for me."

"But he doesn't have to know," Peter argued.

"I'll know."

"And do you love him, Zoe?"

"Yes," I told him without a millisecond of hesitation, and knew it was true.

Peter drove me home. We didn't talk. I rewound my hair into the twist. As soon as he pulled into our driveway, I opened the car door. "I'll see you tomorrow," I said.

"You're not quitting?"

I laughed. "Oh, Peter, don't you understand that it's always been the work—the good you try to do—that's important?"

He smiled. "Damn. All this time I thought it was my ruggedly handsome face."

Reassured that we'd done no permanent damage to our friendship, I was feeling better as he drove away, and I let myself in through the side door. It was then that I noticed the lights on in the family room.

Spence

The sound of Peter's car was unmistakable—and familiar. He'd been at the house often since moving back to Madison. Zoe included him in any social event we hosted that wasn't just family. Even the rare barbecue or potluck Sunday-night supper with close friends included Peter, along with some single woman Zoe had decided was the perfect romantic match for him. I wasn't a kid and I trusted Zoe, so Peter's presence no longer raised any red flags for me. It was just that I understood he was always watching, waiting for any sign Zoe and I were struggling.

Well, he'd have his chance now, I thought as I heard Zoe humming after she opened the side door. Maybe he already had. It struck me that I had no idea whether Peter and Zoe had moved beyond being coworkers. Things between us had deteriorated so much that most interaction focused on either the kids or work. More often than not we were either too busy, too caught up with the kids and their schedules or just too tired to put the work into our relationship.

Now, in a moment of loneliness, self-pity and pure folly, I had gone too far and possibly jeopardized any chance we might have had to close the widening chasm that lay between us. I buried my head in my hands and waited for her to follow the light into the family room.

"You're home," she said with no expression.

"Yeah. I caught an earlier flight." *And you're late,* I wanted to say but realized that I was just projecting my guilt onto her. Just because I'd...

"Did you eat?" she asked, tossing her raincoat over the back of the rocker.

"Airplane stuff. It wasn't terrible," I said, quoting Cami's favorite line when she didn't want to appear too enthusiastic. "How about you?"

"Peter and I went to Zeno's."

My eyebrows must have lifted, because she continued in a flat I-really-don't-owe-you-an-explanation voice. "We finally finished the budget so we decided to celebrate."

I swallowed the comment that Zeno's closed at ten and it was now nearly midnight. Instead I stood. "Well, I'm beat," I said and stretched as if to accent the point.

Zoe was at the patio doors, staring across the lawn and lake to the lights of the city beyond. "Could we talk?" she said in a voice so soft I thought I might have imagined it.

"Is it the kids?" I asked.

She sighed. "If I said no, would you postpone talking to me?" For once she didn't sound as though she was accusing me, just curious.

I shook my head and sat down again. "Shoot," I said, giving her my attention.

She sat on the ottoman close to me, rested her hands on my knees and dropped her bomb. "Peter kissed me tonight."

I swallowed and waited to hear if there was an after-explosion. There was.

"I let him and I kissed him back," she said.

I shifted uneasily. "And?" I waited for the other shoe.

She was going to leave me. She was going to be with Peter and it was no one's fault but my own.

She shrugged. "I just didn't want that to be between us," she said. "It's over. It never got started. Peter understands that there's nothing between us, that—"

"Are you resigning?"

She looked surprised. "Of course not."

"Then it's not over," I said.

Her eyes flashed at that. "I am trying to be an adult about this, Spencer."

I shrugged and sank lower in the chair, not meeting her eyes. I stared out the patio doors and saw nothing except Peter Quarles' triumphant smile the night I'd left her attic apartment on Mifflin Street.

"He's a patient man, Zoe, and he loves you—has always loved you. And with things between us—"

She stood. "What about things between us, Spence? What about the trips and the meetings and the nights you're just too tired and the—"

"You think I'm having an affair?" There. The word was out there between us.

"I don't know," she said, shouting each word distinctly. "I just know that lately when I try to understand what's going on in that head of yours, in your eyes, the blinds are shut tight and nobody's home."

I snorted. "Like you are so devoted. Get over yourself, Zoe. You've dug yourself so deep into this career of yours that you barely know what day it is, much less—"

"Are you having an affair?" she asked now as if the idea had just begun to sink in. "Is that what you're telling me?"

I looked up at her, caught up by the way the lamplight played over her face, devoid of the makeup she always wore these days. I knew that makeup had been effectively removed by the tongue and mouth of Peter Quarles. "I was," I said, getting up and heading for the stairs. "But it's over, and according to you that makes everything okay, right?"

The one truth I knew about Zoe and me was that as angry and hurt as each of us was with the other, we could trust that neither of us would allow it to spill over into the lives of our children. Thankfully Cami—who usually noticed everything—was caught up in the throes of her first real job as a junior camp counselor for the summer. The twins were also attending summer camp, and I could only hope that in the six weeks they would all be gone, Zoe and I could arrive at some understanding about where our marriage was going from here.

But if anything, being in a role of responsibility had only sharpened Cami's skills of observation. When she got home, she helped me put the final coat of sealant on the canoe I'd spent a big part of the summer building—mostly as an excuse to stay out of Zoe's way. It was late August, and the air was hot and still.

I could feel Cami watching me, working her way up to asking whatever was on her mind. She tested the waters a couple of times.

"Did Mom help build this canoe?"

I chuckled. "Not her thing." It wasn't an answer and we both knew it.

We worked in silence for a while.

"Everything okay with you and Mom?"

"Why do you ask?"

She paused in midstroke and stared at me, her mouth open and her eyes wide. "Gee, I don't know. I go away for my first real summer job and come home to find the two of you are barely speaking. One or the other is up and out before anybody else is even awake. Family conversation is a joke. I mean, do you seriously think the boys and I don't get it that something has shifted in this house?"

She paused, and I saw by her expression that she regretted the outburst. On the other hand, now that she had put forth her case, she was waiting for answers.

"Mom and I are like every other married couple, Cami. Sometimes we disagree." I continued stroking the brush across the smooth wood, buying time. But I could feel my shoulders tensing. Here it was—the moment both Zoe and I had dreaded—separately, of course. I could not deny the feeling of victory I felt in realizing that Cami had trusted me first.

"Are you and your brothers worried?"

Cami rolled her eyes. "Todd and Taylor were in my room last night. Of course I got the assignment to 'talk' to the two of you. Are you getting a divorce or what?"

I sucked in breath—the kind of breath you take before you're about to plunge into water and you're not sure how cold or deep it's going to be. The fact was that neither Zoe nor I had been able to bring ourselves to even say, much less discuss, the *d* word. But if our children were using it so easily… "Okay. Here's what we're going to do," I said. "We're going to call a family meeting."

Cami groaned and blinked back the tears that suddenly filled her eyes to overflowing. "You *are* going to divorce," she blubbered.

I dropped my brush and had my arms around her faster than she could put down her paintbrush. I felt the splat of it against the back of my shirt, but nothing mattered except erasing those tears and that panicked expression. "No," I said, and repeated it several times while she held on. "We're not," I told her. "We're going through a rough patch but—"

"Todd overheard Grandma say you had an affair," she managed to choke out.

I went still but did not let go of my daughter. "Well, that's grown-up stuff, pumpkin. Grown-ups can make big mistakes, and I made that one."

"Do you love her—that other woman?" she asked, her voice muffled by my shirt.

"Never did," I said. "Just made a mistake that hurt Mom a lot. Mom knows that just like I know…. Anyway, in those cases simply saying you're sorry isn't enough. If the mistake is big enough—and the hurt you cause goes way deep—it takes time." I loosened the hug but held on to her shoulders, my eyes meeting hers. "Here's what you and the boys need to understand," I said. "Mom and I love you and we love each other. We're a family and we're going to be okay."

"Promise?"

"Promise."

1995

Zoe

In the years that followed the day in 1987 that we signed the contract, our focus turned to the children. Proms, graduation, choosing the perfect college, the right major, the career. Spence and I rejoiced in the accomplishments of our children and celebrated with friends the passages of milestones in all our lives—silver anniversaries, turning fifty, starting the dream second career.

One day I was unhooking and labeling the mass of cords and cables behind the desk that held the computer. Despite the pleas of our children to put the computer someplace less public, Spence and I had stuck to our rule that the computer belonged to the family. As such, we were adamant that it would remain in a shared room—the family room we'd added to the back of the house a few years after the twins were born. Of course our main objective had been to monitor what our children "researched" and the people they formed online friendships with.

Now, on one of my cleaning binges, I had decided that with the children practically grown, I could move the thing and its unsightly and uncontrollable mass of cords to a less prominent place in the house. There behind the desk was the contract. I sat back on my heels and blew away the years of accumulated dust and remembered the afternoon Spence strode into the kitchen, announced, "We should talk," and continued to his study. He had waited for me to follow and then shut the door.

In his direct manner, he told me about the conversation he'd just had with Cami. "So, if you're planning to leave— or have me leave—let's get on with it," he said.

I was stunned. "What on earth gives you the idea that I want you to leave or that I'm planning to leave you?" I asked.

He didn't have to answer. We both knew how things had been between us.

"Admittedly we've come to a crossroads in our marriage, Spence—notice I said 'crossroads' not 'dead end.' Neither of us can honestly say what direction we'll go from here, but I know the old 'staying together for the sake of the children' isn't something I view as a good thing—for us or the kids."

His eyes had widened and I recognized the expression in them as fear. *Please don't,* his eyes said before he turned away to the window. He used the moment to draw in a deep breath and slowly blow it out. "I see," he said softly.

"No, you don't."

I walked around the desk and stood next to him, not facing him but focusing on where Cami sat on the rope swing Spence had hung for her when she was six. She was sixteen now and kicking at the dirt as she twisted the swing chains into a single strand. Then she lifted her coltish legs allowing the chains to unravel and spin her round and round.

I put my hand on Spence's arm. "I am not leaving you and I hope you aren't leaving me," I said. "You and I made a commitment—for better or for worse. This is one of those 'worse' times and I'm not willing to say we can't find our way through it—not yet—not by a long shot."

He looked at me then and this time his eyes were filled with hope—false hope, for I was still angry and hurt and knew that I had miles to go before I could completely forgive him. Before I could forgive myself for the part I was all too aware I had played in letting things deteriorate to this point. "Spence, we aren't there, yet," I told him. "All I'm saying is that I won't hang our marriage on the children. And I won't permit some thirty-something who is smarter, prettier and more in tune with where you are at this stage of your life than I am to count as a reason we abandon the commitment we made to each other. I feel angry and betrayed and guilty and a host of other things I've got to work through, Spencer Andersen. I don't like you a whole lot these days, but I love you and I think you still love me and we will get through this."

He rubbed his palm over his unshaven chin. "Well, that's all fine, Zoe, and you can have all the time you need, but frankly, our children deserve reassurance now."

And that was when we came up with the idea of the contract. At the family meeting—a tradition Spence and I had begun once I went back to work—it was clear that Cami wasn't buying it, but in the absence of anything else, she signed it. I had no doubts that she would use it as proof we'd lied to her if Spence and I didn't find some way to get us all past this.

The terms were simple. Spence and I agreed to be "gentle and sweet"—Cami's wording—to each other. In return, the children agreed to come to either Spence or me with their questions if they had concerns about how things were going. It was Taylor who suggested the final stipulation.

"Every night at supper, we each have to say something nice about every other person at the table."

"Like what?" Cami demanded. "What would you say about me?"

Taylor smiled and held out the pen for me to write in the new condition. "You'll be surprised," he said.

And we were. That night at supper Taylor cleared his throat loudly right after I had taken my place opposite Spence and started to pass the salad dressing to Cami.

"Cami, I noticed your hair is getting really long. It's nice on you."

Todd snorted and swallowed a mouthful of lemonade.

Taylor was unperturbed. "And Dad, you know that defense move you showed me last week when we were shooting buckets on the driveway? I tried it in practice today and Coach was really impressed."

"That's great, Taylor," Spence said, somehow maintaining a straight face while the rest of us sat staring openmouthed at Taylor.

Taylor turned to his brother. "Todd, I have this science thing that has to do with plants, and you're really better at that stuff than I am. Can you help me after supper?"

Todd looked as if he might explode with delight at this unexpected compliment from his brother. "Sure," he muttered.

Finally Taylor focused his attention on me. "Mom, I

think the work you do for the mayor is very important. He's a jerk, but I like telling my friends that my mom is the brains behind everything good that happens in this town."

I glanced the length of the table at Spence, who had taken a sudden interest in cutting his meat. "Thank you, Taylor," I said softly.

Taylor released a sigh of pure relief at having completed the circuit. "See? How hard was that? Okay, who's next?"

In spite of the fact that I knew it still bothered Spence, I kept working for Peter. I did it as much to prove to myself that I had done nothing wrong as I did it for the love of the job. I had admitted the temptation but resisted it while Spence had…. I felt noble and wounded. Oh, who was I kidding? I could accomplish just as much working in a dozen other positions. It wouldn't take much more than the news that I was resigning as Peter's chief of staff for the offers to come rolling in. I knew that and Spence knew that. That Spence and I had arrived at this brink was so scary for me, and when I am scared, I am not the type to burrow under the covers. I fight back and sometimes I fight dirty.

Our little roundtable of compliments had opened my eyes to the realization that if Spence and I were going to get through this, we had to start with what had happened. We had danced around a confrontation for weeks now. It was time to have our say—in plain language rather than thinly veiled smirks and grimaces.

"Can we talk?" I sounded like a poor imitation of Joan Rivers. "The kids have gone up for the night and it's early yet, so I thought…"

Spence looked up from the Sunday paper he'd finally gotten around to reading on this Monday night. "Okay," he said reluctantly. Unlike me, Spence would prefer not to rehash the past, searching for answers we might have missed. Spence is a let's-get-on-with-it sort of guy.

I curled into a corner of the couch. He sat up straighter in his favorite chair and put the paper aside. I tried not to be irritated by the minuscule raising of Spence's eyebrows that said, *Oh, no, not a* talk.

"It's important that you understand that I haven't stayed on with Peter—on the job—as a kind of punishment for you," I began, and bit my lip, realizing I had blurted out the one thing I had wanted to calmly lead up to.

Spence frowned and looked down. "I understand your work is important to you, Zoe."

I waited for more. "But?" I prompted.

"But nothing. I am saying I accept that your work is important."

I hated it when he spoke to me as if I were a patient of his. He was my husband. "You do believe that there's nothing between Peter and me?"

Spence flashed a sardonic smile. "About as much as you believe there was nothing to my fling with Jane Brooks," he said. "The difference is that Jane is absent from the scene. She accepted that job with the pharmaceutical company in Texas. We're not likely to ever see each other again, much less—"

"Much less what?" I sat forward on the sofa, facing the gauntlet he'd thrown down. "Are you implying that because Peter and I continue to work together, that I am incapable of—"

Anger glittered in Spence's eyes. "I am not implying anything, Zoe. I am saying outright that I have apologized for what happened on my part and taken the steps necessary to make sure you aren't hurt any more than you have been. You, on the other hand, seem intent on rubbing my nose in it by dangling Peter Quarles in front of me at every opportunity."

I opened my mouth, but Spence stood up and continued talking. "Well, here's a news bulletin for you—I have known from practically the day I met you, and certainly from the day I first I loved you, that Peter would be there…always be there. I have also known that you find some subliminal comfort in that—having a fallback position just in case things don't work out here. Well, I'm tired of walking on eggs, Zoe. Two people have cheated in this marriage."

"But only one acted on it," I shot back, hating that he had as usual gone to the very core of the issue and laid it bare.

"Mea culpa," he said in a whisper. "I'm going to bed."

I stayed up half the night, wandering through the house, eating peanut butter and then ice cream directly from the containers as I fought against the understanding that Spence was right. We had been traveling separate paths long before Spence admitted the affair. I had realized that he had begun to want different things, united only when it concerned what was best for the children. I had been thrilled to go to work for Peter, to once again find "me"— Zoe, the independent woman with something to contribute beyond the chaos of carpools and school events and wife-of-the-doctor/professor performances. And the truth was that I had settled for the prestige and power that the job with Peter had given me, abandoning any notion of building something on my own. But at what price?

Spence was right that ever since our dual confessions of infidelity, things between us had gone from awful to horrible, and never more so than when I stubbornly refused to resign. And I knew at least a part of that stubborn refusal had been the fact that I was appalled Spence actually believed I had betrayed him first.

"Not physically," he'd argued, "but the late nights, the public appearances where he insisted he must have you at his side. Do you have any idea what it felt like to hear one of my interns identifying you as the mayor's wife after seeing that spread in the paper last fall?"

"So, of course, that was all the justification you needed to take your little research assistant to bed," I'd fired back.

We'd fought dirty and aimed to inflict as much pain and punishment as we could in an effort to keep from examining our own motives. For I knew that there was an element of truth in Spence's accusations about how much I enjoyed Peter's attentions. And he understood that it was his guilt and self-loathing at having succumbed to his own temptation that made him want to defend himself against my righteous anger.

But somehow with everything out in the open between us we were able to move beyond the shouted insults, accusations, prolonged silences and avoidance of being alone with each other. As Cami had made crystal clear, our polite smiles and public displays of solidarity for the sake of the children were fooling no one—least of all our children. And because both Spence and I were united in our determination not to drag the children into our private anguish, we honored that contract while the natural progression of our children's lives drew them out into the larger world—and away from us.

Taylor's nightly compliment fest was obviously a challenge for all of us, but to our surprise, the harder it became to keep inventing fresh compliments, the more fun we had with it as a family.

"Cami," Todd said the night after Spence had walked out on my attempt to talk through our problems, "your—" He paused, obviously racking his brain for something—anything—nice to say about her. Then he smiled. "Your fingernails are very clean."

He was running low on new ideas and we all knew it, but it set off a round of silliness that had us all laughing so hard that we could barely speak.

"Your turn, Dad," Taylor announced after all three of the children and I had made our rounds.

"Okay, here goes." Spencer sat up very straight and focused on each child as he delivered their compliment. "Todd, your love of nature inspires me. Taylor, you're a born entertainer. Cami, your smile could light up a room."

There was a silence as each child digested this enormous praise from their father, who was more given to caution when it came to doling out his compliments.

"And what about Mom?" Cami said.

"Your mom is the best friend anyone could ever hope to have," he said without hesitation as he looked at me across the table, his eyes holding mine.

"Wow," I heard Taylor whisper.

Spence continued to command our full attention. "Maybe going forward we could ease up on the regimen of this compliment thing? I think we've all got the gist of it, don't you?"

Four heads nodded in unison.

"Works for me," I said. "How about dessert?"

As I stood there years later, the dusty, crinkled contract in my hand, I tried to recall how we had spent the rest of that evening. That I couldn't meant that Spence and I must have settled into the truce that allowed us to rediscover the friendship and respect we had once thought could never last.

Remembering that night and what Spence had said, I carefully folded the contract and placed it in the folder I kept for saving such things. My cleaning binge had begun because I'd started to realize that soon Spence and I would no longer have the buffer of the children and their activities, friends and chatter. These days we were tumbling far too fast toward that day when we would be alone—with each other. I wasn't ready. I had no idea how we were going to do this.

That spring, Cami had finished her graduate degree at Harvard and was now living with my parents in Manhattan while she searched for a job and an apartment and toyed with the idea of getting her doctorate at Columbia in her spare time.

"What about getting a life in your spare time?" Spence had teased her.

"This is my life, Dad, and I love it. My work, the city— it's all fabulous."

"So the possibility of a husband and kids any time in this century is…?"

Cami had giggled. "You're going to have to look to Todd and Sandra for those grandchildren—in *this* century," she'd said, and Spence had laughed. She always made him laugh—something I used to be able to do before….

That spring Todd announced that he had proposed to Sandra Alexander, a girl he had met only months earlier. He stated that they planned to be married as soon as possible.

"Is she pregnant?" his brother, Taylor, asked, barely glancing up. He was chewing the end of his pen as he completed the application for the summer broadcasting job he was hoping to land in Minnesota.

"No," Todd replied quietly.

I glanced over at Spencer, who had lowered his newspaper and was watching Todd over the tops of his half reading glasses. He caught my eye. After almost twenty-five years of marriage, he had gotten good at translating my glances into actual words. *Do something,* this one told him.

"Sit down, son, and let's talk about this," he said.

Todd crossed the room and stood by the fireplace. "Here's the deal," he said in a voice that indicated he'd been rehearsing the coming speech for some time. "We're in love. I know we're young, but we know what we want. I mean, I may not have Taylor's brains, but..."

Ah, I thought, and realized that Spencer was also thinking the same thing. Early in the lives of our nearly identical boys, it had become clear that the distinguishing mark between them was to be the ability to learn and comprehend and excel in the realm of formal learning. Taylor had sailed through high school with a solid four-point average, earned a full academic scholarship and would enter his sophomore year at UCLA in the fall. Todd had struggled through every class since third grade. In fact, at the end of that year his teachers had suggested we hold him back a year.

"So he can get some special help. Also, then he won't be constantly compared with his brother," the principal had told us bluntly.

But he was compared. As he followed Taylor year after year, teachers would inevitably make comparisons—subtle, but unmistakable. Todd coped by spending more and more time at the farm, helping his grandparents and enjoying solitary outdoor sports like fishing and cross-country skiing—*silent* sports, he called them.

"Where will you live?" I asked him now, working overtime to keep my emotions—my fear that he was about to make an enormous mistake that would change his life forever—from showing.

"The farm, if Grandma and Poppa will let us. They don't use the upstairs anymore and we could convert that into an apartment. There's already an outside entrance. We'd be company for them and we could help Poppa bring the farm back—make it profitable again. Keep it in the family."

I saw Spence consider this. I was practically twitching with all the objections that pressed to spill out of my mouth without censorship, while he was always so calm in the face of the things our children had sprung on us through the years. Like the time Cami had decided she wanted a tattoo, or when Taylor had rolled the car over, trying to beat curfew one night.

Now I focused on Todd—this young man who was so like his father—this stranger who was my son—and willed myself to form words that would not make things worse.

"Are you nuts?" Taylor said before I could speak. He was completely involved in the drama playing itself out in our family room. "Move to the farm, set up your own place there—great idea. But get married—I mean, you haven't even begun to live yet, man."

I actually felt a smile tickle the corners of my mouth as I blessed Taylor for saying more or less what I'd been thinking.

"This isn't about you," Todd said to his brother. "This isn't about the life you want. It's about what I want." He turned his attention back to Spence. "It's about finding my place in this family of superoverachievers and it's not something spur of the minute."

"Okay," Spence said slowly. "But Taylor has raised one pretty good point."

Todd's grip on the fireplace mantel tightened, but his

features remained impassive. "Why get married?" he asked, and glanced from me to his father and back.

We both nodded.

"Because I love her and she loves me. Because we've both had to find our way in the world alone so far—"

"You've never been alone," I interrupted.

"No, but it's been pretty lonely sometimes," he said. "Look, I know you both love me and you've done everything you could for me, but it's time to fend for myself."

"What about school?" Spence asked. "You and Sandra are graduating in a month, but what about college?"

"We'll finish senior year out there—in Mount Horeb. We'll be living at the farm, so that makes sense."

And on one level it did. He would not have to compete with the memory of his brother for those last couple of months of high school—no one would remember that his brother had been the valedictorian. He would be the new face and judged only on his own performance.

"And college?" I repeated.

He shot me a smile so filled with pity that I had to look away. "Mom, we both know that's not happening. I just don't want to waste four more years of my life trying to do something I'm not good at. Maybe later. Down the road, I can pick up some agricultural courses or something."

"We can get tutors," I began. "At the university, they offer…"

He just stood there shaking his head.

Spence cleared his throat and removed his reading glasses. "Okay, so you move in with Mom and Dad at the farm and finish high school. Doesn't Sandra already go to school there?"

Todd nodded.

Spence stood and began pacing—a sure sign that he was working through the logistics of this thing. I only hoped that his plan included some way to keep our son from throwing away his life by marrying before he was even twenty.

"So the two of you can be together for what's left of your senior year. During that time a lot can change, but even if it doesn't, you'll be more prepared and more sure—"

"We're sure now, Dad."

I could see that Spence was floundering in the face of Todd's determination. "You're just nineteen, Todd," I began. "Sandra is only eighteen. People in this day and age simply do not get married when they are still teenagers and still growing."

Taylor let out a hoot of laughter, which he stifled as soon as I threw him a look. I was well aware that my argument was full of holes, but Spence was getting nowhere. "Your father and I have to have some time to consider this, Todd," I said firmly. "End of discussion."

Todd shrugged and crossed the room to the stairway. "We'd really like your blessing," he said, and I understood that what he was not saying was that with or without our blessing he was going through with this. "And as long as I'm dropping bombs tonight, I joined the National Guard."

My mouth opened and closed. I shook my head, hoping I hadn't heard that right. "You c-can't," I stuttered. I felt Spence beside me, his hand on my shoulder.

Todd stepped back into the room. "Mom, I'm not doing any of this to hurt you—it's not about you or Dad. This is my life, and I want to start taking charge of it and planning a realistic future for myself. Please understand that."

I was shaking and chewing my lip to keep the howls of protest at bay. I stared at my clenched hands and heard

Spence say in a voice that all three children were aware meant the discussion was far from closed, "We'll talk about this tomorrow, son."

I stayed where I was, mentally counting out the heavy footfalls as Todd climbed the stairs. When I heard the familiar click of his bedroom door, I drew in one long shuddering breath and stood.

"Taylor, go to bed," I snapped at our other son, who was now leaning forward, fully prepared to engage in the discussion that would follow Todd's dramatic exit.

Spence

After our teenaged son announced his decision to join the National Guard and plans to marry and move to the farm, we stayed up most of the night debating the best plan for stopping this insanity. Somewhere around three in the morning as she was brewing a fresh pot of coffee, Zoe said, "Okay, let's address one issue at a time here. What if we're wrong? I mean about them marrying?"

I was bleary-eyed. Zoe's staying power for these sorts of discussions had always been superhuman. She looked as if she could go on for hours. "Zoe, they're kids."

"In many ways, so were we," she reminded me softly. "Look, Spence, all we've been doing is thinking about this thing from *our* point of view. He made some good arguments," she added as she refilled my coffee mug.

"Name one."

"College would be agony for him—I don't care where he went or how many tutors we hired."

"Name another."

"Both he and Sandra are mature beyond their years.

Sandra's dad died when she was only three and her mother has been the family's sole job. Sandra's worked in some sort or other since she was twelve—babysitting or such. Marie thinks the world of her."

"She's a terrific young woman—I'm not denying that. But is she ready to be a wife? Is Todd ready to be a husband?"

The slightest tug at her lips told me she was fighting a smile. "Were we?" She sat in the chair opposite mine. "Think about it. We'd known each other for only a few months before you went to Vietnam. Most of our so-called courtship was carried on through the mail."

"We were adults," I argued.

"Semantics. We were in our twenties—me barely. Did that make us any wiser when it came to having any idea what it meant to be married?"

"You need to switch to decaf," I said, reaching for her coffee mug. She stopped me by putting her hand over mine. I looked into her eyes. "You're actually considering saying yes to this insanity?"

"I'm seriously saying that it isn't up to us. Our son has reached a decision about his life—he's clearly not arrived at this lightly. Just because we've only had tonight to talk it through doesn't mean he hasn't been working it out for months already. Did you appreciate the way he handled himself tonight? The way he handled Taylor? That shows planning—strategic planning. At least we've taught him that."

I couldn't argue. "And what if it doesn't work out?"

She shrugged. "Hey, life doesn't come with a warranty for happiness." She continued to keep her hand on mine. "We learned that," she added softly.

Then she was up and rinsing out the mugs and turning off the coffeemaker.

"So we're decided?" I asked, watching her, enjoying as I hadn't in months the efficiency and grace of her movements. "I mean about the marriage?"

"I am," she replied. "You have to make your own decision."

"If I say okay, can we go to bed?"

"Oh, Spence, don't give in—I want you to believe this is best for Todd. He—and Sandra—deserve our complete support."

The woman who stood at the kitchen sink folding the dish towel and making this impassioned plea was the same woman I'd first noticed that day on campus nearly twenty-five years earlier. It was hard to refute her arguments and it was impossible to turn away.

"Besides, Todd's always dreamed of someday managing the farm," Zoe reminded me. "Your dad has counted on that."

"He doesn't have to get married to take over the farm," I said, but there was no energy left for the debate.

"He loves her," Zoe said in almost a whisper, "and she loves him more than she can bear sometimes." Her voice shook with emotion, and when I looked up, she was crying. "It's right there for the whole world to see. It's like…"

I got up so fast that the kitchen chair teetered on two legs before tipping over and hitting the floor. But neither of us noticed. I stood in front of Zoe as she leaned against the sink, her chin practically on her chest as huge tears plopped onto the front of her denim shirt.

It had been so long since I'd held her—really held her. Over the months and years since my affair, we had not only signed a contract with the kids, we had carefully built an imaginary picket fence between us. It was the kind that good friends or neighbors might exchange news over without ever stepping through the gate to be together on the same side. Oh, we had hugged and even resorted to giving each other a quick dry-lipped kiss on our way out the door in the morning. In bed we groaned with pleasure at the comfort of the bed after exhausting days filled with work and social commitments, but not in the ecstasy of lovemaking. We were polite and gentle and still too shaken by what we had almost lost to risk anything.

So as I stood in front of Zoe, watching her cry, wanting nothing so much as to take her in my arms, I hesitated. And in that hesitation, the moment was lost. She raised her hands to her face and laughed as she moved around me and busied herself straightening the place mats on the table. "I'm losing my baby," she said with a wry laugh, "or one of them, anyway." She glanced around the kitchen as if seeking some other task she could tackle. "I suppose we ought to get some sleep," she said finally.

"What about the National Guard?" I asked.

Her eyes and mouth tightened. "If we agree to the marriage, then…"

"He can't turn back that clock, Zoe," I said, and when I saw her regrouping for battle on this topic, I added, "Whatever strings you're thinking of trying to pull—or asking Peter to pull—I won't be a part of it," I told her.

Through all our years together Zoe and I had compromised on many topics, but not this one. She had remained steadfastly antiwar, while I continued to support the idea of a strong military as vital to maintaining the peace and security that Americans too often took for granted—as if it were an entitlement, not something to be earned.

She started to debate my logic, then caught herself. "Well, it's the National Guard and they do good work—tor-

nadoes, floods, civil disobedience. I mean, it's not like…"
She glanced at me, her eyes pleading for reassurance.

"Todd'll be fine," I assured her. "Let's get some sleep."

"You go on," she said. "I'll be up in a bit."

Zoe

Thursday, March 15, 1995

It's been a long time since I wrote anything. I used to think the point of keeping a journal was to record my life— the events of that life whether grand or minuscule. But it seems the only times I resort to putting my thoughts down in writing is when I can't find answers—can't find a solution. Like tonight.

But it's not a solution for Todd and Sandra that I need. It's not even about Todd joining the Guard. I don't like it. No, that's too mild. I hate it, although I suppose I should have seen it coming. Growing up, he was always more like Spence and Hal than like me. And he was also like Ty in so many ways—serious and thoughtful, gentle but at the same time quietly determined. The way he sits at the dinner table, saying nothing while I rant on about whatever new perceived injustice has caught my attention. Like Spence, he nods and even smiles. Usually once I run out of words to hurl at the problem, I just stop, expecting my children—if not my husband—to agree. Cami always plays devil's advocate—deliberately adding fuel to the debate. Taylor shrugs with the "whatever" indifference of the times and Todd concentrates on eating.

"What do you think, Todd?" I ask.

He finishes chewing his food, then offers me that incredible smile that so mirrors his father's and replies, "As you would say, Mom—they didn't ask you."

How many times had I raged on and on about some issue, only to add after I finally ran out of steam, "But as my grandmother used to say, 'They didn't ask me.'" The implication being that if they had, things would not be in the mess they were in.

This time Todd isn't asking me, either. Not about joining the Guard and not about getting married. So I can rant and rave and howl at the moon, but I will not change what he has decided to do—what he has done. My choice is clear. I can either support his decisions and do everything I can to help make them the right decisions for him. Or I can refuse and risk losing him.

But I already knew all that halfway into the discussion Spence and I had earlier in the kitchen. That was the point. I knew that what I needed to do was move from denial to anger to acceptance in a place where Todd would not hear or be hurt. I knew that I could only do that with Spence.

Only Spence.

Always Spence.

Why do I continue to reject him? Why—after all this time and after everything he does that shows me every day his love for me—do I run from any overture he makes? All I had to do tonight was take the tiniest step forward and we could have—would have... What? Made love? Turned back the calendar? Torn down the tangles of wire barbed with our individual hurts and hysteria or self-righteousness that allow us to be with each other but not connect?

I realized tonight that I was ready to let Todd and Sandra do this thing because I remembered nights sitting on the steps of the Mifflin Street house with Spence. We'd warm our hands on steaming mugs of hot chocolate and plan our tomorrows. Thinking back on my life, there have been many moments of high excitement, even ecstasy. But for sheer simple happiness, nothing compares with those quiet nights when most everyone up and down the street was asleep and Spencer Andersen and I saw the whole world—our whole lives—ahead of us.

We've traveled so far from those days and I appreciate how blessed we've been—I've been. We have three magnificent children, a home we have loved from the moment we first walked through the front door, life's work that we never could have imagined would be so fulfilling. But somewhere along the way we lost each other. It's become a day-by-day thing haunted by the past for us. We've lost the ability to look forward, to dream. That's what I heard Todd telling us tonight—about his dreams for the future, about seeing what lies ahead—not backward.

Tonight I stood at the kitchen sink and thought about Todd and Sandra and how they are just beginning with everything in front of them—with everything possible for them. In a perverse way I even saw Spence and me in them—Sandra is a very strong young woman. Even the National Guard thing began to seem like a safe parallel to what Spence and I had been through. But most of all, I wanted that precious time back for Spence and me. I wanted "us" back. And yet when he stepped closer and I realized that he would hold me, I also knew that he hesitated because of all the occasions I've rebuffed him openly or pretended not to see the signs.

I could have made that new beginning for us. I could have moved that tiny step, raised my eyes to his, lifted my arms. But I didn't...again. If I long for us back together again, then why? Because the risk that we might reach that cliff again and this time go over terrifies me. Safer this way.

Spence

I was still awake when Zoe finally got into bed. The sky was already losing its blackness and I could hear birds stirring. She eased herself under the covers, trying not to wake me. I stretched my arm across the expanse of our king-size bed until I felt her shoulder.

"They'll be okay," I whispered.

Zoe was quiet for a long moment, then her fingers curled over mine. "I know." She rolled toward me and curled against my side. "And so will we," she said as she smoothed my hair away from my forehead.

It had been so long since I'd cried, but I did nothing to stop the tears that seemed to wash over my cheeks in a river as I reached for her.

I studied her in the moonlight that filtered through the lace curtains of our bedroom and saw every facet of her beauty as clearly as if we'd left every light in the room on. "You're exquisite," I told her.

I stroked her hair, still long but now streaked with gray and sunlight, nudging it away to expose her bare shoulders. Shoulders that were sprinkled with freckles in spite of the sunscreen and wide-brimmed straw hat she wore religiously. I followed the line of her gown, a river of green batiste. But her beauty was not in her hair or the body beneath the gown. Her beauty was in her eyes and her smile—both ripened by the years, the experiences she had had, the choices she had made, the wisdom she had cultivated.

The kiss seemed to last forever and at the same time be over in a millisecond. The familiar taste of her, the fullness of her lips and mouth opening to mine. The delicate cotton nightgown that was no match for the silky smoothness of her bare arms and shoulders. It was as if I was home at last.

"Spence," she whispered, her head lowered so that I couldn't see her eyes. "Maybe we should take a page from our son's book."

I kissed her throat. "I'm listening."

She laughed and lifted her head to give me better access to her neck, her ear, the curve of her jaw. "You're not, but I'm going to say it anyway."

My heart tripped, fearful as always that we had made this small step but not the large leap I so longed for us to take. I rested on one elbow. "Say what?"

"Let's make a fresh start—like Todd and Sandra. Let's let go of the past and just—live."

"The past—good and bad—is part of who we are," I reminded her.

"I know. For better or worse, but we can get back to focusing on the better."

I grinned. "Works for me."

Our lovemaking was a remembered waltz, the music filled with memories of an attic room on Mifflin Street, a waterbed above a bookstore, and this house—this wonderful place where we had once again found "home."

Winter 2007

Zoe

The new regimen of medication proved to be the miracle we had all prayed for. I felt wonderful—so much so that late in October Spence and I made that trip to Vancouver with Ginny and Jon. So much so that during the whole of the trip no one had to ask if I was "doing okay." In fact, having been assigned the role of tour leader, I packed our days and evenings so full that the rest of the group begged for a little downtime.

"Jon, you look exhausted," I said one afternoon as the four of us sat in an outdoor café enjoying cups of herbal tea. "Are you doing okay?" I placed my hand on his and offered him my most concerned gaze.

I noticed how Spence and Ginny held their breaths

at my use of the phrase that had become everyone's mantra for reassuring themselves about my well-being.

Then I laughed, pointing at the three of them, barely able to speak. "If you guys could see your faces," I said.

The joke morphed into a kind of secret code that only we four understood. "I'm not doing okay," Ginny would shout from her position far behind the rest of us as we biked around the city. It was our cue to slow down and give her a chance to catch up.

One night after we'd gone to our hotel room for the night, Spence kissed me and murmured, "I'm doing okay."

"Would you like to try for better than okay?" I asked.

It had been months since we'd made love with the abandon that had been our trademark in our youth. The times we'd tried either I was too exhausted from the meds or chemo, or we were both too scared—too tentative.

"You sure?" Spence asked, his eyes sparkling with wanting me, wanting this.

"I won't break," I said, and led him to the bed.

But I did—or at least, my rib cracked. The following morning I could not hide the fact that I was not doing okay, but I shrugged it off as overexertion. Jon and Ginny, still safe in the magic of the time we'd had together, believed me. Spence had doubts, but when I insisted that I'd only pulled a muscle during the night and winked at him, he let out a breath of relief.

He knew better and so did I, but when you love someone and accept that time is finite for all of us, you will sometimes look the other way just so the two of you can have one more day—one more hour—before the next challenge.

On the plane trip home, I switched seats with Ginny

and told Jon what I suspected, while Spence explained the situation to Ginny. By the time we touched down, an ambulance was waiting to take me to the university medical center, where Jon had arranged for the various scans and tests he needed to evaluate this latest development.

"What's the damage?" I did not like the frown on Jon's face, but I appreciated the fact that he had long ago stopped trying to maintain a "professional" impassive expression when talking to me.

"Osteoblastic metastases," he said, and Spence turned away.

"In English," I coached.

"There are two types of bone metastases," he said, pulling up a chair so that he was knee to knee with me. "Osteolytic eats away at the bone, forming holes. Osteoblastic actually increases the bone density, making the bones more susceptible to fracture."

"And the treatment is?"

"A class of drugs called bisphosphonates. One currently available can be administered intravenously. But there's another that's under study. It's actually stopped the progression of bone metastases in mice—as well as the formation of new metastases."

"Go for it." I heard myself say the same words that Spence and I had offered our only daughter when she'd called from New York to tell us she was pretty sure she'd be offered a job in the financial district. Advice that had brought her to the north tower on that September day that changed the world. It was advice rooted in the certainty that we only get one life and the key is to fill each hour of it to overflowing so when it's the end there are no regrets.

Spence sat with me. "What is it?"

I shrugged as I stared out the window at the floor of white clouds. "Nothing. I was just thinking about Cami—about how we—"

"This is not the same thing, Zoe."

"Yeah, it is," I replied. "Cancer is the terrorist this time, striking without warning because you never realized it was there."

The real question following this latest discovery was, of course, whether or not I was up for one more battle. The answer? I honestly didn't know. All I knew was that Spence rushed home—a week after the confirmation that the cancer had spread to my bones—beaming, his eyes filled with excitement.

"I ran into Jon at the hospital," he told me, excitement coloring every syllable.

His exhilaration was contagious. I laughed without knowing why. "That's not so unusual," I reminded him.

"Yeah, well, sure, but he'd just heard about a new clinical trial—a new treatment that could help you—us." He picked me up and swung me around. "It's already in the final phase."

"I don't understand."

"If all goes well in this last test group, it's a slam dunk for approval by the FDA—maybe as early as March."

My smile wavered. Although I was feeling better than I had in months, the facts could not be ignored. The cancer had spread again from my lungs to my bones. Who could say where else cells were lurking?

"Will you try it?" Spence asked as he put me down but did not release his hold on me. His eyes were soft, reminding me of our sons when they were small and longed for something desperately. In that moment I thought about Cami. I thought about Todd and Taylor. I thought about our beautiful grandchildren. And I peered into the eyes of the man I loved and nodded.

"Sure," I said, for what else do I have to offer him but the precious gift of hope?

Spence

I knew it was a long shot, but for whatever reason, the new drug worked for Zoe. In the midst of a Wisconsin winter she blossomed like a sunny daffodil. Her energy was up. Her spirits were high. And for the first time since we'd heard the news of her cancer recurring, life got back to normal.

She returned to her work and clapped her hands in delight when she saw the lift chair her friends had chipped in to buy her when it became nearly impossible for her to climb the steep stairway. Day after day I walked into our home and found Zoe being Zoe—humming as she stirred a pot of homemade soup. Sitting in the study with Sara or Liz, a glass of wine in hand, watching some talk show and offering their own commentary on the topic and guests. She even accepted a position on the board at the botanical gardens.

"I may not be around for the full term," she said with a grin, "but I have a couple of ideas that might shake things up as long as I'm there."

"Heaven help them," I said, and meant it. Seeing her excitement over the appointment to the board at the gardens, I was torn between trying to preserve her energy and giving her encouragement to go out there and live full-out. We all understood that once Zoe got the idea to create something there was no stopping her. She did not know the meaning of the word *impossible*.

"Just don't overdo it," I said before I could stop myself.

She sighed with exasperation. "Make up your mind, farm boy. A couple of months ago you were pushing hard for me to pick myself up and get out into the world again and now—"

I kissed her and it had the anticipated reaction. The pseudo-frustrated woman became the girl I had fallen in love with. She curled closer to me, resting her mouth just below my ear as she whispered, "Or I could let the garden board do their own thing and we could see what blooms here."

"I have a meeting at the hospital," I said as she ran her tongue along the side of my neck. "On the other hand—"

"Here's a rain check," she murmured, and kissed me. Then, giggling, she escaped my arms and collected her coat, scarf and mittens from the closet. "Tuna casserole okay for supper?"

"How about I pick you up at the gardens and we'll go out?"

She grinned with obvious relief. "Boy, you sure do know the way to a girl's heart."

I kissed her forehead. "I'm just setting the stage for that rain check you promised me. I'll meet you at the gardens at five?"

Zoe smiled. "So in real time that would be five-thirty," she teased.

I had long ago given up trying to get Zoe to be on schedule and had compensated by setting appointments half an hour before the actual time we needed to meet. "When did you figure that out?" I asked.

"Oh, about two years ago. But it works."

"Most of the time," I agreed.

When I got to the gardens' welcome center that afternoon, Zoe was nowhere in sight. It had started to snow and huge fragile flakes landed on the grass and flowerbeds as I parked and went to the door.

The building was locked and there was no sign of anyone inside. I'd passed Zoe's car on my way in so she had to be there. "Zoe!"

The snow was beginning to stick to the sidewalks and paths as I walked around the center and back into the actual gardens. Daffodils and tulips had begun to fight their way through the frozen ground with the promise of an early spring. I paused and looked around, trying to decide which of the multiple paths to follow. I turned up the collar on my leather jacket and thrust my hands into the pockets. One closed around my cell phone.

I dialed Zoe's number. Voice mail. I checked for messages on my phone. Nothing. My heart started to race and my feet began moving in rhythm with its pounding. "Zoe!" I called as I ran. Choosing the most logical path, I crossed a wooden footbridge.

There in the distance, red and gold against a white landscape, stood the Thai sala. The project that had consumed Zoe's every waking moment in the months before 9/11. The place where she dealt with her sorrow in the weeks after our return from New York. I slowed to a walk as I saw her standing alone under the shelter.

Her hands were folded in front of her and she was facing toward the reflecting pond, where abstract floes of ice circled like water lilies on the surface. My breathing steadied as I allowed the balm of pure relief to wash over me. Of course this was where she had come. She always ended any day she spent at the gardens here— alone. Of course she had lost track of the time, for who wouldn't in a setting of such pure beauty?

"Zoe?" I kept my voice low, as befitted the hallowed ground of a place meant for meditation and reflection.

Zoe turned at my voice and glanced at her wristwatch. "Oh, Spence, I'm so sorry. I just— Five years, Spence. We were almost there," she whispered, and I held out my arms to her.

Almost there. Cami had said the same thing.

2001

Zoe

"**M**om, I got it—the job. I got it!"

Cami's voice was filled with confidence rather than the amazement that I might have anticipated given her anxiety about whether she was qualified.

"That's wonderful, Cami," I said, even as I marveled at how this bright young woman who not only understood stocks and bonds and other assorted mysteries of the economic world but also relished the chance to play that game had come from me. "When do you start?"

"I'm not sure. I'm going in this morning to complete the stuff for HR—human resources," she added, obviously certain that someone like me who had never darkened the door of a corporate American enterprise, would need the jargon explained. "I'm wearing the gray Armani—you know, the one Gramma Kay insisted I buy?" she continued, and I could hear the sounds of the city coming to life and going to work in the background.

"Okay, so even though that suit cost a fortune, I have to admit that it's paying off now," I said, reminding us both of my reservations about spending that kind of money for one suit. I'd commented that it was ridiculous at best and obscene at worst.

"I'll let you borrow it next time you go begging for money for the botanical gardens," she joked, then her voice changed. "I'm so nervous, Mom. Not sure what that's about. Could you just talk to me about stuff there? It might help."

This was the daughter who rarely had turned to either Spence or me for help, so if she asked, we understood it was serious. "Let's see," I said. "Well, the artisans that designed and built the sala are arriving today," I added.

"What's a sala, anyway—some kind of religious temple or what?" She already sounded more at ease.

"Not religious at all. In Thailand it's a shelter for people from rain or heat."

"Like bus stops?"

"Well, I haven't noticed any American bus stops that feature gold leaf with bright red lacquer, but I suppose that's one comparison."

"So, the crew is coming to set it up and you're no doubt going to be right in the thick of it," Cami said.

"The crew—as you call them—arrives at O'Hare this morning. I'm putting the finishing touches on tonight's reception. We're holding it here at the house—in the garden. And tomorrow we start reassembling the pavilion. It'll be all done when you're in for Thanksgiving. You are coming for Thanksgiving, right? I mean, this new job…"

"I wouldn't miss Turkey Day, Mom. Thanksgiving and the Fourth of July are my favorite holidays."

"No presents, no fuss and you know the menu," we said together.

"Mom, do you ever have regrets? I mean, about leaving when Peter ran for governor. You probably could have ended up the mayor or a senator or something."

"I have no regrets," I said. "I have filled my life with so many wonderful people and projects, and you and your brothers are certainly up there near the top."

"Right below Dad?"

I laughed. "Right below Dad," I assure her.

She sighs. "I can't help it, Mom. I want it all. Career, kids, a man like Dad who thinks the sun rises and sets on me. I had this crazy feeling this morning that I was on my way, you know?"

I felt something deep inside in that moment that made me pause in my normal multitasking any time I was on the phone and sit down at the kitchen table. "Cami, Dad and I are so very proud of you," I said, and was surprised at the emotion that filled me as I thought about this child who was perhaps more like me than I had ever dared to hope. Cami had always been independent and determined to succeed at anything she did, no matter how difficult. She wasn't as smart as Taylor or as practical as Todd, but she had gotten to where she was all on her own.

Her voice wavered. "Thanks, Mom. You don't realize what that means to me—especially today." There was some static on the line, and, afraid that I was losing the connection I said, "Are you on the subway or…"

The line cleared. "...concourse," she said, obviously finishing a sentence I hadn't heard. "Do you want a play-by-play?" she teased.

"As a matter of fact I would like one," I replied. "It's not every day that the daughter of a throwback hippie lands a major job at one of the world's top investment firms before she hits thirty."

"World's top firm might be stretching it, Mom," she said. "Okay, on the escalator on my way up to the main lobby—prophetic, don't you think?"

"Very. What floor are the offices on and do you get a window?"

"Seventy-fourth and practically everyone gets a window."

In the background I could hear a jumble of movement and voices. "Impressive," I said. "How many underlings will you be supervising?"

She giggled the way she had when she was thirteen and on the phone with her girlfriends dissecting the merits and pitfalls of the latest crop of boys in her class. "I do have an assistant," she said. "Imagine me ordering somebody around?"

"Well, your brothers certainly could."

She laughed. "How are the monsters?"

"Your brothers are grown men, Cami. Show a little respect." But I was smiling as I chastised her.

"Well, they turned out pretty great, didn't they? My influence, no doubt."

"No doubt." I hooked the receiver between my shoulder and ear as I placed the chicken pieces in the marinade, covered the bowl and put it in the refrigerator. "One of them is talking about making you an aunt."

Cami squealed with delight. "Sandy and Todd? Really? That's way beyond cool."

"Where are you now?" I asked, laughing because she suddenly sounded far too young to be climbing the corporate ladder.

"Elevator doors opening—express, of course." Her voice dropped to a whisper. "It's packed, Mom, and I don't want to get labeled a total geek. I'll call you back, okay?"

We hung up and I gathered the notes and materials I needed for the meeting scheduled later that morning at the botanical gardens. It occurred to me that in many areas I had achieved so much more than I had dreamed I would ever do in my lifetime. And none of it was what I had planned. Spence and I had raised three children who were actually sane and well-rounded and on their way to successful and happy lives. I had finally found work that gave me the sense of accomplishment I'd always sought—even if I was no longer being paid to do it. On top of that—to everyone's surprise, including my own—I had become a passable—if not a gourmet—cook and a master gardener. I paused for a minute and gazed out at the gardens—resplendent in the colors of autumn—reds and golds and purples against the backdrop of the still-green trees and the deep, clear blue of the lake. Beds were arranged in the kind of organized chaos that I preferred in stark contrast to the formality of my neighbor's equally impressive yard. Yes, life was good, I decided as I turned to load the files and papers I would need for the day into my tote bag.

In the background Al Roker delivered the weather report for *The Today Show*. He was speaking in mime, because I always muted the sound when one of the children called. I glanced at the time, automatically calculating what Taylor would be doing in California—sleeping—as well as what

Todd would be doing thirty miles away on the farm he and Sandra now managed for Hal and Marie. I called Spencer's office and reminded his assistant to get him out of there no later than five so he could come home and change before the reception. It crossed my mind that Cami's express elevator was certainly taking its time.

As soon as I hung up the phone rang. "Slow elevator," I said, ready to pick up the conversation with Cami where we'd left off.

"Mom?" Her voice sounded far away and scared.

"What is it?" I was on instant alert, a dozen scenarios racing through my mind in the split second before she answered me. Had she been attacked on the elevator? No, she'd said it was packed. Maybe the elevator had stalled. She never could stand tight spaces.

"Mom, there's..." Her voice was obscured by the shrieks of panic and screaming. My heart actually stopped for a split second.

"Cami! What's happening?"

"Move on," I heard some stranger say close to the phone. "Can you walk?"

"Sure," I heard my daughter reply. Then I only heard her breathing—hard and fast as if she was running a marathon.

"Lose the shoes," I heard the same man say.

"Cami?"

"I'm here, Mom. I think there's been a fire on the floors above us and the smoke is pretty intense and... Okay, we're in the stairway—also packed and smoky..." She forced a laugh and I heard voices around her.

I turned to the television and saw a picture that would haunt me for every day of the rest of my life. One of the twin towers of the World Trade Center was indeed on fire.

I forced myself to remain calm. "Now, Cami, I'm watching the television, and yes, there's a fire, but it's well above you. Just take your time, stay calm and keep heading down the stairs, okay? And stay on the line," I added.

"Well, at least we're not having to go *up* the stairs." Her voice was shaky.

"Are you hurt?" I asked, my eyes glued to the television as I tried to think of ways to keep her talking while I made some sense of the fact that Matt Lauer was telling me that a plane had flown straight into the building—an enormous jet plane.

On the other end of the line I heard a thunderous reverberation—like a sonic boom that had just happened in your own backyard. "Cami?"

"Mom?" she shrieked at the same time. "What was that? Do you have the TV on? What are they reporting?" Then I heard her talking to others around her as the news spread. "Mom? People here are telling us that planes are flying into the towers—huge planes. What's happening?"

"Keep moving, Cami. The fire and police departments are on the scene. The best thing you can do is get out so they can do their jobs."

"Stay on the phone, okay?" she begged. "Don't talk. Just stay on, okay?"

"I'm not leaving you," I promised, and knew it for the lie that it was. I was safe in my kitchen in Madison, Wisconsin. Minutes passed as I chattered on about the weather and the news at home. Outside it was a glorious September day—one of those stereotypical Americana mornings you see in the movies—blue skies over the calm waters of the lake with the flag over the Capitol building. As the flag rippled lazily in the light autumn breeze, the situation in New York suddenly seemed surreal. My daughter—my firstborn—was trapped in a stairwell filled with panicked people and smoke, while above her the fire raged and an ominous black pillar of smoke obliterated an identical blue sky in Manhattan.

I felt the tears I'd been holding back start to spill over as the signal faded. "Cami?"

"Right here—[crackle]—and here—[crackle]—are the good guys."

For endless minutes all I could hear were other voices ordering people to stand aside and then the trampling of heavy feet and shouted commands.

"Firemen," Cami explained after they'd passed. "Hope they—"

The line crackled and I prayed our connection would hold. "Cami," I shouted as I watched the second hand tick off the minutes.

After what seemed like forever, I heard Cami say, "Okay. Making some progress now."

Another boom—this one prolonged and so loud that I nearly dropped the phone. I spun back to the TV in time to see the south tower collapse like the blocks that Todd and Taylor had delighted in knocking over as children. At that same moment I heard Spencer's car in the driveway.

I stumbled to the door as he ran to the house, leaving the motor on and the car door open. "Have you heard from Cami?" he asked, and I understood that my face must have mirrored what I had just seen.

Spence

I pried the phone from Zoe's fingers as she held it toward me. Her face was ashen and she seemed incapable of breathing, much less speaking.

"Cami?" I shouted, then more calmly added, "It's Dad."

"Daddy? What's happening? The walls are cracking like enormous zippers and there's so much smoke and—" She started to cough.

I followed Zoe into the kitchen and blinked at the television replay of the collapse of the south tower. My daughter was trapped in a stairwell in the north tower. How much time did she have to get out? "Cami, keep moving," I ordered. "Just keep going. I'm right here with Mom and we're not going to leave you, okay?"

Above the thousand other voices around her I could hear my daughter breathing. *Just keep breathing*, I pleaded, whether to Cami or God or both I couldn't have said. *Keep moving. One foot, then the other, then...*

I forced away from the horror repeated incessantly on the television and focused on the lake. I remembered the day I sat in the old rowboat we'd inherited when we bought the house. Cami swam alongside. *Breathe—stroke—breathe—stroke*, I'd coached.

"You breathe," she'd snapped back when she'd gulped a healthy mouthful of lake water instead of air and emerged coughing as she clung to the side of the boat. Then, with the mischievous twinkle she'd gotten directly from Zoe, she tipped the boat so that I landed with a splash next to her.

"Cami?" Zoe had picked up the portable phone from the family room and returned to stand next to me. "We're here, Cami," she yelled.

"Just tell me what that noise was," Cami yelled back, her voice breaking in the separate syllables laced with panic.

"The south tower collapsed, Cami," I told her as my eyes met Zoe's. "You have to get out of there."

"I'm trying, Dad. But..."

"Cami, remember that time you were training for the swim meet and I was in the boat and—"

To my relief she laughed. I exchanged a look with Zoe and saw that she understood what I'd just realized. If this was our daughter's last hour on earth, we were not going to waste it reprimanding her. Zoe gave a quick nod.

"That was the same summer you decided to take up cooking. Remember?" Zoe said. "Grandma Marie taught you how to make her famous coconut cake? How about making one when you're home for Thanksgiving?" Zoe stretched out her hand to me.

I flicked off the television and grasped Zoe's hand.

"Almost there—losing you," Cami shouted. "Almost there…"

I suddenly could not speak around the enormous lump that had formed in my throat or the weight that pressed down on my chest. *This is what it feels like when your heart breaks,* I thought. Zoe took the phone from me and kept shouting Cami's name and redialing the number as I switched on the television. Minutes later we watched as the north tower crumbled to the ground. In the silence of that perfect day, the only sound I heard in that house where we'd raised our beautiful daughter was the phone hitting the granite counter. When I turned, Zoe was sliding to the floor, her legs liquid, her face a mask of grief and disbelief.

Zoe

By noon the house and yard were crowded with people—family and friends who had all watched as the un-imaginable had happened. But for most of them this war had not yet hit as close to their homes as it had to ours. And so they came or called. Neighbors, coworkers, Spence's students and former students deposited their offerings of food in the kitchen with Marie and Todd's wife, Sandra, who had arrived and taken charge of the kitchen seemingly within minutes after we lost contact with Cami. The guests would say a few words to one family member or another and then wander out to the lawn to speak quietly in small groups of their own disbelief and shock.

The chair of the committee in charge of the sala called to tell me that the Thailand delegation had been on the last plane allowed to land at O'Hare before they stopped all air traffic. As if that would somehow comfort me. Of course he hadn't heard about Cami yet. I glanced at the sky and realized how quiet the day had grown. In contrast to the chaotic sounds of the morning—the screams, the shrieks, the sobs and the sheer thunder of supposedly indestructible buildings collapsing like playing cards—had been replaced by this silence. As if the world were holding its breath, waiting for what would happen next.

Todd—so like his father—stoic and unflappable in the face of any challenge—moved from group to group, thanking people for coming, enduring their expressions of sympathy while I stood at the window of our bedroom, observing the scene. Taylor had phoned to say he was driving cross-country and would drive through the night to be home as soon as possible.

I had excused myself, citing the need to keep trying to reach my parents in New York. Understandably the lines to the city had been jammed for hours. The truth was that once I reached the safety of our bedroom and closed the door, I had spent the entire time dialing Cami's cell phone.

"She isn't dead," I muttered as I stood at the window, observing the mother of one of Cami's closest friends break down in front of Spencer and have to be led away by her husband. "We don't know that yet," I added, wanting to shout it at all of them as I let the blind tumble back to the sill.

I prayed for Spence to do something, to assume command, to reassure us all by putting on the mantle of leadership he had worn so well in Vietnam and in his career as a doctor and professor. I watched him through the slats of the blind. He stood off to one side of the yard—the same way he had stood on the fringes of the gathering after my brother's funeral. He looked the way my father had—shell-shocked and broken.

I threw the portable phone on the bed and cast about for something concrete I could do, some action I could take. My daughter called out to me. I stood in front of the closet, staring at the contents, seeking answers in whatever had made me cross the room and stand there. Finally I took down a duffel from the top shelf and positioned it on the bed. By rote I opened dresser drawers and deposited items in the duffel— underwear, socks, T-shirts for Spencer, then the same for me. I turned to the closet, ignoring the tap on the door.

"What are you doing?" Spence asked as he walked in and closed the door behind him. His tone was lifeless and held no real curiosity, just weariness for what craziness he might be called upon to deal with.

"Packing," I replied, and continued depositing clothing in the duffel, stretching it to accommodate each pile. "Should I pack your electric shaver or a regular blade?"

"Zoe?"

I looked at him then, his handsome faced aged at least ten years in just the past few hours. His eyes red-rimmed from the tears he refused to allow others to witness but had shed freely behind the locked door of his study. His shoulders stooped with the weight of the day's events.

"We don't know, Spence. We don't know anything. We'll go to New York. We can stay with my parents. And we will find Cami," I pleaded. "If we drive through the night, we'll be there by morning. Todd and Sandra and your folks can stay here in case Cami calls. We'll have our mobile phone."

Spence gave a dry shuddering sob and nodded. "Let's go bring our daughter home," he said.

We traded off driving—two hours on, bathroom and coffee stop to switch drivers, then back on the road. We talked only if there was some question about a detour for road construction or a way around a city that could be bypassed. The one who wasn't behind the wheel slept or pretended to. The driver plowed on, with the strains of Vivaldi's *Four Seasons* playing repeatedly on the audiotape that had already been in place when we began the trip. Marie had packed a hamper with enough sandwiches and bottled water and fruit to sustain us for several trips between Wisconsin and New York, but we devoured them hungrily and without much appreciation along the way.

When my shift at the wheel came around just after midnight, Spencer crawled into the backseat and curled himself along the width of it. I tossed him the small pillow that he kept at the small of his back when driving. In minutes I heard the soft rhythm of his breathing and knew that I was alone with Vivaldi and my thoughts for the next couple of hours at least.

How can he sleep? I fumed, the anger I'd felt throughout the day finding a target at last. Then I recalled when

Cami had asked the same question, probing for answers I neither wanted nor could give her.

Earlier that summer Cami had burst into the house, clearly expecting the usual frenzied activity that had been the hallmark of all our years as a family. But with Taylor off at college in California and Todd married and living on the farm, it was just Spencer and me. "How can he sleep?" Cami had asked me that night after supper when Spencer had settled into his den on the pretense of watching the news and promptly fallen asleep. What she left unsaid was *When I'm here for just a couple of days?*

"Your father works hard," I told her. "And neither one of us is getting any younger, in case you haven't noticed."

She studied me for a long moment. "So, are you two okay? I mean, please don't tell me that you stayed together for the kids and now that we're all out of the nest, you're falling apart."

That was the night that I saw her across the kitchen table where we had conducted a thousand mother-daughter talks and accepted that she was no longer coming home to seek our guidance and advice. That was the night that I realized that without my being aware of the exact moment—as I had always been aware of milestones in the lives of my children—she had evolved into her own person, made her own life. That was the night that my daughter and I talked until four in the morning about everything that two grown women might entrust to each other upon realizing that they had passed the parent-child milestone and blossomed into the best of friends. That was the night that Cami had dared me to go into the den, wake Spencer and announce that the three of us were going out for breakfast—at four in the morning, as he and I had done in those days when we'd been students...and madly in love.

Spencer stirred in the backseat, unfolded his lanky frame with much grunting and groaning and leaned over the console between the front seats. "Zoe, it's almost four. You must be beat. Why didn't you wake me?"

I shrugged and pointed to a billboard advertising a truck stop that served breakfast twenty-four/seven. "How about some pancakes?" I asked.

Mom and Dad were waiting for us when we pulled up. Dad had called in every favor he could to get us through the detours and barriers that had locked down the city. Now he arranged for the doorman to handle parking the car while we rode with them in the elevator to their penthouse—a place Cami had always adored.

"Gramma Kay has the most incredible taste!" she would exclaim after spending summers working in the city and living with my parents during her college years, implying that I was definitely lacking in that department. "I mean, the way she uses antiques and mixes them with contemporary art. I mean, wow!"

In the living room, a large canvas that usually occupied the wall opposite the sofa was missing. It was Cami's favorite, and I felt a sudden need to make sure that it hadn't been sold. "What happened to the Pollock?" I asked.

Mom glanced at the empty space on the wall, burst into tears and left the room. "We gave it to Cami for a housewarming present when she moved into the loft," Dad explained.

The loft. I glanced at Spencer and saw that we were thinking the same thing. It hadn't even occurred to us to try the loft. If Cami had made it out of the north tower before it collapsed, she might have found her way back there. She might be lying there hurt, unable to call us. I grabbed the phone and dialed. A disembodied voice informed me that the number was temporarily out of service.

Mom returned, carrying a tray with coffee mugs and a plate of breakfast rolls. "I made some herbal tea," she said. "You've both probably had enough coffee to keep you going for days, but you need your rest. You'll be no good to Cami if the two of you collapse."

This was the mother I had always leaned on in hard times. The no-nonsense, let's-be-practical woman who could chair any committee or group and turn it into an institution through the sheer force of her organizational skills. I glanced at Spence and saw him manage a smile as he accepted the mug of tea that Mom handed him.

"What's your plan?" Dad asked as we all settled around the coffee table.

Spence waited for me to answer, but I really hadn't thought much beyond where we were now. Get to New York and find Cami.

"Ah," Dad said. "Perhaps your mother can help."

To my astonishment, Mom produced a folder of neatly printed papers—names and numbers of hospitals where survivors had been taken; names and numbers for rescue groups and hastily organized survivor contact groups. "I've called them all at least once," Mother said. "With no luck, I'm afraid, but everything has been such a mess," she added.

Dad reached over and pulled out more papers—at least fifty copies of a single sheet that featured the heading: *HAVE YOU SEEN THIS WOMAN?* Underneath was a recent color photo of Cami, along with information about age, hair and eye color, height and weight and what she was wearing when last seen—the Armani suit. Then, in bold print at the bottom, *IF YOU HAVE ANY INFORMATION, PLEASE CONTACT*: with three phone numbers I didn't recognize.

"Your father has set up a phone bank at the office," Mom explained.

"Have you heard from anyone?" Spence asked.

My father nodded. "We've had dozens of calls, but only one seems to relate to Cami—so far."

Spence and I both leaned forward, and Dad's eyes skittered away.

"Someone saw her get onto the elevator," Mom said. "Someone who worked with her from her previous company."

Spence slumped back on the sofa and focused on his hands. I got up and roamed the room. "We already know she got on the elevator," I ranted. "We know she got off the elevator. We know she made it all the way down to at least the nineteenth floor before…before we lost contact. Where is she *now?*" I spun around toward the fireplace and pounded my fist on the marble mantel. "Where is my daughter?" I said once, but did not stop pounding the cold white stone until I felt Spencer's hands on my shoulders.

"Lie down for an hour, Zoe, and then we'll go there. We'll go to the loft. We'll go to every hospital. We'll go to every temporary shelter. We'll go together, okay? We will find her."

I watched the antique clock as it ticked off each second. "It hasn't even been twenty-four hours," I whispered. "Why does it seem like forever?"

2001

Spence

Zoe stayed in New York for weeks. I returned home after ten endless days. We had both known from the time Zoe started packing that the search was futile, but we had to try. Those days ran one into the other with all the fluidness of a nightmare. One of those horror shows of the mind that's determined to play itself out no matter how often you hope to end it by waking up.

Those first days had a bizarre routine all their own. After checking every list, every hospital and shelter, we stood with hundreds of other parents, spouses, siblings, lovers and friends behind the television journalists reporting from Ground Zero. We held up the picture of Cami and the boldly printed phone numbers. We got calls—crank calls from sick souls who claimed that the death of our daughter was somehow God's will, as well as calls from people who wanted to be helpful but knew nothing.

But it was the day we went to Cami's loft that I think both Zoe and I understood that our daughter was truly gone. Because of the dust—the thick gray powder that permeated everywhere—I was suddenly back in Vietnam, where there had also been dust, blinding, choking. Even our footsteps on the stairs leading to Cami's third-floor loft were silenced as we climbed over the miniature dunes that had formed on each step. The power was out, and suddenly Zoe said, "Remember when we took the Immigrant Museum tour with the kids and the guide told us how the landlord would make the people sign the lease before they saw the apartment?"

Her voice shook and I knew she was remembering Cami's comment that day—the comment that had made everyone, even the tour guide, laugh: "No landlord would have gotten away with that if my mom had been there. She'd have marched right up these stairs and checked out everything from the plumbing to the view before she signed anything." She'd been ten years old.

"Yeah, I remember," I said.

"Fifteen minutes, folks," a policeman called from the downstairs entrance.

Once again Zoe's father came through for us, pulling the strings necessary to gain us access to Cami's building just days after the attacks. No one was being allowed into the area because the authorities were still assessing structural damage to surrounding buildings, but Mike Wingfield's firm had offices on the first two floors of the converted nine-story building that sat right on the border of the quarantined area. The top seven floors had been converted into lofts. Cami's was on the third floor.

"She left the window open," Zoe said as we walked across the large undivided expanse to where a bamboo shade tapped out a rhythm like a wind chime against the window leading to the fire escape. "It's so *Breakfast at Tiffany's*," Cami had told us over the phone. "All I need is my hair in a towel, a guitar and the words to 'Moon River,' and I'm Audrey Hepburn," she added, giggling with the pure delight of someone who had moved into her first real home.

I stared at the window and knew that we both saw that it was not just raised—it was gone.

"She always liked fresh air," I replied.

"Likes," Zoe corrected, but without conviction. "She likes fresh air." She was in the galley kitchen area, running her finger along the sink, then peering into drawers and cabinets. "She was running late," Zoe said, more to herself than to me, "but she washed the dishes."

"Maybe she was too excited to eat," I suggested.

Zoe picked up a dishtowel that had been spread across the edge of the sink. Dust flew everywhere. "No, see? She left the towel to dry."

I felt something twist inside me as I pictured my beautiful daughter blissfully going about her routine, never realizing that outside that door, on a perfect September day when she had the world before her...

Her whole life before her, I thought, and understood what those people at Ty's funeral had meant. Cami had not lived her whole life—not by a long shot. Those people had been right. The knot inside me twisted another half hitch.

Zoe was standing in front of Cami's desk, her fingers resting on the laptop computer we'd bought her as a celebration of her new place. Next to it was a pen—a traditional fountain pen given to her by Zoe's father—the only writing instrument that Cami ever used. Zoe picked it up and wiped it free of dust on the side of her jeans before putting it in her pocket.

"For Dad," she said when she saw me watching her.

I wandered into the curtained-off area where Cami had set up her bedroom. Evidence of her excitement was everywhere—piles of discarded clothing on the bed, open pots of makeup on her dressing table, a bath towel dropped on the floor. It should have been a scene filled with splashes of vivid colors—the oranges and yellows and reds our daughter preferred. Instead everything was coated in the gray ash. In fact, the entire scene was monochromatic. If Zoe and I had not been wearing color, we might have convinced ourselves we were players in a black-and-white film—one that would end and the lights would come up and—

"Folks, you've got to get out now." The officer stood at the door, his eyes weary with all that he had seen and experienced in the past forty-eight hours. "You should be able to get back in after a few days." He held a mask to his face, protection from the dust he'd been breathing in for the past forty-eight hours.

I saw the trail of footprints that Zoe and I had left. I studied the little puffs of fine ash that followed Zoe's steps as she moved more quickly around the space, her eyes searching for signs, evidence, that our daughter was alive. And then I spotted the small carved elephant I had given Cami the day after she'd broken the news to Zoe and me that she was pretty sure she was a Republican. She'd been fourteen years old.

"Mom, Dad," she'd said, nervously edging into our

room late one night. Zoe had been reading while I watched the news.

"What's wrong?" Zoe asked, immediately putting her book down and half getting out of bed. "Are you sick?"

"No." Cami's adolescent voice shook and she appeared to be miserable. "Look," she said, rushing her words, "there's no way to do this but to jump right out with it. We're having a mock election at school tomorrow and I'm voting for Mr. Reagan, okay?"

Zoe glanced at me, the corners of her mouth twitching slightly. I faced Cami.

"You're sure about this?" I asked, mustering all the sincerity I could in the face of our daughter's obvious distress at delivering this news.

She nodded. "Not only that, but you might as well get ready for it. I've been studying the differences between conservative and liberal ideas and philosophies, and frankly, I have to think that the conservatives have a better chance of getting things right—at least for my generation."

"Okay," Zoe said.

"Yeah, well, you say, okay, but—"

"Your mother and I have always taught you and the boys to consider both sides," I interrupted. "You've apparently done that. You've reached a decision based on knowledge and serious consideration of the facts and we respect that," I told her.

"Mom?"

Zoe nodded, her face composed. "Even if we don't agree, Cami. We can agree to disagree, okay?"

Cami searched our faces, obviously waiting for the catch. "Okay," she said as she turned to go. "Besides," she said, "it might not be forever—I vote for the person, not the party." And with a smile on her face she marched out of the room.

It had been Zoe's idea to get the elephant. "You have to find some token that will prove to her this is okay," she insisted after we had both smothered our laughter at what we had thought Cami might say, and how obviously relieved we were that it was a matter of politics.

The next day I'd brought the elephant home and earned for myself Zoe's approving smile and Cami's delight.

Now I picked up the small carved figure, my fingers closing tightly around its middle. I shut my eyes and saw the images of the towers on fire, heard my daughter's frightened voice on the phone, replayed the collapse of the buildings, so unreal on the small television screen in our bright, sunny kitchen as the phone line went dead. I jumped as I felt Zoe's fingers on my shoulder.

"We have to go," she said, her voice hoarse—a combination of emotion and the fine powdery dust we'd been breathing in since entering the area.

I nodded and showed her the elephant. She folded my fingers around it and took my arm as we followed the police officer back down the stairs and out into the devastation that had been our daughter's neighborhood.

I stayed the rest of the week and then told Zoe it was time to go home.

"I can't," she said, her eyes welling with tears. "Not yet."

"Zoe, she's gone." I managed to get the words out around the huge rock that seemed to have become a permanent fixture in my throat.

"You go," she said, and there was no accusation in her tone. "I just need to… Maybe I can…do something."

So I made the long drive home and Zoe stayed. She

spent her days—days that more often than not stretched well into the night—at Ground Zero. She handed out water and food to the rescuers, she answered phones and consoled others who like us could not yet get their brains around the idea that on a glorious fall morning their child, spouse, loved one had left the house and simply vanished.

"I think we can do more," Zoe told me one night, her voice weak with the exhaustion of too much emotional pain and too little sleep. "Spence, I was thinking. This is post-traumatic stress—maybe not battlefield stress, although an argument could certainly be made for that—but these people need help. There are counselors, of course, but you're the expert in this. You wrote the book, for heaven's sake."

In fact, I had written several books and articles, all for the cause of raising funds to keep the work of the counseling center on track. "What are you thinking?" I asked.

"Could you send out a team to do in-service work with the counselors they have? This isn't the usual grief process—it's so much more."

"Sure, but, Zoe, that's only half the job. The people directing this thing have to want our help."

"Dad talked to the mayor's office this afternoon. Have you got a pencil?"

I reached for my day planner and a pen. "Shoot."

Zoe recited a name and number, along with the path for getting past any gatekeepers who might be screening calls. "They'll be waiting to hear from you," she instructed.

"Okay. I'll call first thing in the morning."

"Don't forget the time difference—you can reach them an hour sooner, you know."

"Got it." We both went quiet. "When are you planning to head home?"

She hesitated. "Soon," she said softly.

"Well, that's a step up from 'I don't know,' so I'll see it as a good sign," I said. "Are you eating and getting at least a couple hours of sleep?"

"I'm okay," she said. "Spence, I have to do this. I mean, in a strange way, it's helping."

"I know." And I did. The fact that Zoe was developing ways we might offer concrete help was a good sign. That she had gone into what Cami had always referred to as her "battle mode" meant that Zoe was fighting her way through this thing and we would—eventually—be all right.

Our holidays were understandably nonexistent that year. Zoe returned the second week in November and slept for most of the first two days. Mom and our daughter-in-law, Sandra, took charge of Thanksgiving. And even though no one in the family was much in the mood for giving thanks, we gathered at the farm and made every attempt to remind ourselves that we had many blessings.

Ever since her return from New York Zoe had been unusually quiet. Because she had spearheaded the plan to get a team from the rehab center out to New York and involved in coaching counselors, I had expected something different. Like her usual whirlwind of activity as she set in motion half a dozen projects to provide more assistance and support to survivors or families.

Instead, within a couple of days of her homecoming, she had gone back to her volunteer work at the gardens. I knew that she spent long hours working on the new Thai garden. I knew she often stayed after everyone else had left, alone in the now-completed pavilion, sitting cross-legged under the red-and-gold lacquered arches, staring out at the calm waters of the reflecting pool, her scarf wrapped tight around her neck against the prewinter chill of November. For Zoe this Thai shelter had become a place of meditation and in some strange way a connection to Cami.

Trying hard to create some environment of normalcy, I left the house every morning for either the center or my lectures at the medical college. At home we discussed our day, carefully skirting anything that would naturally lead to talking about Cami, then settled in with work or reading for the evening. Occasionally, we would agree to meet friends for dinner at one of the local restaurants that had opened after Cami moved to New York—one that held no memories of her.

On the weekends we rigidly stuck to our traditions. Early on Saturday morning we drove downtown to the huge farmer's market on the Capitol Square, where Todd and Dad had a booth selling pumpkins and Mom's dried-flower arrangements. We followed that with a late lunch on the terrace of the Union and a walk on the lake path. It was almost as if we both clung to this structure, these ties to the familiar. On Sundays we traded sections of the *New York Times* as we picked at the oversized cinnamon breakfast rolls we'd bought at the market.

We broke with tradition in one way only. We did not attend church. As thousands of Americans filled the pews of churches and synagogues and mosques, Zoe and I spent most Sunday mornings working on the house, telling ourselves that with the promise of a hard winter and the amount of time we'd been away, we really must attend to these repairs and chores.

That gut-wrenching twisting of my insides that had started that day we went to Cami's loft and stayed with me for weeks afterward had begun to ease. Then, on Thanksgiving, we gathered at the farm around the dining room table that had occupied the same space for three generations. Mom had set the table without using the extra table leaf, so we were sitting shoulder to shoulder. I understood that she hoped this sensation of a jam-packed table would take our minds off the gaping hole in our lives that had been Cami's place. My stomach knotted.

"Spencer, would you lead us in grace?" Dad said.

My head shot up. Every eye around the table was locked on me, but I saw only Zoe. Her face was the mirror of everything I was feeling. Her eyes sunken and without expression, her skin pale, and when had she gotten so thin? She coughed, studying the decorative pattern of Mom's best china.

"I'll do it," Todd said, and clasped hands with Sandra to his left and Zoe to his right. He waited until the chain of joined hands had made its way around the circle of the table, then bowed his head. "Dear God, thank You for this food that we are blessed to receive. Thank You for the strength You have given each of us to guide us through these terrible times. Help us to find our way from wandering in this wilderness of our pain back into the light of grace and goodness. Amen."

Taylor cleared his throat and released my hand to pull a bandana handkerchief from his back pocket. Mom left the table, murmuring something about forgetting to fill the gravy bowl, and Sandra followed her. Dad reached over and placed his callused stubby fingers over Zoe's long slim ones as he looked at Todd and said, "Beautifully done, Todd." Then he cleared his throat loudly and stood. "Now, let's see what kind of damage we can do to this turkey."

Gradually, conversation settled into a more or less normal pattern. "Pass the salt." "Sandra, did you change the recipe on these baked apples?" "How about some more stuffing, Taylor?"

Zoe and I remained silent, smiling and nodding on occasion but not really contributing to the conversation. We were like two outsiders, who understood that this place and these people were safe and kind but who were still cautious about trusting that any of this could last.

"Save room for dessert," Mom urged as Dad went back for third helpings on the sweet potatoes. "Zoe made her wonderful pies—pecan, pumpkin *and* mincemeat."

Taylor chuckled and glanced across the table at Todd, who also started to smile.

"What?" Zoe said, her voice more normal than it had been in weeks. "What's so funny?"

Now Todd and Taylor were both laughing in earnest. Finally, Taylor gained control of himself and said between snorts of laughter, "It's just that when we were little and you made the mincemeat pie?"

Zoe's lips twitched. Everyone leaned forward, eager to hear the story—perhaps more eager than was really warranted because it promised to lift the mood.

"Well, you know, the name—*minced meat*—it sounded suspicious so Todd and I figured we'd better check this out."

Now everyone was smiling, anticipating the punch line as Todd took up the story. "So we decided to ask Cami…."

Every smile froze as Taylor and Todd exchanged panicked glances and everyone realized it was the first time our daughter had been mentioned that day. The room went absolutely still.

"And she told you that I used the innards of the chickens, cows and pigs that Grandma Marie saved for me from the farm," Zoe said quietly. Then she smiled at our sons. "She told you that I mashed them up in the food processor—blood, guts and all—then tried to cover it all up by adding a couple of apples, some raisins and brown sugar."

There was a long silence, as if we'd all stopped breathing for a moment. Then Zoe chuckled. "It was her favorite pie, and since I really only made it once a year, she was determined the two of you would not have a bite if she could help it." Then she looked around the table, her eyes alive with her usual enthusiasm for a good story. "Of course, that doesn't hold a candle to the time Cami…"

And we were off, sharing stories, educating our new daughter-in-law to the shenanigans her oh-so-serious young husband and his brother had often pulled on their elder sister. Zoe nudged me, pointing to the way Sandra kept one hand on her stomach during all of this.

"You'll find out soon enough," she said as she polished off the last bite of her pie, her appetite seemingly restored after weeks of barely touching her food. "Or am I reading this all wrong?" She glanced toward Sandra's protective hand.

Sandra blushed scarlet and so did Todd.

"Well, well, well," Taylor said, and let out a low whistle. "You guys are preggers, right? The Toddster is about to be a dad?"

"Just a few months," Sandra protested, and everyone burst out laughing.

When the women began discussing names and then moved on to the more graphic issues related to having a baby, I stood up. "Gentlemen, I believe we have a touch football game to play," I announced.

Zoe laughed. "Yes, right after you men clear the table and get the dishwasher loaded and running. Marie and I will set up the boundaries for the game. Sandra, you should sit this year's game out—how about keeping score?" She went to the door, then looked back and said, "Oh, yes, guys. In light of Sandra's 'condition,' we need an extra player. We choose Taylor."

"No way," Todd protested. "The guy was All-State and—"

"Now, Todd, it's only fair," Sandra said quietly, and I couldn't help smiling as our son went silent. "Come on, I'll help you men with the dishes." She stood on tiptoe and kissed Todd's cheek and I knew the boy was a goner.

Zoe

Perhaps it was the safety-in-numbers factor that made Thanksgiving bearable—even memorable. Certainly the news that Todd and Sandra were expecting our first grandchild helped distract us from Cami's absence. *Cami's death. Cami's murder.*

"How do you feel about being called Grandma?" Spence asked as we drove home after the touch football game and a second feast of turkey sandwiches, wild rice soup and the last of the pie.

I made a face. "Like I'm a hundred and five. How about 'Grammy'? Isn't that more youthful?"

"Too much like you won a music award—and sweetheart, we all know you can't carry a tune in a bucket."

I laughed. "Oh, sure, farm boy. Well, how do you feel about Grandpa?"

Spence laughed. "Like I'm a hundred and five," he agreed. "Can you see Todd as a father?"

"He's a baby himself—they both are. Thank heavens they have Marie around to guide them."

"And you—they have you," Spence said as he reached over and took my hand.

"They have us and each other and two sets of great-grandparents, who are going to spoil that baby rotten," I said, intertwining my fingers with his. "They'll do just fine."

Later that night, after I'd put away the food Marie had insisted we bring home and Taylor had gone out to meet some of his friends who were also home visiting, I wandered through the house. I walked into the living room, where I rearranged throw cushions on the furniture, then into the dining room, where I redid the centerpiece of silk flowers on the table. In between I started a load of laundry and went through the pantry, making a shopping list.

"Hey," Spence said as I stood in front of the open refrigerator, surveying the contents, a pen and notepad in one hand. "Need some help?"

"What would you think about our taking a cruise over the holidays—you know, leave maybe the day after Christmas for ten days or so?"

Spence watched at me for a long moment, then shut the refrigerator door. He placed his hands on my shoulders. When I refused to meet his eyes, he tilted my chin up with one finger. "I'd say that it won't help to run away," he said. "We'll get through it, Zoe, just like we got through today."

"I know, but today everybody was here, and Christmas… Well, Taylor's already said he's going to stay in California—I mean, you can't blame him. With Todd and Sandra going to see her mom and stepfather in Minnesota and Marie and Hal spending Christmas with your brothers and their families in Colorado—"

He hugged me and kissed the top of my head. "It's a day, Zoe—just like any other day, except it has all this stuff attached to it. We don't have to play just because the world tells us we should. We can sleep in and spend the day reading or watching old movies or taking a walk in the—"

"You know better than that." My words were muffled against his sweater.

We stood there, rocking slightly for a while. "We could go to New York and spend the holidays with your folks," he said. "See a couple of shows. Go to the museums."

It was a good solution, I realized. Mom and Dad were almost as devastated as we were over Cami's death. They had been so close to her—much closer than they were to either of the boys—and losing her must have brought Ty's death back to haunt them. "We'd be there with Cami," I added.

Spence rested his chin on my head. "We're always close to Cami," he said. "We don't have to go to New York for that."

"Yeah, I know." I rested my head against his chest for another moment. "Thanks, Spence."

Spence

The holidays had at least been a distraction. Neither Zoe nor I was the type to resent the happiness of others. We attended a couple of small gatherings with friends, then headed for New York. The thing about New York is how easy it is to be alone there—alone with your thoughts and memories. Alone in the midst of thousands of people—who are also alone. Zoe and I enjoyed long walks in Central Park, deliberately reliving the good times—the night we'd walked there after Ty's funeral, our wedding day. We attended a concert at Carnegie Hall with her parents and saw the exhibits at the Metropolitan and the Museum of Modern Art. On New Year's Eve morning we set out for a walk.

Before we knew it, we'd walked all the way from Mike and Kay's apartment building across from the park down Fifth Avenue and over to Broadway then on through the theater and garment districts. We stopped for lunch at a bistro in the East Village just past Washington Park.

The closer we'd walked to Lower Manhattan, the tighter Zoe's features had grown. She resembled a person using every bit of energy she possessed just to hold herself together. "Should we get a cab and head back?" I asked as we finished our espresso.

"No. let's go on. We've gotten this far."

We both knew the destination without actually speaking the words. We were on a pilgrimage to Ground Zero. "Zoe?"

She looked at me across the small wrought-iron café table. I took her hand. "You don't have to do this."

She nodded and I breathed a sigh of relief, thinking she had agreed to abandon the quest, but she said, "Yes, I do. If you don't want to, I understand. I'll be okay, really. Go ahead. I'll be along later." She patted my hand and put on her jacket.

"She's not there," I reminded her.

"But she was—she was." She wrapped the knockoff of the designer cashmere shawl I'd bought her on a street corner somewhere around 42nd Street around her shoulders.

I stood and laid out enough to cover the bill, plus a generous tip. We nodded to the waiter as we left. Outside I took Zoe's hand in mine as we headed south.

The void where the buildings of the World Trade Center had been was as good a parallel to our lives without Cami as I could have imagined. The area was barricaded by a thick chain-link fence and cleanup of the site had been stopped for the holiday.

"This way," Zoe said as she worked her way along the

fence, seeking something. She found it in the form of a small opening and squeezed through.

"Zoe, it's dangerous—the ground might still be unstable and—"

She was gone, making her way down into the pit, working her way over rubble, pausing now and then to glance around and choose her path. I saw what she was trying to find. The north tower—or what had been the north tower. I tried to force the opening wider so I could follow, but it was useless. I was too big and all I could do was stand and watch.

Finally she stopped, and I saw her kneel and remove something from her pocket. Then I saw her scoop up a handful of the rubble and dust and place it in the container.

"Hey!" a policeman yelled at Zoe as he made his way around the perimeter at a trot. "Lady, you can't be there," he shouted, and as he reached the place I was standing, he shook his head and stopped to catch his breath. "Crazy woman. She could get herself killed," he muttered between heaves of breath visible in the cold winter air.

"She's my wife," I said. "Our daughter…" My voice cracked and the policeman's features turned to mush, his own eyes filling with tears.

"My son—a firefighter—rookie," he said.

We stood side by side as Zoe slowly made her way back, her hands jammed in her pockets as she picked her way over the ruins.

"North or south?" the policeman asked.

"North," I replied. "Coming down the stairs."

"Yeah. Benny was on his way up." Silence and then, "Maybe they saw each other—you know, passed on the way."

"Maybe so."

Zoe glanced up and saw the man waiting with me, and her expression changed to defiance as she lifted her chin and strode up the final ridge.

"Zoe, this is Officer—"

"McCoy," he supplied as he helped her through the hole in the fence. "Sorry for your loss, ma'am," he added.

Zoe was confused. She'd been prepared for a reprimand. Then she focused on the policeman and their eyes met and she rose on her toes and hugged him. "And yours— partners, friends?"

"Both. And my son," McCoy said. He was making no attempt to hide his tears now. "But he died a hero," he responded with the pride of a man who clings to anything that provides a reason for his loss.

Zoe patted his back as she looked at me over the man's shoulder and I saw her mouth tighten. "I'm sure he was a wonderful young man," she whispered as she gently broke away.

McCoy cleared his throat and got control of himself. Readjusting his hat, he nodded. "You get what you came for?"

Zoe smiled slightly as she removed a small box from her pocket. It was a box of birch bark, which Cami had made for her one summer while at camp.

"Just don't be going down there again, okay?" McCoy sniffed as he waited for Zoe's solemn assurance that she had no need to ever go there again and walked away.

"Dad?"

As was common for me these days, I had been lost in memories when I saw Todd standing in the doorway of my office at the counseling center. Todd rarely visited Madison during the week, so I knew something was up. From the expression on his of his face, it wasn't something I was going to like hearing.

"Sandra okay?" I asked, indicating a chair across from my desk and closing the door behind him.

Yeah. He sat forward, with his hands dangling between his knees. He glanced around the office. "You've made some changes."

"Mom," I said, and we both smiled. "Yours, not mine," I amended quickly. "Zoe seems intent on redecorating the world one room at a time since we got back from New York."

Todd did not smile. In fact, he looked worse. "I got called up—my Guard unit," he said, his face averted and the words muffled so that I prayed I was hearing them wrong.

"Your unit?" I repeated dumbly. "To where?" I mentally ran through the news stories that had flashed across the TV screen that morning. There was a blizzard in the Rockies—in Vail. Taylor had been skiing there and had phoned to reassure us that he was safely back in what he called "smoggy California."

"Afghanistan."

I shut my eyes, squeezed them to rid them of the other images I'd seen on the morning news. Images of bombed-out military vehicles and people screaming in anguish and panic as they ran through the streets of Kabul.

Todd raised his face to mine. "How in the world am I gonna tell Mom?"

I put my hand on his shoulder. "We'll tell her together," I said.

Todd let out a shuddering sigh. "She's gonna freak," he muttered.

"Yeah. Probably so," I agreed. "When do you go?"

"Two weeks."

"Have you told Sandra?"

He nodded and then released another of those heart-breaking sighs. "The baby…" He swallowed hard. "I won't be here."

"Your mother and I will be here—and Grandma Marie and Poppa…" I stopped. It wasn't the same and I knew it. I reached for my coat. "Let's go tell your mom."

As soon as Zoe saw us, her face turned to stone.

"Look who I found wandering around campus begging for a free meal," I called out as Todd and I stopped in the laundry room to remove coats and wet boots.

"Is it the baby?" she asked, rushing forward to take Todd's scarf and spread it over the washing machine to dry.

"No, Mom. Sandra and the baby are fine—just fine," Todd said as he hugged her and then moved past her into the kitchen. "How about I make us some grilled-cheese sandwiches?" he said as he stood in front of the open door of the refrigerator.

Zoe glanced at me, her eyes full of questions.

"Sounds like a plan," I said, following Todd's lead. "Hand me that carton of tomato-basil soup—I think there's enough for three."

Zoe leaned against the doorway between the laundry room and kitchen and watched us prepare the lunch. I could see that she wasn't fooled but that she had decided to allow us to get to the point in our own way. "As long as no one's on fire or not breathing," she used to tell the kids, "it can wait." Todd and I were clearly testing that theory big-time.

"All right," she said when the three of us were at the table and Todd and I were making a production of blowing on the hot soup and moaning over the perfection of the sandwiches. "Enough. Tell me."

Todd put down his spoon and cleared his throat. "You're not gonna like it, Mom, but there's nothing to be done. There's…"

"Todd's National Guard unit has been called up. He leaves for Afghanistan in two weeks," I said, and everything in the room went still. The hum of the refrigerator was the only sound. I don't think any one of us was even breathing.

Slowly Zoe got up from her chair and took her dishes to the sink. She'd barely touched her food. I heard her scrape the dishes and run the disposal. There was a pause, during which Todd and I stared at each other, wondering what to say. Then we heard the shattering of the dishes as Zoe systematically destroyed her plate, bowl and glass against the sides of the stainless-steel basin. "It's enough," she murmured with each thrust of her arm. "Enough. No more. You cannot have another child of mine. Send your own if you must, but you cannot have mine."

Todd stood up. "Mom?"

Having finished demolishing the crockery, Zoe remained at the sink, her fingers gripping its edge as her lips continued to move. Todd and I both knew this wasn't some rant at God. This was her stating the facts for the powers that be—those people in Washington deciding who would go and who would stay.

Todd put his arms around her and turned her into his embrace. I stood by as our son—well over six feet—a giant of a man in so many ways—tried to comfort the diminutive woman who had given him life. "I have to go," he was saying, then his voice was muffled as he put his face next to her ear. I heard *duty* and *responsibility* and saw Zoe's shoulders stiffen under the gentle barrage of his logic.

When Zoe raised her face to his, she had visibly aged.

Her mouth and eyes were lined with exhaustion and something else that at first I couldn't name. I only knew it wasn't
an expression I had ever seen on Zoe's beautiful features
until now. And then, as she placed her palm against Todd's
cheek, I understood. The expression was surrender. Zoe
had no fight left and nothing in my life had ever frightened
me quite as much as that realization.

2002

Zoe

The winter that followed Cami's murder, I could never seem to get warm or over one cold and hacking cough before the next hit me. Spence built fires for me each night. I lay on the couch, wrapped in one of Marie's handmade afghans mindlessly watching the flames as I surfed the channels and caught sound bytes of a variety of the mindless reality shows that were all the rage. How could people embrace such drivel? Where was their anger, their passion, their determination to make a better world?

But I was no different from those who gathered in homes and offices all over America to analyze the latest person voted off the island or sent packing by perfect-bachelor Mr. Right. I considered abandoning my volunteer work at the gardens. It was time for the younger crowd to take up the cause, I told myself, a thought more like one from my seventy-eight-year-old mother than myself. I couldn't seem to focus on anything—reading, making a meal, putting food in my mouth. I lost the weight I had finally started to regain over the holidays and cringed when my friends marveled at how fabulously thin I was and asked for my secret.

My secret? One child dead and another in constant danger halfway around the world. My secret? I was scared to death by the total lack of control we seemed to have over our lives these days. My secret? I was disappearing physically because nothing I had ever believed seemed to make sense anymore. I wandered through my days and nights without purpose. I was fifty-three years old and wondering how it was possible that I could be middle-aged—beyond middle-aged—and still not have a clue.

Spence was understandably worried and tried to help. He suggested that perhaps I wanted to go back to work or back to school by bringing home announcements of workshops for writing and art classes that he saw on campus or by reading aloud an interesting part-time job description from the Sunday paper.

"Are you looking for another job?" I asked him one Sunday morning as he scanned the employment ads and I stared blankly out the window without seeing the ice on the lake or the piles of snow that had drifted to cover the lawn furniture we'd never put away last fall.

Spence folded the paper and took off his reading glasses. "No," he said quietly. "What I'm looking for is my wife—my Zoe."

"Sorry—haven't noticed her lately," I said, and left the room.

Later I made Spence his favorite Sunday-night supper—a cheese-and-mushroom omelet with hashed brown potatoes, and fresh-fruit salad. We both understood it for the symbol it was—an apology for being bitchy when he only sought to ease things for me. We ate in front of the TV, watching a British comedy we liked on public television.

When the show ended, Spence flicked off the television and came to sit with me on the couch. "Let's talk," he said, and I pulled the afghan up to my chin as I scooted into the corner of the couch to make room for him.

"I'm worried about you."

"I know." I swallowed and pounded my fist against the arm of the sofa. "Sorry," I muttered as I forced my fist to unclench. "I just don't know what's...I just don't know how to...I just..." The tears escalated into sobs.

Spence wrapped his arms around me and pressed my face to his chest. "Sh-h-h," he whispered. "We'll find a way, Zoe. We will."

"I'm just so scared all the time," I said.

"Yeah. Me, too," he admitted, and tightened his grip on me. After several minutes, he said, "Zoe, what would you think about getting some help?"

I made a face. Shortly after returning from New York, I had followed Liz's advice and attended several meetings of a support group for mothers who had lost a child. At first I had found comfort in the shared emotions and the tips for getting through the tough days. We had laughed and prayed and held hands and offered words of encouragement when the going got beyond rough for one of our members. But when one of the women—a charter member of the group—failed to show up for the meeting one night, I asked where she was.

"Oh, Zoe, didn't anyone call you? Sally's son was

killed by a roadside bomb in Afghanistan. The memorial service is next Friday."

It was impossible. Sally's son had been two weeks away from the end of his tour of duty. He had beaten all the odds. Sally and I had gone out for a glass of wine to celebrate. Now she had lost not one but both of her children. I had gone to the service—we all had. But Sally's rage had turned on us. We still had at least one child.

"Zoe?"

I refocused my attention on Spence, who had obviously been talking to me.

"I said how about talking to somebody at the center?"

I went completely still. "At the center?" I managed finally. *Post-traumatic stress,* I thought. But it wasn't *post*—the trauma wasn't in the past or after the fact—it was here and now and always every day.

"It might help," Spence said.

"Couldn't hurt?" I added automatically but without conviction.

Spence put his finger under my chin and urged me to look up at him.

"You think I'm losing my mind?" I asked.

"No. I think you're trying to find your way through something that's very serious and very scary and not something you should have to go through alone."

"I have you," I said, and snuggled back against him, burying my face once again.

"But I'm struggling, as well," he said, and his voice cracked.

I was stunned that he was crying. "I don't know what to do, Zoe and I can't stand seeing you waste away—

physically and in every other way. I'm so afraid that I'm losing you. Tell me what to do."

Not since the memorial service for Cami that we'd agreed to hold just before Thanksgiving—the service that Spence had convinced me was necessary for her friends and the rest of the family—had I seen Spence this close to the edge. In the weeks following that service, he seemed to have found a certain resolution and peace. I had envied his ability to move forward—not only to miss her and grieve for our loss, but to live. More than once he'd observed that getting back to our lives—refusing to allow this horror to change who we were at our core—was what Cami would want. What she would expect of us.

And I had tried. Following his example, I told myself that every invitation accepted, every act of charity delivered, every tradition observed was for Cami. For a while I actually thought it was working, but before long I was emotionally exhausted—empty of anything worth getting up in the morning for. I knew that Spence was right. I was getting worse, not better. Sinking deeper and deeper into the void those planes had left in the souls of every American that day. Disappearing as I attempted in vain to hide from life, afraid of what it might hold in store for me next. The enemy was winning—and I didn't have the strength to fight back.

"I'll find a way," I said, reaching up to caress Spence's wet cheeks with my palms. "We'll do it together—really," I added.

Spence held me closer and kissed my forehead. We stayed that way through the rest of the afternoon. It started to rain, and there in that house that had always been our refuge, with Spence's arms around me, feeding me the strength and courage I had lost, I made a promise to myself—to look forward and not back.

"In just three short months, you're going to be a grand-father," I said.

Spence chuckled and kissed my temple. "And you are going to be the sexiest grandma who ever lived."

Spence

Formalized counseling had never been Zoe's thing. Maybe it was all the years of living with me, talking shop over breakfast or dinner. Whatever it was, she probably knew more about what was going on inside her than anyone else. I was aware of that when I kept pushing her. Aware that the only hope I had for bringing her back from this brink of depression was to give her the challenge of handing over her problems to someone else. I knew she would hate that and I was right.

"Spence?" I heard her calling one afternoon as she rushed in from the garage, doors slamming behind her—not in irritation but in haste. She rushed through the downstairs like a whirlwind. "Spence! Where are you? I've got to talk to you."

I met her in the front hall. Her cheeks were flushed with the cold and her excitement. She was practically vibrating with the energy of whatever project or idea she was so eager to share.

"Right here," I said.

"I was on State Street today and—remember the book-store?" She shrugged out of her coat and tossed it onto a straight-backed chair in the front hall. Then she began rummaging through her bag.

"Where our first apartment was?"

She nodded and waved a sheaf of papers, then led the way to the study. "Well, it's been converted into commercial space and it's for rent and I don't know—sentimental reasons, I guess—I went in to take a tour."

"Okay," I said, not at all sure where we were headed.

"And that's when it hit me—the perfect memorial for Cami."

I must have appeared every bit as dumbfounded as I felt. "I don't understand."

She spread the paperwork on the coffee table and knelt next to it, indicating that I should take a seat on one of the two leather sofas flanking it. "A living memorial," she said. "That's been a big part of my problem, you see. It's as if Cami is disappearing and I want people to remember her—remember that vitality and sparkle. I didn't want some kind of statue. I wanted something alive and thriving."

"And the converted apartment fits in how?"

"I rented it—here's the lease. I can get out of it within thirty days, so we'll have somebody who really knows real-estate law to check it over to be sure we're not signing away our lives. But it seems pretty clean to me and it's month to month, with reasonable rent that includes all the utilities. We'll need furnishings, of course," she said, her voice falling into talking-to-myself mode as she burrowed through the papers and turned up a yellow legal pad that already contained half a page of notes.

"Okay, so you rented this space and now what?"

She sat back on her heels and her face brightened in a way I had not witnessed in years. She was so radiant and beautiful that I missed the opening words and caught up as she was explaining.

"A center—a kind of a... A think tank where we would bring the best and brightest to offer seminars and lead discussions on working for peace… A Place for Peace," she announced, triumphant in her vision.

"It's going to take more money than you think," I cautioned, but I was smiling because her enthusiasm was contagious and the idea was exactly right for honoring our daughter.

"I may have been hiding out for a while, but I still have a few contacts," she said haughtily. "I can make some calls, write some grant proposals…." She added notes to her list, muttering all the while.

"A Place for Peace," I repeated. "I like it." I cupped my palm around the back of her neck. "How can I help?"

Zoe

"Mom?"

Todd sounded as if he were across the street, not half a world away.

"Todd! What a wonderful—"

"The baby's coming. Sandra's en route to university hospital. She was at the farm by herself and—"

The connection faltered.

"Dad and I are on our way," I screamed into the phone, motioning frantically for Spence to get up, get coats and keys. "Can you call back on Dad's cell?"

"…got the ambulance…too soon…okay…cell."

I put down the phone and thrust my arms into the sleeves of the coat Spence held for me, grabbing my purse in the next gesture as I led the way through the house and out to the garage. "Sandra's on her way to the hospital by ambulance. She was alone at the farm and…oh, I don't know what happened, but somehow she must have gotten hold of Todd and…"

"Maybe he called her," Spence said with maddening logic as he backed the car out of the garage and headed for the hospital. "Phone Liz and tell her to meet us there."

I was tempted to argue that Todd would be trying to call back, but then nodded and dialed Liz's number. "Where are your folks?" I fumed after Liz's service assured me that she'd been notified.

"They had that reunion in Milwaukee, remember? They were staying overnight."

"Oh. Right." I sat on the edge of the seat, mentally urging the car forward. "It's way too early," I said more to myself than Spence. "Maybe it's a false labor. Maybe…"

Spence put his hand on my knee. "We're almost there."

The cell phone rang and vibrated at the same time and I jumped. "It's Todd," I said before answering. "Todd?"

"Right here, Mom. Okay, here's the deal. I've been on with the emergency tech riding with Sandra. Her water broke and contractions have started. About twelve minutes apart. They just got to the E.R. so she's being admitted."

"How…"

"We were on the phone when her water broke. She called 911 on her cell, then we were on the land lines until they got there." His voice shook with more excitement than fear. "She'll be fine. Baby's signs are strong. You're gonna be a grandma!" Then he whooped with pure delight. "And I'm going to be somebody's dad!"

In spite of everything I grinned and held up the phone so Spence could hear Todd's cheer. He laughed.

"Dad and I are at the hospital, so the cell is not going to work. I'll get to a phone and call you back, okay?"

Spence held out his hand for the cell. "Todd? Liz is already here. I see her car. It's going to be fine, okay?"

"I want a play-by-play," Todd said. "You and Mom right there—where I would be, okay?"

"Right there, son, every step of the way," Spence promised.

Spence

Our first grandchild—a beautiful girl with lots of coal-black hair like her mother and her father's expressive eyes—arrived in the world just five hours after we arrived at the hospital. In the middle of everything, Todd had been sent out on patrol. A doctor who heard about that from a nurse running between birthing rooms brought in the video camera she'd just bought to give her parents for their wedding anniversary and filmed the entire delivery for Todd to see and hear.

"Hello, Millie Andersen," Sandra cooed as she held her sleeping daughter for the first time, the pain and exhaustion of her labor already a distant memory.

Zoe and I glanced at each other, then clasped hands as we stared at the miracle of our granddaughter.

"Is that okay?" Sandra asked. "Millie? Short for Camilla? Todd and I were going to talk to you about it, but then she was early and…"

Zoe swallowed hard and nodded. "It's wonderful," she whispered. She cleared her throat and gathered herself. "Is there a middle name?"

Sandra nodded. "Rae—with an *e*—short for Rachel. My dad's name was Ray—with a *y*."

"Sounds Southern—Millie Rae," the obstetrics nurse said as she took the baby from Sandra. "Okay, show's over." She directed this at the doctor wielding the camera.

"Let's get Mom settled and then Miss Millie Rae can visit later, okay?"

"Camilla Rachel," I said once the nurse had left with the baby. "It's perfect." I bent and kissed Sandra's damp forehead.

"Anything you guys have to say to the father before we wrap this up?" the doctor turned cameraperson asked.

Zoe and I moved in close to Sandra and leaned down so the doctor could get all three of us in the frame. "Mom and I are going for a little break while they get this new Mom settled," I said.

"Your daughter is gorgeous, Todd. Stay safe and hurry home," Zoe said.

"I love you, sweetheart," Sandra said.

"And that's a wrap," the doctor announced.

Zoe and I stayed at the hospital until dawn just to be sure that Sandra and Millie were really all right. When Sandra's mother and stepfather arrived after driving through the night from Minnesota, we decided to go home, shower and catch a couple of hours of sleep.

At home Zoe made us eggs and toast while I showered. We relived every detail of the birth while we ate. We laughed over the time that Sandra had fought her way through a particularly long and hard contraction and suddenly yelled at the camera, "Todd Andersen, this is going to cost you big-time when you get back here—all the 4:00 a.m. feedings are yours."

"She's always been so sweet and mild-mannered," Zoe said.

I cleared the dishes while Zoe went to shower. When I got to the bedroom, she was humming. It had been so long since I'd heard that off-key voice that I thought I'd imagined it, until I eased open the bathroom door and heard her voice crack on a note she had no hope of hitting.

I stood there, grinning, feeling something I hadn't felt in months—relief, normalcy, the wonder of ordinary.

When Zoe shut off the water and pulled the towel across the top of the shower enclosure, she was still humming—and I was still standing in the doorway. She opened the shower door, rubbing the towel over her naked body in time to the tune she was humming—something I thought might have been from a show we'd once seen on Broadway. *Thoroughly Modern Millie*, I realized, and smiled.

Our eyes met and I felt suddenly shy, but couldn't stop looking at her—couldn't disguise wanting her. Zoe placed her palms on my cheeks. She kissed me, and in the sweet tenderness of that kiss, I believed that everything was going to be all right. We were going to be all right. I wrapped my arms around her, my lips moving over her eyes, her cheeks, her mouth. She was smiling.

"You're getting all wet," she protested without any real concern, since she was laughing.

"Wet? Good idea," I said as I maneuvered her back into the shower and turned on the faucets. I blocked any attempt she might make to escape as I quickly stripped out of my clothes and threw them on the floor before shutting the stall door. We were enclosed in a steamy cocoon and there was some question whether more heat was coming from the water or from the desire that steamed between us.

"Spencer," Zoe shrieked with delight as the water cascaded over both of us and I began soaping her breasts, stomach and hips. "We're grandparents, for heaven's sake."

"And your point is?" I murmured as I massaged her ear with my tongue.

Zoe moaned and stood on tiptoe to press her body the length of mine as she slid her hands over my hips. "I mean, it's just that…" she whispered, her breath hot against my ear.

I put both hands under her hips and lifted her until she wrapped her legs around me. "For a grandmother, you're pretty limber," I said.

She smiled, smoothed back my wet hair from my forehead and then lowered herself onto me. My knees threatened to buckle from the jolt of sheer ecstasy that shot through me. I held her and saw all traces of playfulness had disappeared.

"Love me," she said.

I braced myself against the shower stall wall and together we found the rhythm that had always been uniquely ours. Words were unnecessary as we rediscovered the intricacies of our lovemaking, the way we fit, the way we moved, the touch that made us arch and pause and stop breathing.

Afterward we washed each other slowly, lovingly. Zoe dried me with the oversized towel. I rubbed her skin with the lemon-scented bath oil that was her signature fragrance. Then she took my hand and led me to the bed, where we curled against each other spoon-fashion. My hands and arms covered her breasts and stomach and her hands crossed over her shoulders and my arms.

We slept deeply until the ringing phone roused us.

"Hello?"

"Could you let a guy know he's become an uncle or what?" Taylor demanded.

I felt Zoe's arms around me, felt her naked breasts against my back.

"Dad?" Taylor prompted when I hesitated.

"Yeah, I'm here," I said. "Mom, too."

"We forgot…" Zoe muttered. We had planned to call

Taylor as soon as we had both showered and eaten something. Zoe had been concerned about the time difference and not waking him.

"Wanna guess how I heard?" Taylor said, still obviously miffed. "Todd reached me from halfway around the world. I had to hear it from him."

"Well, he is the father," I said logically, and Zoe giggled.

"And I'm the godfather." He paused. "Are you two okay? You sound…weird."

"We're fine," I assured him, and as Zoe wrapped her arms around me and bit the lobe of my ear, I added, "Just fine."

"When's he getting time off?" Zoe coached.

"Mom wants to know when you're coming to meet your niece?"

"I'll be there this weekend—might have some news of my own to share," he added. "Might be back to stay. Is my room still available?"

I held the phone out to Zoe. "Your son—the one who is completing his doctorate in Film Studies—wants to know if he can move back home."

Zoe's smile lit the room as she grabbed for the phone. "Taylor? Of course, you can stay here." Her smile wavered. "Is everything all right?"

Taylor laughed. "Well, I have this interview with the film department at UW, and assuming they like me—like my work…"

Zoe let out a whoop of delight. "That's terrific." To me, she added, "He's going to be on the faculty at the film studies department."

"Slow down, Mom—it's an interview."

"Details," Zoe said with a dismissive wave of her hand. "Here's your father."

She handed the phone back to me and scurried off to the bathroom. I asked Taylor a few more questions, learned that he was almost finished with his dissertation but could work on that anywhere. "Might as well save some money by living at home at least until classes start next fall—I mean, assuming I get the job and all."

"You'll get the job," I assured him. Of all our children Taylor had always been the extrovert, the class clown as well as the team leader, and yet in so many ways he was the most insecure of the three. It had taken him three changes in majors to decide on a course of study, and even then he'd ended up graduating summa cum laude with a double major. The kid was brilliant—so much so that Zoe and I had often wondered where those superbrains had originated.

"Thanks, Dad. Hey, Dad, is the kid cute or one of those red-faced, wrinkly newborns? Just need to prepare my happy face so I don't blow it."

"She's precious, and she's going to have her godfather completely wrapped around one tiny finger in the first five minutes. She's already got your mother and me."

I heard the toilet flush and Zoe came out of the bathroom wrapped in my terry-cloth robe. It trailed on the floor as she crawled onto the bed and motioned for the phone.

"Taylor? They named her Millie—after Cami."

"You okay with that?" Taylor asked.

"We're very, very touched," Zoe said. "So e-mail us your flights and we'll meet the plane."

Taylor obviously agreed, and they said their goodbyes and Zoe put the phone down on her bedside table. When she rolled toward me, she smiled, and it was that same shy uncertain smile she'd given me that night after we'd first made love. That smile that then had said, *What have we done?*

"Good morning," I said, snuggling next to her and loosening the tie on the robe so I could run my hand over her stomach. "You know, lady, for a grandmother, you're in pretty terrific shape."

"I've still got a few moves in me," she replied with a sassy grin.

I laughed. It felt so incredibly good to laugh with Zoe again. "Really? Care to show me?"

Our lovemaking before had been filled with tenderness and rediscovery. Serious, tentative, savored. But with the sun streaming through the blinds we'd never gotten around to shutting and the hours of deep, peaceful sleep providing a fresh supply of energy, we became playful. We were young again—flirting, challenging each other to invent new ways to surprise and delight, to hold back and tease, and finally to surrender.

"I love you, Zoe Wingfield Andersen," I said as we lay facing each other, our arms and legs so intertwined it was hard to say where one began and the other ended.

Zoe touched my face, her smooth palm against the stubble of my beard. "Oh, Spence, when I think of all the weeks I've wasted wallowing in my grief. So much time. You were right. We need to live—every day, every hour. Fill them to overflowing the way Cami did—the way we taught all our children to do."

"Could we start with breakfast—or rather lunch? I'm starving."

Zoe grinned and rolled to a sitting position. "Sure. I'll take peanut butter and banana sandwiches." She placed her hand over her stomach. "People have been telling me I need to fatten up."

I reached for her and drew her back on top of me.

"You're fine as far as I'm concerned." And in an instant all the teasing playfulness was gone, replaced by the pure passion we'd known in those early years of our marriage when we simply could not get enough of each other. And this time as I explored every inch of Zoe's body, I found the one thing that could destroy everything.

Zoe

The moment Spence went completely still, I felt my heart skip a beat. I had become so attuned to the potential for tragedy that it was like a sixth sense. Spence's fingers rested on my left breast. He explored gently close to the nipple and I flinched.

"Tender," I said with a smile.

"Zoe, there's something there," he answered. Then he took my fingers and guided them to the spot.

Dozens of times I had sat in the exam room of a hospital waiting for the technician to perform the one test every woman dreads—a mammogram. Like thousands of other women I had passed the time fingering the model breast on the table in the dressing area, searching for the lumps the sign told me were there.

Squish…squish…then something unmistakably hard like a tiny pebble that works its way into your shoe and can't be ignored if you want to keep on walking. I found every lump every time.

But this was no fake breast—no tiny pebble or pea inserted to simulate a lump. This was real—familiar as those samples. I blinked and sat up, examining the rest of my left breast and then moving on to my right.

"You haven't felt it before?" Spence asked.

"No," I said, regretting my own laziness and stupidity for putting off a self-exam month after month and settling for an every-few-years mammogram.

"When was your last mammo?"

"I'm due for one next month." I put on my robe and got out of bed. "Hey, we should be getting back to the hospital."

Spence watched me as I dressed. "Zoe? Call Liz," he said.

"Yeah, I will. Now, move, Grandpa."

"Today," Spence insisted.

I nodded and went into the bathroom and shut the door.

It was late afternoon by the time we made it back to the hospital. At first no one seemed to think it odd that the promise to go home, catch a quick shower and a couple of hours' sleep had stretched into almost the entire day. Sandra and her folks were too mesmerized by the baby. Hal was equally smitten with his great-granddaughter. It was Marie who noticed.

She and I were on the elevator, headed for the hospital coffee shop, later that evening. "Well, Grandma," she said.

I smiled. "She's beautiful—perfect—isn't she?"

Marie laughed. "For the moment. She'll give them a run for their money and there will be days when *beautiful* and *perfect* are the last words anyone would use to describe her. But she's the first girl and that secures her special place in this family forever."

We got mugs of tea and found an empty table.

"I'm thinking, though, that there's more to the story than Millie," Marie said as we sat across from each other stirring our tea.

I had never been able to fool my mother-in-law. "I found a lump," I said. "Or rather Spence did."

Marie took my hand and gripped it. "I am so sorry, Zoe.

You don't need this after all you've been through. How can I help?"

"Just be there for me," I said. "I'm not as young as I used to be and the battles seem to get harder."

To her credit Marie resisted the instinct to assure me that everything would be all right and finished her tea. "Let's go see that baby," she said. "Best medicine in the world for when you don't know what lies ahead."

Over the next few weeks friends once again gathered round. These were the people who had stood by us both through everything, refusing to judge either of us or take sides as we struggled through the aftermath of our near separation and then quietly stepping back to allow us time to mourn Cami's death. They showered us with gifts and love as we celebrated the birth of our first grandchild and Taylor's homecoming. It was as if the clouds had lifted. And while two clouds remained—Todd in Afghanistan and the lump in my breast—we were determined to live in the moment. Millie represented a new era.

Sandra's parents stayed with us for the two days she spent in the hospital, then went home with her to the farm. Taylor returned and moved back into the room he'd shared with Todd. We said nothing about the lump Spence had discovered. Only Marie knew and she held our secret close, assuring us that it was our news to share when and where we were ready.

We called Jon and Ginny and Liz. Liz ran the necessary tests to confirm what we feared but assured me that it was well defined and that we had caught it early on. Spence and I debated the merits of a lumpectomy versus a mastectomy. Jon confirmed Liz's assurance that the choice was ours to make and that if I chose lumpectomy and the cancer returned in that breast or the other one, then we could do the mastectomy.

For all sorts of reasons I chose the lumpectomy, even as my mind was screaming, *Get rid of it—it's just a sack of flesh hanging there.* But I didn't want to take the spotlight off Millie and I didn't want to have her birthday always associated with the day Spence had found a cancerous lump.

"Here's what we're going to do," I announced one night as Spence and I stood side by side in our bathroom, brushing our teeth at bedtime. "I'll have the lumpectomy and the radiation. With any luck no one has to know—at least for a while."

I spit out the toothpaste and rinsed. Spence continued brushing rhythmically up and down, staring at me via the mirror.

"Marie will cover for us with the family and Ginny can handle the friends. By the time we tell them it'll be over and I'll be good as new." I folded the hand towel precisely and placed it back on the rack. I noticed that my hands were shaking. "What do you think?" I said, but my voice sounded childlike even to me.

I heard Spence spit, rinse and turn off the water. Then I felt his fingers close around my shoulders. "I think that as usual you are taking care of everyone else. I think that it's time you took care of you. The only question here is this—are you sure this is what you want to do for you— not me or the kids or our friends, but you?"

I nodded and leaned back against the solid wall of his chest. "Will you go with me?" I whispered.

"Try to keep me away."

The lumpectomy was performed the following afternoon. I was home in time for dinner and heard Spence assuring Sandra that I would be out to see Millie in a day or so, once I was sure I had gotten over this bug.

By the end of the week I was driving out to the farm every day and returning each evening with news of Millie's latest accomplishments.

"She grasped my finger today and smiled."

"I thought you told us a baby's 'smiles' were more likely gas," Taylor said with a wink at Spence.

"Not this smile," I assured him. "This was real."

"Whatever you say," Taylor said. "Want another smile?"

Spence and I paused, forks in midair.

"I got the job," Taylor said, and his voice held the wonder of having achieved something he'd never really believed possible. "It's one of the best film departments in the country," he'd told us when we'd gone overboard in our assumption he was a shoo-in for the position.

"Congratulations, son," Spence said.

I got up and hugged him. "We are so proud of you."

Taylor hugged me back. "Does this mean I can stay?"

"It means you can start paying some rent," Spence said.

Taylor continued to attract people like a pied piper. Through the summer the house and yard were often filled with students, fellow faculty from the film department and independent filmmakers from all over the region. These lively and fascinating young people represented all kinds of backgrounds—ethnic, religious, economic. Some were students in the U.S.A. on a student visa. Several were from the Middle East—Israel, Syria, Pakistan. Others were from African nations that seemed to be constantly in the news and not in a good way.

"What are you chewing on?" Spence asked on a rare summer afternoon when he'd left work early. Taylor was away in California, defending his dissertation, and we had the house to ourselves. Spence handed me a glass of sangria and sat on the lawn chair next to mine.

"Have you noticed how much all the young people Taylor brings home have in common?"

"They all love film—they all live and breathe their screenplays or the latest technical—"

"I mean as people—even if they weren't all interested in the same profession."

Spence sipped his sangria. "Such as?"

"They're from all over the world—some of them have seen incredible horrors. That young woman from Darfur, for example."

"I can see the wheels turning," Spence said, holding my hand. "Keep talking."

"But when they talk—like around the table or just in casual conversation—about their families and their friends and their plans for the future, there's no real difference. The pigment of their skin or the way they talk to God, or the shape of the house they grew up in—all that may be as different as night and day, but their souls—their dreams for the future—those are the same."

I was working this through even as I was telling Spence. I could feel excitement building inside me. I sat forward and stared out at the lake and the city skyline beyond. "What if…" I muttered, almost without realizing I'd said the words.

Spence sat forward, as well, but he was looking at me. "What if what?"

"I don't know. I can't quite see it." I felt as if I were reaching for something in a dream and it was just beyond my fingertips—there, but not yet.

"What if the way we see these young people—the way they are here with us and each other…" Spence coached.

I faced him and there it was. "What if that were real?"
He was confused. "It is real," he said.

"I mean, for the world—what if we could make others—governments and political leaders—see what we see in these kids?"

"Through film," Spence said softly.

"Through a film festival. What if we established a film festival that focused on the films of internationally diverse filmmakers telling the stories—personal stories about real people, families with kids and grandkids and jobs and hopes and dreams even in the midst of famine and war and…"

Spence bought time by sitting back and taking another swallow of his wine. "Taylor's going to have his hands full, Zoe. A film festival when he's just getting started in the department…"

"I'm talking about the peace center," I said, watching him. "And the film festival would become an annual thing—a fund-raiser as well as a showcase for these brilliant young people to get out their messages to the world."

Spence continued to pretend an interest in the lake, but was more than a little excited. "How about this? The awards could be called—" I made the sound of a trumpet fanfare and together we said "—the Cammies."

We both turned at the sound of car doors slamming. We ran across the lawn as soon as Sandra, carrying Millie, hurried toward us, with Marie and Hal close behind.

"He's coming home," Sandra shouted, her face alight with relief and happiness. "Todd's on his way."

Zoe's Letters to Spence

October 31, 2007
All Saint's Eve

I *have never been a fan of Halloween—as you well know.*
When the kids were small, I put up what I hope was a
good front as I pieced together whatever costumes they
decided they absolutely could not live without each year. I
don't think they were completely fooled, because it was you
they always wanted along when they went to trick-or-treat.

But tonight I saw the magic that others find in this night.
It's almost as if ever since we got the diagnosis, I've been
getting worse. Almost as if simply because the cat is out of
the bag so to speak, this aberration feels it has the right to
simply take charge. So, we've barely gone anywhere but
back and forth to doctor appointments since we returned
from Vancouver.

I was feeling scared and frankly more than a little sorry for myself, hiding away on the sunporch—defying the unseasonable cold to make me even sicker. And then you appeared, dressed in a hippie wig, peasant blouse and almost-to-the-floor skirt. You'd accessorized the whole look with round wire-rimmed glasses, sandals and a placard that read TREATS NOW!

I couldn't help laughing. You looked so incredibly ridiculous. Then you handed me your old uniform jacket and hat and insisted I put them on.

"Why?" I demanded.

"Because we are going trick-or-treating."

"Are the grandchildren here?" I asked, for surely that would be the only sensible explanation and you have always been the sensible one in this partnership.

"Let them get their own candy."

"What are we supposed to be?" I asked, even though I already knew.

"We are going strictly as ourselves—enough of the masks and subterfuge. Of course we are switching places, but people will just have to figure that one out on their own."

You helped me into your uniform, then into the wheelchair I had refused to admit any need for and off we went. Door to door. The expressions on the faces of our neighbors and friends when they opened the door to us was priceless and something I will remember with delight again and again. In the end we became a bit like the pied pipers of Sunset Lane—kids lined up behind us as we made our merry way up and down the driveways. In chorus we shouted, "Trick or treat," at the top of our lungs—you even made us rehearse. It worked, because we came home with a pillowcase filled with goodies.

And the thing we both noticed was that with all the

laughter, I barely coughed. I was barely aware of being in the wheelchair and, best of all, I completely forgot about being sick. You, my by-the-book husband, lover and best friend, found this wild and crazy way to remind us both that we have a life—and it is right now—not yesterday's news or tomorrow's forecast. In the black of the starless nights and the blinding rain of the return of my cancer, I had forgotten that.

Back at the house, we stuffed ourselves with chocolate bars and the kinds of gummy sticky stuff the kids go wild for. We laughed and giggled over each step of the adventure and we stayed up way past midnight, sitting by the fire—holding each other and reveling in the pure joy of "us."

And then this morning, I woke to find you there, watching me, but without the fear and worry I've grown so used to seeing.

"Hi," you said. "Welcome to the first day of the rest of our lives."

Corny? You bet. But it made my day. We may have a few months or a year or maybe more, Spencer Andersen, but we won't count our time in what's down the road. We'll savor the moment and let the rest take care of itself.

New Year's Eve, 2007

What if you knew you were about to enter the last year of your life? What would you change? Mother Teresa once said, "In this life we cannot do great things. We can only do small things with great love." That works for me, and as I begin to take stock of the life we've shared, I think maybe—more often than not—we succeeded at that. So if this turns out to be the last year of my life, then so be it. I *mean that, Spence. Looking back, there is nothing I would change about the way you and I faced life's joys and sorrows together. I know that I could not have done it without you. I know that you made me a better person than I ever dreamed I would be.*

So, to answer those opening questions and my resolution for this coming year...

Nothing is for sure, but I suspect that I will not make another New Year. What would I change? NOTHING, except to remind myself to savor the moment—each precious and seemingly insignificant moment—and to keep doing more small things with greater love.

Thanks for all the happy years—new and old!

Z

February 14, 2008—Valentine's Day

One glance from you and my heart sings
The sound of your voice instantly brings
A love that few are given
At least this side of heaven.

Look, farm boy, I've been thinking about this, and there's not a reason in the world that you should sit around in sackcloth and ashes for weeks and months after I go. I want you to get out there and live, okay? I'll be watching and believe me, I will let you know if you pick someone to be with who is totally wrong for you, so don't mope around. Remember, you're not getting any younger yourself and it would really bring me a greater peace to know that someone is making sure you eat right and remember to take your blood pressure meds. And if some nosy-Rosie criti-

cizes you for not waiting, show her this letter and tell her to mind her own business.

All my love,
Zoe

March 12, 2008

And in this winter of my discontent you came home yesterday with a gift—the possibility for yet another new treatment—a possible miracle.

"Let someone else have a chance," I told you.

"Why?"

"Because a younger person would have time to do so much good—"

"What about the good you can do?" you asked, exasperated and clearly disappointed that I had not received the news with enthusiasm.

I mentally ran through all the arguments—I even uttered some of them. But we'd already had this discussion. You knew what I felt about this. In the end, I simply said, "No," leaving no room for debate. But what I should have said is, "Maybe the good I can do is to give this other person their chance—their chance at happiness and a life spent loving someone and bringing children into the world to keep the circle going."

I didn't say that, and tonight as you sit over there reading and I lie here in the hospital bed we've added to the converted study, I feel the distance between us—and the admission we're both facing that you have offered me my last best hope. And I have turned it down. I search for words, but none come. I love you so much and see daily the toll that this takes on you. And it occurs to me that what I really want is the chance to give something back to you—

the chance for you to live your life. Yes, you will miss me, but I am always with you—you know you can't get rid of me. After all, think of all the times I've popped up again and again when it looked as if we were through!

You glance at me over the tops of your reading glasses. I watch as your features soften. I see forgiveness. I see acceptance. I will put down this pen, for we don't need words. I will simply hold out my arms to you and you will be there.

June 9, 2008

Sara was here today—not just for one of her usual visits but for work. She said she needed me to review the entries for the festival. I know it was a ruse to lift my spirits, but it worked. It felt so fantastic to focus my limited attention and energy on something so positive—so creative—so filled with hope for the future of this country and the world.

Oh, Spence, my whole life all I wanted was to work for peace—to find ways to put the concept of peace out there— to give it equal time with the idea of revenge or outright war. Even after 9/11. Even after Cami. Because of Cami.

And it occurred to me that we did this—our love did this and so much more. Were there ever two more different people? From backgrounds to philosophies to the way we react to everyday happenings? Yet neither of us could have realized these things in the same way without being together. Even the lessons that grew out of the bad times— the sad times—they came from "us," Spence—not from me or you alone but "us." Maybe I'm just being philosophical because the clock is running down, but, Spence, the love we have shared has created a kind of magic—for us and for others. That's something, don't you think?

2006

Zoe

In spite of the fact that the larger world around us was in chaos and disarray, Spence and I understood that these were our "golden years." I had been cancer-free for four years and saw no obstacle to grasping the magic five-year ring. Spence had handed the reins of the counseling program over to others. He maintained two lecture classes at the medical college and spent more time at the farm. On Saturdays, he helped Todd with the booth at the farmer's market on Capitol Square, where Spence took enormous pleasure in selling the birdhouses he'd made from the dried gourds he grew from seed and that Sandra and Millie helped him paint.

As grandparents we felt the responsibility to respect

our son and daughter-in-law's choices. Because their faith was central to their lifestyle, Spence and I returned to church. Todd and Sandra had now given us a grandson—Noah—and had designated Sundays as Gran-Day—meaning Spence and I had both children for the day. Early on Spence and I planned elaborate outings—Sunday school while we attended church services, followed by lunch and a museum or trip to some local historical site.

"Gram? Could we just be?" Millie asked one Sunday after church.

"Be?"

"You know, just be home—go to your house and just—you know, be?"

Spence and I looked at each other. We had begun to run out of ideas for these outings, and frankly, it was exhausting to keep Millie and Noah entertained all day.

"From the mouths of babes," Spence muttered and grinned as he turned the car around and headed for home.

"I am not a baby," Millie corrected. "I am almost four and a half."

"Cookie," Noah crowed, pointing to the sign above a bakery.

"Would just 'being' include making cookies?" I asked.

Millie considered this, then gave a sigh no doubt to demonstrate that this would be for me, not her. "I guess."

And just like that, the pattern changed. Baking became a favorite pastime—a surefire way of getting both children to agree to a nap before donning the aprons and matching chef's hats Sandra made for each of us. Spence bought the children child-sized rakes and put them to work in the fall helping him with the leaves. More often than not this ended with both children leaping into piles of red, gold and purple leaves and scattering them all over again.

In the spring my father had died, quietly in his sleep after returning from his traditional Saturday afternoon in the park and settling in for his nap. Hal suffered a stroke, but with Spence and Todd encouraging him and Taylor attending every session of therapy with him, filming the exercises so he could replay them on his VCR, he made an almost full recovery. Marie—like my mother—seemed destined to outlive us all. Both women were smaller in stature, but no less a presence than they had always been.

Like them, I wasn't ready to "retire." I wasn't sure women ever really did retire. Maybe they left jobs and careers, but it seemed to me that they kept on doing things—necessary things—that held their families and their communities together and kept both moving forward.

I stood outside the entrance to the building that housed A Place for Peace and the headquarters of the now respected but still struggling Wingfield Andersen Film Festival. The dream was finally solid bricks and mortar— a reality I could not even have imagined five years earlier. In September Spence and I would go to New York to attend the fifth anniversary of the attacks of 9/11. We would stand at a podium as we had done on the first anniversary and read out Cami's name. We would look out at the sea of bereaved faces—those who belonged to this unique and eternally painful society of those who had lost a loved one that day.

I opened the door that led to the stairway, heard the familiar chatter and laughter coming from the staff in the open space at the top of the stairs and started up. But halfway, I had to stop. My chest felt tight and I was breathing heavily.

"I have got to start getting some regular exercise," I muttered, and forced myself the rest of the way up the stairs. At the top, I smiled and waved to those who caught my eye before going on with their business. I turned the handle of the door that led to the conference room, walked inside, and collapsed in the nearest chair.

"You okay?"

My oldest friend and former housemate, Sara, stood in the open doorway. When I'd decided to open the center, Sara had been the first person I contacted. She'd been living in a suburb of Chicago, divorced, her kids, like mine, grown and off on their own, rambling around in the massive house she and her husband had built, and bored to tears with planning charity balls and galas so she'd have some semblance of a social life. It had taken her less than a month to sell the house, find a small condo in Madison and show up to work with me.

"Just a little winded," I said, gasping for air and coughing.

"That's a lot winded, my friend. Maybe it's the pollen count—it affects some people this time of year."

"Could be," I agreed, thinking of the hours I'd spent in my own gardens, not to mention the years of volunteering at the gardens when there'd been no hint of allergies. "What's up?"

Sara gave a nervous laugh and trailed her finger over the smooth wood of the conference table as she sat in the chair across from me. "You'll never guess who called."

"I give up. Who called?"

"Peter—as in United States Senator Peter Quarles," she added with emphasis on the title.

"I know who he is and what he is," I said. "What did he want?"

"He's just returned from a fact-finding trip to the Middle East and he wants to put together a symposium to present his findings."

"Here?"

"Well, not here per se," Sara said, indicating the small space. "But here as in Madison. He's thinking perhaps at the Orpheum Theater."

"And we fit into this how?"

"We would host it."

"We don't have that kind of money," I said. "The calendar's full."

"He's got the funding." Sara tapped her nails on the tabletop. "It would give us national exposure," she pointed out.

I laughed. "Oh, Sara, this is Peter. There's one reason he wants to do this—he's going to run for president."

Sara lifted her eyebrows. "And?"

"You know I can't do this without first talking to Spence. I realize that may appear mid-Victorian to you, but…"

"So talk to Spence," Sara said, standing and heading for the door. "But do it today, okay? The senator-who-would-be-president wants an answer and we could use the media coverage."

I spent the rest of the morning thinking how I would introduce the reemergence of Peter Quarles into our lives. Spence and I had agreed to meet for lunch on the terrace at the Union. He was conducting an in-service for new volunteers at the rehab center. The longer the wars went on in Afghanistan and Iraq, the more lives they touched. The center was now counseling not only the men and women returning from the front, but also their families—and, in too many cases, their survivors. Recently Spence and I had established a fund to expand the services of the center to include job training and financial counseling, in addition to the psychological counseling the center had become nationally known for.

He was waiting for me on the terrace. He'd chosen one of the small metal tables for two in the shade. When he saw me, he stood, his eyes following me as they always did, making me feel beautiful and desirable, practically broadcasting his love for me to anyone watching.

"Sorry, I'm late," I said, a little breathless, although I had taken my time walking there—time I needed to form the words I would say.

"You're not late," he said, glancing at his watch. "Sit down and catch your breath. I'll get the sandwiches. Lemonade?"

I nodded and he crossed the terrace to the outdoor service bar, where he ordered burgers and lemonades for each of us. In spite of his years, he still had that same elegance of movement that I'd first noticed at Ty's funeral. I smiled. We had found a way out from beneath the aftermath of 9/11 and now breast cancer. Compared with all that, the reappearance of Peter Quarles was little more than a blip on the screen that was our lives. We were fine and I was worried for nothing. As soon as he brought the food, I told him.

"Peter Quarles wants the peace center to host a symposium so he can present the 'facts' from his mission to the Middle East," I said while we unwrapped the burgers, added mustard and—in Spence's case—ketchup.

Spence took a bite and spoke around chewing. "Where? Here? In Madison?"

"He's working up to a run for president—I'm sure that's behind it all," I said.

"That and the chance to work with you again. That guy never did know when to quit," Spence said, and grinned. "I assume this is on his budget?"

"So Sara says."

Spence laughed. "Now, there's a thought. Sara and Peter—I mean, doesn't a presidential hopeful need a wife?"

I couldn't help it. The very idea of Peter Quarles—the man who had gone from a hippie's torn jeans and tie-dyed T-shirts to designer suits and monogrammed cuff links— matched with Sara—the woman who had thrown off the anchor of her *Desperate Housewives* persona to lose herself once again in long flowing skirts, peasant blouses, sandals and a gray-streaked braid that reached her waist— was ludicrous.

"I don't think either of them is in the market," I said.

"It'll be good for the peace center," Spence said. "Could bring you some first-rate national attention. And if you time it around the film festival..."

My eyes widened. Of course. We could take Peter's symposium and use it to showcase the film festival—the festival that had struggled to find its audience. But with Peter's symposium attracting some big names, the media would be everywhere and—

"Oh, no," Spence said. "There's that glazed-over look, and that means you are processing at least a gazillion new ideas and—well, all I can say is, poor Peter."

I focused on Spence, studying him for signs of the slightest glimmer of doubt—the slightest thought of the past.

"It's fine, Zoe," he said, reading me like a book. "We're fine. Call the senator and tell him to—what's that line his former boss likes to use—'bring it on'?"

We both exploded in laughter for Peter Quarles—

rabble-rouser extraordinaire, who had sat perhaps at this very table, plotting the overthrow of the government—had announced just before running for the U.S. Senate that he was switching parties.

I pulled my cell from the pocket of my slacks and punched speed dial. "Sara? Call the senator and say, yes, but be sure he understands the terms—the symposium and this year's film festival go hand in hand and he's paying—for both."

Spence reached for the phone. "And tell him I said hi," he said, and I could still hear Sara laughing as she hung up.

Spring 2008

Zoe

Although the new treatment from the clinical trial has had some positive effect, I am past fooling myself. The truth is that I am in almost constant pain these days. And I feel brittle—as if any little move might cause something to snap.

I'm not fooling Liz, either. I feel her watching me closely one February afternoon as I putter around, throwing together a kitchen-sink salad for us to share. She's stopped by unexpectedly.

"Spence is in Boston at a seminar," I tell her, and my suspicions are confirmed. "But you knew that because he asked you to check on me, right?"

Liz smiles. "Guilty."

The gesture would have irritated me just months

earlier. Now I recognize it for what it is—a gesture of caring and love and friendship. "Thanks."

I continue mixing the salad, then reach for plates and utensils. "Let me," Liz says, moving around my kitchen with familiar ease.

We sit in the breakfast nook, an alcove that overlooks the lake. Grass peeks through patches of snow left over from the most recent storm. "Maybe we'll have a real spring this year," I say wistfully.

"Zoe, there's no reason you have to grit your teeth and bear the pain."

"I know. I just don't want meds to dull me any more than I already am. We've got a couple of things cooking at the center and I hate falling asleep practically the minute Spence gets home and—"

Liz stops my babbling by covering my flailing hand with hers. "We can titrate the meds so they offer you relief without dulling that overcharged brain of yours."

We go back to eating our salads, aware that nothing has been decided.

"Okay," I say after a while.

Liz gives an audible sigh of relief. "It's for the best," she says, as each of us spears veggies with undue concentration.

"I'm pretty sure I'm coming to the end of any benefit there might be from this new treatment," I confide. "I haven't said anything to Spence yet. He's been so happy and relaxed these past several weeks and I just hate to—"

"Don't sell him short," Liz advises.

Another silence.

"Has Jon mentioned hospice?" Liz asks.

"Yeah—once. I wasn't ready, but maybe—"

"It's not like the old days when it meant a vigil around your bedside, Zoe. It doesn't mean it's the end."

"I know. Jon said there are all sorts of services—social services, homemaker services—Spence might like that." I smile and Liz gives a hoot of laughter.

"Someone in a French maid's outfit, perhaps?"

I pick at my salad.

"There's no rush, Zoe. Just know it's an option—like the pain meds. When you feel you're ready."

"It won't buy us time," I say sadly.

"But it will buy you quality for the time you have," Liz replies. "And that's something, isn't it?"

She's right, of course.

After Liz leaves, I weigh the dwindling range of choices before me. Limited as they are, I do have options. I still have time. I pick up the phone and dial Spence's cell.

"Hi."

"Hi," he says, his voice filled with subliminal fear that something is wrong.

"Have I told you today how much I love you, farm boy?"

He chuckles. "I don't believe you have and I was just sitting here feeling sorry for myself—thinking nobody loved me."

"Well, thank goodness I called, because I love you, Dr. Andersen. And if you'll hurry back home, I'll be happy to show you just how much."

Spence laughs and I close my eyes, reveling in the pure blessing of this man in my life.

By late March I am spending most of my time at home. My world is slowly shrinking mostly to the kitchen, sunporch and the study, which has now been outfitted with a hospital bed and a variety of other equipment to meet my needs and make life easier for the parade of friends and family who daily come and go.

As depressing as it all is, I am stunned to realize that I am not despondent. Rather, I focus on using every minute of my time to make sure that all the people who have touched my life know how much they have meant to me.

"Let's have a grand party," I say to Spence one night as he sits in his easy chair next to my bed and we watch the news together.

"Okay," he replies.

"Don't patronize me, Doctor. The Fourth of July. Let's invite everyone we know and just have a blast of a party. Write this down so I can discuss it with Marie and Sandra when they stop by tomorrow with the kids. Oh, and you'll need to book a flight for Mom. Flights will fill up fast for a holiday weekend so don't put it off."

"Yes, ma'am." Spence gets a legal pad from the desk and a pen and sits down, poised for taking orders. "Start with the food," he says.

"Start with the guest list," I correct and, seeing that there are only a couple of sheets of paper left on the pad, add, "You're going to need more paper."

This morning I ask the home health aide to help me out to the sunporch and bring me a box of materials I had stored in Cami's former bedroom.

"Grandma!" Millie cries as she races through the house, her small feet pounding on the hardwood floors. "You're up." She throws herself at me and hugs me hard.

"We have work to do," I say, hugging her back.

"We have work to do, Noah," she reports to her

brother, who has been a step slower to reach the sunporch. "You sit there and Grandma will tell us what to do." She motions to one of two small chairs at the bright green child's table set Spence brought home one day. Noah glances at me for confirmation.

While Marie and Sandra busy themselves in the kitchen, filling our freezer with wholesome meals that Spence can easily prepare, I motion for the children to move closer. "We're going to have a party," I whisper. The eyes of both children grow wide with excitement.

"Is it a secret?" Noah asked.

"For now, yes. I want the two of you to help design the invitations."

Noah is confused.

Millie sighs. "That's like those paper things Mommy gets when we're invited to a birthday party."

Noah nods. "Whose birthday is it?" he whispers.

"Well, it's your dad's and Uncle Taylor's but it's also a big birthday party for America and everyone who lives here," I say and once again the eyes focused on mine are enormous.

"Wow."

"So it has to be a big invitation," Millie tells him.

"Not so big, but colorful," I tell her. "Can you help?"

Millie's dark head and Noah's blond one bob in unison as they hurry back to the table, dump out the entire big box of crayons and feverishly set to work.

For the next half hour I soak up the energy of these tiny dynamos. "How's this?" Noah asks, presenting me with a page scribbled with ribbons of color in one tight corner.

"I can do better," he assures me before I have the chance to comment.

Millie's creation is a collage of glued paper strips in the abstract form of a flag with one purple stripe. "I ran out of red paper," she says with a frown.

"It's perfect," I assure her. "We'll use yours as the cover and Noah's for the inside, where the message will go."

Millie and Noah both dance around my chair.

"Time for Grandma Zoe's nap," Sandra announces from the doorway. And they are off, lured away by my assurance that they will be the very first to see the completed invitation, and Marie's suggestion that she is just starving for a cheeseburger from the local drive-in.

How I cherish such days. But the times I cherish most are those late nights when Spence and the night aide are both sleeping and I am feeling fully alive in a way I have never appreciated before. I know that I have only a small window of energy, but I take it when it's there—two in the morning or high noon. I reach for the little hand recorder my friend Sara bought for me and dictate another of the letters she has agreed to transcribe and one day give to Spence.

Summer 2008

Spence

On the Fourth of July Zoe was at home and our annual party was about to get started.

"Mom," Taylor said, as he sat on the side of her bed late that afternoon. "I'm getting married."

Zoe's eyelids, heavy with the drugs she took to keep her comfortable, opened. "It's about time," she croaked. Then she reached up and cupped Taylor's chin. "Wait a minute. Is this an abstract idea or do you actually have someone in mind?"

Taylor had long been on the receiving end of family jokes about the confirmed bachelor, so set in his ways that no sane woman would have him. "It's Nora," he said.

Zoe smiled. Of all the filmmakers Taylor had brought

into our lives, Nora was our favorite. From the beginning she had been comfortable stopping by, whether Taylor was home or not, and of all the women surrounding Taylor, Nora was the only one he could depend upon to offer an honest and critical opinion of his work—and his attitude.

"Good choice," Zoe said. "You should have someone who doesn't think the sun rises just because you woke up this morning."

"Mom," Taylor protested.

"Have you asked her?"

"Not yet."

"You know, we could use a little joy around here—the place is so somber with me just lying here and everybody tiptoeing around." Zoe sighed. "And I expect you haven't gotten a ring?"

"Not yet," Taylor admitted.

Zoe pulled off the engagement ring and wedding band she had worn every day of our thirty-eight years together. "How about these?"

"I can't," Taylor said.

"You can't or don't want to? Those are different, you know."

"Can't," Taylor muttered.

"Look, kid, let's be practical here. You'd like to have them. Nora has often admired them. What are you going to do—scatter them with my ashes over the lake? What a waste!"

I saw the corners of Taylor's mouth lift even as he swiped at his cheek with the fingers of one hand. Zoe caught his hand and pulled it firmly to her. She dropped the rings into Taylor's palm and wrapped his fingers over them. "Now, stop stalling and go ask her. You are not getting any younger, kiddo—and neither is she."

That evening, I slipped into Zoe's room just before dark and lifted her out of the bed. The aide we'd hired brought the wheelchair close, but I shook my head and carried Zoe out the French doors of the study we'd converted into her bedroom and onto the sunporch. The party she'd planned with me and the grandchildren was in full swing.

I gently laid her on the huge chaise for two that she'd brought home from an estate sale the summer after we'd reunited. "For watching sunsets and fireworks," she'd explained when I had pointed out we already had a chaise, not to mention those lawn chairs we'd bought at the art fair.

"We can't snuggle on lawn chairs," she reminded me with a wink as she curled onto the new chaise.

On the table next to it I had placed a bowl of her favorite chocolate ice cream custard, with pureed raspberries from our garden on top. The aide covered Zoe, then stood. "Dr. Andersen?"

"Go enjoy the fireworks with your family and the others," I told her.

She smiled and bent to kiss the top of Zoe's head. "Thanks, for including my kids and me tonight," she said.

Zoe formed a word. "Family."

Our "family" knew no bounds as far as Zoe was concerned. Almost from the day our first grandchild was born, Zoe had seemed determined to share her joy with everyone she met. Where the kids had occasionally brought home a stray cat or injured bird, Zoe showed up with people—people in need, people in pain, people she admired and wanted me to meet.

Out on our lawn and encroaching onto the neighbors' lawns were all the members of our beloved immediate family, plus people from the university and rehab center—staff and patients we'd gotten to know through the years. Sara waved on her way past the sunporch and on across the lawn to join others from A Place for Peace. There were people from the botanical gardens and all the other charities that Zoe had found time to support with time and money through the years. They mingled with neighbors, friends—ours and our sons'. There might have been some total strangers out there who had simply wandered in off the street, for all we knew. Zoe would have loved that idea.

"Open," I said settling next to her on the chaise and placing the tip of the spoon near her mouth.

"Mmm," she murmured, although I wasn't sure any of the ice cream had actually made it past her chapped and dry lips.

I set the dish aside and snuggled her into my arms as the first flash of light appeared over the lake.

"Disappointing—no more than a two," I said, using the rating system Zoe had created to keep Cami's mind off the fact that she didn't like the noise of the fireworks at first.

The show got better after that. Once Zoe held up the fingers of both hands following an impressive display of the white gold spirals and popcorn-popping firecrackers that she'd always loved.

"Ten? You're so easy when the subject is fireworks," I teased and tightened my hold on her. I felt her push away the blanket so that her hands could rest on mine.

"Ah, the grand finale," I said when the sky went dark and silent for a moment.

And then it was like the brightest morning—the sky alive with color and sound, the children on our lawn squealing with delight and the adults cheering and applauding. But Zoe was still—more still than ever before, and I knew that she was gone. Just when it seemed that the show was over, I saw a single gold light rocket high in the sky. At its pinnacle, it burst into a thousand twinkling gold lights and gently floated down to the calm water of the lake.

I sat there holding her for a long time. In the background, I could hear family and friends rehashing the spectacle of the fireworks as they helped themselves to the make-your-own-sundaes that Zoe had always made available for our parties. And to the background music of their laughter and almost innocent delight in such simple pleasures as fireworks and ice cream sundaes, I thought about the seasons of our lives—mine and Zoe's. Taylor and Nora strolled across the lawn to the secret garden Zoe had created when the boys were kids. He would propose to Nora there. I turned to the musical laughter of our grandchildren and saw Todd swinging Millie up and onto his broad shoulders, while Sandra lifted a half-sleeping Noah into her arms. And suddenly I remembered what Zoe had said to me the last time we'd lain together on this chaise—the night after we'd gotten the diagnosis that her cancer had spread.

"You know something, farm boy?" She'd squirmed around until her face was very close to mine. "I'd be willing to bet that there're no two people who have loved each other as much or as well as we have—at least, not this side of heaven."

I looked out at the clear sky and saw two bright stars. And thought, *Maybe not that side, either.*

* * * * *

"Kitchen closed until further notice," read the note propped on the counter beneath the telephone. "The cook ran off to join the circus."

Jake Marshall squinted and read it again as he groped for a mug to fill with lifesaving coffee—

Which…wasn't there. The carafe was all but empty and stone-cold.

"Lilah?" he called, but he'd already sensed that she wasn't home. The house had a different feel without her in it—too still, somehow. Lifeless without her unbounded energy.

He glanced out the window and saw Puddin' sniffing around. Though the dog was nominally his—found by him, yes, but named courtesy of their daughter's favorite dessert—Lilah was the one who babied the old guy. If she had really run off to join the circus, she'd have taken Puddin' with her.

Jake grinned sleepily, shrugged and began assembling the makings for a fresh pot. She was pulling his leg, but Lilah's sense of mischief went down better after his brain was clicking. She was wide-awake the second her eyes opened; he hated mornings altogether.

The filters took a while to hunt down. When was the last time he'd had to make coffee? She was always up before him. He muttered a little before he finally succeeded. Was it one extra scoop for the pot or—

He set everything down, shoulders drooping. He needed caffeine, tanker-loads of it. Now. Last night had been a long one, with an emergency surgery lasting until nearly 2:00 a.m. *Okay, you can do this.* He dumped in two extra scoops for good measure, then shuffled off to hit the shower while it was brewing. On the way, he passed the dining room—

Oh, hell. Their anniversary. He'd missed it. No wonder Lilah had sounded funny when he'd called her to say not to wait up.

Man…everything still sat there—wilted salad, melting dessert. His favorite pot roast petrified in congealed grease. Lilah liked her house in order; she wasn't one to leave dishes soaking in the sink, much less food going bad on the table.

He was in deep doo, no question. He'd always been lousy with dates, but this one was sacred, the anniversary not of their wedding but of the night they'd first made love. Our Day, they called it. The tradition had been special to them both. Even during the tumultuous child-raising years they'd never missed it.

He could plead the press of work, which was admittedly crushing since he'd switched to the trauma team. He was so tired half the time he could barely remember his name.

His colleagues thought he was crazy to give up a solid

private practice, but he loved this work. Medicine interested him now in a way it hadn't in a long time.

Not more than Lilah, though.

Kitchen closed. Suddenly the note wasn't quite as funny. Lilah loved to cook and was so gifted that friends had often urged her to open a restaurant or catering service. She might not be kidding, and for her to shut down her beloved kitchen…not good. He had some serious amends to make. Thank heavens it was nearly Valentine's—he could remember that connection, only three days after Our Day. He'd have to go the distance to dig himself out of this hole.

As soon as he showered, he'd get busy cleaning up the dining room as a gesture of good faith. Lilah would be home soon, surely, and he'd grovel, if necessary—

Upstairs, he heard his pager go off. And groaned. He was on call. Not a chance he could ignore it. He cast another glance at the mess, painfully aware that he'd barely have time to throw on clothes. He'd have to shut off the pot. No coffee until he reached the hospital.

Not good. Really not good.

But Lilah was a reasonable woman, and she loved him, too. They'd work it out.

Wouldn't they?

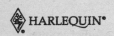

EVERLASTING LOVE™

Every great love has a story to tell™

The Valentine Gift

featuring
three deeply emotional stories of love that stands the test of time, just in time for Valentine's Day!

USA TODAY bestselling author
Tara Taylor Quinn

Linda Cardillo

and
Jean Brashear

**Available just in time for Valentine's Day
February wherever you buy books.**

www.eHarlequin.com

HEL65427

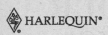
Olivia Banks and James McElroy were high
school sweethearts until James succumbed to
family pressure to end the relationship. He
unknowingly left Olivia pregnant with his
child…. But despite that betrayal, despite the
decisions they each had to make in their lives,
they never forgot each other…and eventually
discovered that love really could last.

Look for

Heart of My Heart

by
Stella MacLean

Available February wherever you buy books.

REQUEST YOUR FREE BOOKS!

2 FREE NOVELS PLUS 2 FREE GIFTS!

HARLEQUIN®

EVERLASTING LOVE™
Every great love has a story to tell™

YES! Please send me 2 FREE Harlequin® Everlasting Love™ novels and my 2 FREE gifts. After receiving them, if I don't wish to receive any more books, I can return the shipping statement marked "cancel." If I don't cancel, I will receive 4 brand-new novels every other month and be billed just $4.47 per book in the U.S. or $4.99 per book in Canada, plus 25¢ shipping and handling per book and applicable taxes, if any*. That's a savings of about 15% off the cover price! I understand that accepting the 2 free books and gifts places me under no obligation to buy anything. I can always return a shipment and cancel at any time. Even if I never buy another book from Harlequin, the two free books and gifts are mine to keep forever.

153 HDN ELX4 353 HDN ELYG

Name _____ (PLEASE PRINT) _____

Address _____ Apt. _____

City _____ State/Prov. _____ Zip/Postal Code _____

Signature (if under 18, a parent or guardian must sign) _____

Mail to the **Harlequin Reader Service®:**
IN U.S.A.: P.O. Box 1867, Buffalo, NY 14240-1867
IN CANADA: P.O. Box 609, Fort Erie, Ontario L2A 5X3

Not valid to current Harlequin Everlasting Love subscribers.

Want to try two free books from another line?
Call 1-800-873-8635 or visit www.morefreebooks.com.

* Terms and prices subject to change without notice. NY residents add applicable sales tax. Canadian residents will be charged applicable provincial taxes and GST. This offer is limited to one order per household. All orders subject to approval. Credit or debit balances in a customer's account(s) may be offset by any other outstanding balance owed by or to the customer. Please allow 4 to 6 weeks for delivery.

Your Privacy: Harlequin is committed to protecting your privacy. Our Privacy Policy is available online at www.eHarlequin.com or upon request from the Reader Service. From time to time we make our lists of customers available to reputable firms who may have a product or service of interest to you. If you would prefer we not share your name and address, please check here. ☐

HEL07

*Inside*ROMANCE

Stay up-to-date on all your
romance reading news!

Inside Romance is a FREE quarterly newsletter
highlighting our upcoming series releases
and promotions.

Visit
www.eHarlequin.com/InsideRomance
to sign up to receive our complimentary newsletter today!

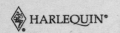

EVERLASTING LOVE™

Every great love has a story to tell™

When a long-lost file lands on Lieutenant
Colonel Anne Dunbar's desk, she's stunned
to find it contains a recommendation
for a medal for Marie Wilson, one of the
Hello Girls who served in France during
World War I. At the same time, Anne faces
dissolution of her marriage to D.C. attorney
Brian Dunbar. Marie and her lieutenant
form a bridge that helps Anne and Brian
overcome their painful past.

Look for

The Hello Girl

by

Merline Lovelace

Available March wherever you buy books.

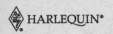

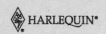

HARLEQUIN®

EVERLASTING LOVE™
Every great love has a story to tell™

COMING NEXT MONTH

**#25 THE VALENTINE GIFT by Tara Taylor Quinn,
Linda Cardillo, Jean Brashear**
*Valentine's Daughters. The Hand That Gives the Rose.
Our Day*—three special stories from three acclaimed authors.
Three different versions of what Valentine's Day really
represents…and how it celebrates everlasting love.

#26 HEART OF MY HEART by Stella MacLean
Olivia Banks and James McElroy were high school
sweethearts—and like all young lovers, they believed their
love would last forever. But they ignored the real world as
it existed in their small East Coast town during the 1960s,
the world of parental power and social propriety. When
James succumbed to family pressure to end the relationship,
he unknowingly left Olivia pregnant with his child…. But
despite that betrayal, despite the decisions they made, they
never forgot each other…and eventually discovered that love
really *could* last.

www.eHarlequin.com